Shadow

Histories

of the

River

Kingdom

Shadow Histories
of the
River Kingdom
Juliet E. McKenna

WIZARD'S TOWER

Wizard's Tower Press
Trowbridge, England

Shadow Histories of the River Kingdom

First edition, published in the UK November 2016
by Wizard's Tower Press

Stories first published as follows:

"Walking Shadows" in *Imaginary Friends* edited by
John Marco & Martin H Greenberg, Tekno Books/DAW
Books (2008)
"Noble Deceit" in *Subterfuge* edited by Ian Whates,
NewCon Press (2008)
"Remembrance" in *Anniversaries* edited by Ian Whates,
NewCon Press (2010)
"Truth, Lies and Consequences" in the
FantasyCon Programme Book (2015)
"Do You Want to Believe in Magic?" in the
Satellite 4 Convention Souvenir Book (2014)
"The Legend of the Eagle" in *Legends* edited by Ian Whates,
NewCon Press (2013)
"The Ties That Bind" in *Aethernet Magazine* edited by
Barbara Ballantyne, Tony Ballantyne (2013)

ISBN: 978-1-908039-65-1

Cover illustration and design by Ben Baldwin
Map by Sophie E. Tallis
Book Design by Cheryl Morgan

Printed by LightningSource

http://wizardstowerpress.com/
http://www.julietemckenna.com/

Contents

Foreword

A new fantasy world emerges from the shadows

From the outset, writing The Tales of Einarinn and subsequent series, I had a very clear concept of magic in that world. For a start, everyone with or without magical skills knows that it exists. Elemental wizardry and mages are organised and hierarchical because any lack of control can have disastrous consequences. Aetheric magic is its opposite in many ways but without control and understanding, Artifice is similarly useless, if not quite so potentially destructive.

As a writer though, you're always asking yourself 'What if...?' and that's often spun off what you're currently writing. What would it be like to write in a fantasy setting very different to Einarinn? What if magic wasn't fully understood? What if it was so mysterious and dangerous that it had to be kept hidden while its practitioners unravelled its secrets piecemeal? What if those with magical talent had to be watched and controlled, maybe made an offer of training they could not refuse? What if the consequences of the wider populace learning that magic is real are too disastrous to contemplate?

Invitations to write short stories offer an ideal opportunity for writers to explore such ideas, especially when an editor asks for something that's not set in an author's established world. I began exploring these ideas in 2008, when I was invited to contribute to the *Imaginary Friends* anthology. Since then, I've written half a dozen short stories set in this new setting, the River Kingdom, exploring and expanding on that original concept. In 2013 the invitation to write a serial novella for the new *Aethernet* e-magazine edited by Barbara and Tony Ballantyne offered me the opportunity to write a longer story. Naturally I seized that chance.

JULIET E. MCKENNA

Readers who've come across one or other of these stories have often contacted me wondering where they can find other stories set in this new and very different fantasy world. As it turns out, the original publications where some of these pieces appeared are not particularly easy to track down. So I am very pleased to be offering this collection gathering together these different insights into the River Kingdom. Once again it has been a pleasure working with Wizard's Tower Press, as well as with Ben Baldwin for the cover art, and Sophie E Tallis for the map.

I am also indebted to Julia and Philip Cresswell for going over the collected text and highlighting the inconsistencies and continuity issues inevitable when stories have been written over such a long period with the underlying concept evolving as I did so. Accordingly there are have been some edits and clarifications to a few of the stories for this collected edition.

I look forward to continuing to write about this new world.

Juliet E. McKenna

Map

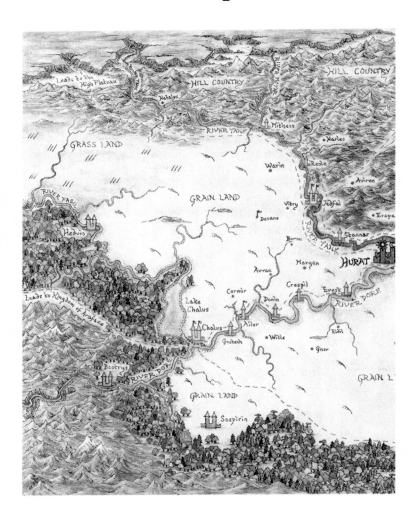

Walking Shadows

'Leshina! Stop flirting with the troopers!' The old woman's bark ripped through the clamour like a knife through silk. Everyone froze; servants, delivery boys and all the horsemen making ready to depart.

'Wait a moment.' Creases deepened in Sarese's gaunt face as she closed her eyes. A low murmur ran around the room.

Leshina half-smiled. 'What will nosy ears hear you saying?'

'Don't expect any sympathy when you're all tears and swelling belly.' Sarese wasn't amused. 'Well? What did you learn?'

'There were several keen to get a hand in my bodice.' Leshina sat down on the low stool by the hearth of the little chamber and retied the blue ribbon in her long blonde hair. 'Out to impress me with their closeness to their highnesses.'

'I know you don't like playing the tease.' Sarese laid a consolatory hand on the young woman's shoulder. 'But we'd be fools not to take advantage of the way you look.'

'Never mind.' Apprehension clouded Leshina's azure eyes. 'Only Kemeti still concerns us.'

Sarese wasn't pleased. 'Jastro?'

'No.' Leshina was certain

Sarese frowned. 'Jastro was pretending he had a hound-whelp—'

'His majesty gave him a brindle from the spring litters,' Leshina said helplessly. 'He has no need to imagine a puppy now.'

Sarese clicked her tongue, exasperated. 'And Kemeti?'

'She's still so young.' Leshina knotted her hands in her lap. 'Can't we wait? This time next year, the question might not even arise'

'This is her ninth summer. If she were going to outgrow imaginary companions, she'd already have done so. Jastro's barely out of his sixth winter.' Sarese's faded eyes were hard as diamond. 'And she's the paramount king's daughter. If she truly has the magic within her, think what it will mean? The rest of us can come out of the shadows and see our defence of this realm acknowledged.' She laughed without humour. 'Cavalry captains boast about their swift horses but we're the ones who really watch the distant borders out in the empty plains, making sure no-one encroaches—'

'I may be new here but I know that much.' Leshina stared at her lap.

Sarese sniffed. 'So the sooner we know if Kemeti has the magic within her the better. The sooner she can be taught its strengths, warned to keep its secrets. Is her imagined friend still the same?'

'It's still the river-boy.' Leshina looked up. 'Why is it so often a river-child?'

'If you're six or seven summers old at everybody's beck and call, realising everyone else's wishes are consulted before your own?' There was some sympathy in Sarese's fleeting smile. 'Wouldn't you want a friend who's seen realms so far upriver that minstrels have barely heard of them? Who knows what's truly in the lands downstream beyond the Nilgeh Mire that no two tales can agree on? Prince or peasant, children envy the river traders' freedoms.'

'Maybe.' Leshina was unconvinced.

'What's his name?' Sarese demanded. 'What does he look like?'

'Like any river-boy. Yellow hair, dark eyes.' Leshina twisted her fingers together.

'Does he have a name?' snapped Sarese.

'She calls him Achel.' Leshina closed her eyes. 'And he has a dog.'

'If that appears...' Sarese looked thoughtful. 'That'll mark the strength of Kemeti's imagination.

'But she's so small.' A tear ran down Leshina's cheek.

'No matter.' Not a pin shifted in the iron-grey twist of her upswept hair as Sarese shook her head 'We'll only have to-night before the barons start paying court to their majesties.'

Leshina shivered despite the spring sun warming the room. 'What if she fails?'

'White Pastures is a big castle.' Sarese folded her arms tight across her bony breast. 'With servants used to caring for Rasun.'

Tears welled in Leshina's cornflower eyes. 'He was older than Meti when he faced his trial—'

'Don't you wonder if we'd intervened earlier, perhaps his magic could still have been safely shaped?' Sarese snapped. 'Not testing Meti won't save her from herself, if the magic within her is strong enough.' She broke off to lay her hand gently on the girl's shoulder again. 'It wasn't your fault though, what happened to Rasun. You must believe that.'

Leshina managed to nod but couldn't speak.

'Get about your usual duties until their majesties arrive.' Sympathetic, Sarese was still implacable. 'Then spend as much time as possible around Kemeti. Whenever you catch a glimpse of her friend, fix him in your mind's eye.'

Leshina nodded, still silent. As she went out, she let her fearful tears fall. Since weeping would convince everyone she'd taken an undeserved tongue lashing from the old crone.

The rest of that day kept her too busy to fret. Housekeepers set every maid of all work to polishing the bedchambers and making up beds with fresh, scented linens. Every dust sheet was removed and the fine furnishings beneath brushed regardless of such precautions while the footmen fetched fine silver, glass and statuary out of storage. Bare-chested yardmen beat carpets hung on racks out beyond the gates while the girls swept hearths and polished fire-irons and servant boys replenished log baskets against the evening chill still coming off the river. Dusk was falling by the time the white stone steps of the main entrance were finally scrubbed.

While the other girls slept, unheeding, exhausted, Leshina stared at the ceiling of their garret. What if Meti failed the test? What if she passed? What would she think when she learned what power she had within her. Would she realise what had happened to Rasun? Would she ever know that Leshina...?

The slam of the door startled her awake. The uncurtained window was pale with dawn light and the other girls were already pouring icy water from the ewers to wash away lingering sleepiness.

They breakfasted in the servants' hall watching the yard-men unloading barrels and sacks and provisions wrapped in muslin or oilcloth. Errand-boys brought baskets of more precious foodstuffs, wrapped and sealed in the coarse yellow paper the river-traders brought from some downstream land.

Then the maids were set to work ornamenting every room with fresh-cut flowers and wiping away any trace of dust brought by night breezes. Leshina had barely returned to the lower hall for noon's bread and cheese when the first outriders' arrival echoed around the courtyard.

'Klyssa, Isette, Asteri, to go to the front of the house and attend to the children's carriages.' Sarese clapped her hands. 'And you, Leshina. And stop yawning!'

Leshina hurried after the other girls, scarlet-faced.

'You weren't here this time last year, were you?' Isette slid her a sympathetic look. 'Don't worry. We've done all the really hard work.'

That's what you think, Leshina thought silently.

They ran up the stone stairs to the heavy door separating the lower halls from the castle's upper reaches. Eyes demurely fixed on the black and white floor tiles, they walked swiftly to the front entrance.

Leshina hoped anyone noticing her nervousness would put it down to the searching scrutiny of the two senior housekeepers already waiting there.

It seemed like an age before the first carriages crunched around the broad gravel sweep to draw up in front of the steps. An age, and yet, far too soon.

The housekeepers acknowledged the children's attendants with cordial reserve before welcoming the princes and princesses.

'Highness, what a beautiful gown.'

'Prince Perisen, you'll soon be as tall as your sister.'

As elegant as her mother, Princess Giseri swept past with a rustle of lace-trimmed skirts, perfumed ribbons coiling amid her auburn ringlets. Tarifa followed, doing her best to mimic such poise. Perisen spared the gathering a good-natured, short-sighted smile before returning his attention to the book he carried.

'I have a hound pup.' Tousle-headed, shirt rumpled and breeches creased, Jastro ran up the steps. 'Mirich, I'm training him myself.'

One of the other footmen nodded at the girls. 'Go and help with the luggage.'

Leshina looked hard at the empty air behind the youngest prince. Not even the slightest trace of his once-imagined dog lingered at his heels. Disappointment hollow in her stomach, she followed the other girls out into the spring sunshine.

A prudently aproned maid of honour was helping Kemeti out of the second carriage. Another was bundling muslin into an incongruously plain pail. The acrid smell of vomit momentarily rose above the spice-studded scent pomander thrown on top.

'Everyone keeps saying I'll grow out of it.' A blush of embarrassment stained Kemeti's pallor. 'I'd like to know when.' The faintest echo of her father's famed temper coloured her tight words.

Sarese knew how ill travel made the child, Leshina thought with silent anguish. How could they put her to the test?

Then she glimpsed the shadow behind Kemeti. A shadow strong enough to defy the sunlight. Looking around. For an instant, looking straight at Leshina. Then he vanished.

'Quickly,' another maid of honour scolded, standing by the first carriage. 'Before their majesties arrive.'

Leshina hurried to take Jastro's toys and games, Giseri's jewel casket, Perisen's books and Tarifa's embroidery basket.

It was wholly dark when Kemeti woke. Where was she? Then the sourness at the back of her throat reminded her of the horrible journey.

Why couldn't they just live in one castle, she thought crossly. Why did she have to be jolted over endless leagues with the turn of every season? Because her father had to make his presence felt in every corner of his vast kingdom, yes, she'd been told that often enough. Because the great river was the kingdom's heart not its boundary. But why didn't Jastro ever get sick?

At least she felt better now she had slept. If she could just rinse away the foul taste in her mouth. As she sat up, she was puzzled to realise her bedroom was unusually dark. Who had laid the fire so badly it had left no glowing embers? As the feather-stuffed quilt slid down to leave her exposed to the night chill, Kemeti shivered.

'Feia?' Her words fell oddly in the dead air. 'Feia, I want some cordial!'

There was no reply and Kemeti realised no light from her night maid's candle was edging under the door. She scowled and swung her legs over the side of her soft warm bed. Feia was supposed to stay awake in case she was needed.

As her bare feet found the rich wool carpet, she realised her bladder was uncomfortably full. She dropped to her knees, reaching beneath the carved bedstead for the chamber pot.

A hand fastened on her wrist. 'Meti?'

She screamed and tried to pull away but the grip on her wrist didn't yield. She screamed again and again, so hard she tasted bile, her heart pounding.

A spiteful chuckle in the darkness silenced her. 'No one's coming.'

It was true. All she could hear was her own rasping breath. No cries of alarm, no running feet, no guard throwing open her door.

'It's just you and me, Meti.' The iron grip released her and she fell backwards.

Horrified to feel a hot thread of urine between her legs she clamped her knees together. 'Who—' Words stuck in her throat. She scrambled to her feet, stumbling on the hem of her long cotton nightgown.

Whoever had been hiding beneath the bed crawled out with another soft laugh. 'It's me, Achel.'

'What?' She stood uncomprehending in the darkness. Then she ran to the window to wrench open the shutters and moonlight streamed in. Outside, the wide silver loop of the mighty river embraced the castle park's carefully nurtured copses. The city sprawled beyond the outer wall, beyond her mother's pleasure garden. Everything was just as it should be outside. But something was very wrong in here.

Long fingers fastened on her shoulder and pulled her back around. 'I was talking to you.'

Kemeti shoved the hand away, clumsy with fear. 'Who are you?'

He was taller than her, older, blonde hair drawn back from his sallow, angular face. His dark eyes were hard beneath scowling sandy brows.

'I'm Achel, your friend.' Irritated, he planted his hands on his hips, bare-armed in his long leather jerkin and coarse breeches, barefooted as every boatman standing proudly on his deck. 'You don't seem pleased to see me.'

'But—' If some curious boy from the river traders had managed to sneak past the gates and the guards, incredible as that might be, how did he know to call himself Achel?

'I'm dreaming,' Kemeti realised aloud.

His sudden slap stung her face. 'Are you?'

As she gaped at him, she couldn't deny a shock of recognition. How could that be? She searched her memories of all

16

the times she'd watched the river boats, out in the gardens, from the towers of the other castles the seasons took her to. No, she hadn't ever seen him, not really.

But somehow she knew deep inside her that he was the boy she'd imagined so often by her side. But he wasn't the friend she had longed for.

'Go away!' She couldn't help glancing beyond him towards the closed door.

'No one's coming.' He laughed, cruelly amused.

'You're not real,' she protested. 'You can't be.'

'No?' He reached forward and pinched her upper arm, twisting the tender flesh through the cloth of her nightgown.

'Ow!' The unexpected pain redoubled the ache in her bladder.

'You wanted me here.' He scowled.

'What do you want?' She was not going to wet herself. Pressing her thighs together, she blinked away furious tears. 'What are you going to do?'

'Whatever I please.' He looked idly around and picked up one of her books from a side-table. 'To pay you back.' He started tearing out pages with slow malice.

'Stop that,' she shouted, outraged.

'Afraid you'll you get into trouble?' he sneered. Dropping the book, he swept a fine china dish from the mantelshelf into the hearth. 'You will, you know.' Laughing, he smashed a crystal tree hung with necklaces beside it. 'Because no one else can see me but you.'

Kemeti rejected the futile hope of saving her treasures and ran for the door. She slammed it behind her, fumbling for the lock. As her fingers fastened on the key, Achel threw his shoulder against the other side. The jolt threw her backwards, the key lost in the darkness.

'You won't get rid of me that easily,' he promised ominously as he pulled the door open.

Kemeti didn't waste breath replying, bolting from the antechamber into the corridor. But everything was wrong.

There were no lanterns. Window shutters that should be safely closed stood wide, uncaring moonlight pooling on the narrow carpet.

She rounded a corner, then another, shivering with cold and fear. Was there anyone here? She threw open the door to Giseri's rooms but the ante-chamber was empty.

Kemeti pushed the door shut without actually latching it. She bit her lip as she hitched up her nightgown and used a shapely vase as a chamber pot. This had better be a dream, otherwise she'd have some explaining to do. She was just setting the vessel down when a deep-throated bark startled her. A dog?

'Seek, Scaff, seek.' She could hear Achel encouraging it.

Dry-mouthed, she remembered imagining a dog at his heels, one of those rangy brindled curs that leapt from deck to deck. But she'd never imagined a name for his dog, she thought bemused.

Panting echoed louder as the dog turned into the corridor. She shoved the door all the way shut with a frantic whimper. The river-cur barked triumphantly and she heard its feet thud on the floorboards. Its claws scraped at the wood as it growled, low and menacing.

Memory paralysed her. She couldn't breathe. That terrible night when Rasun had been taken ill, he had had shrieked about birds in the room, birds that no-one else could see.

He'd screamed for his servants, for Giseri, for their mother and father. When they'd already been standing there. Rasun's empty gaze had slid straight over them, unseeing. He'd blundered about, weeping for fear of the darkness, when their father was summoning countless branches of candles.

She knew from servants' whispers that Rasun was still lost in his incomprehensible madness. Had she gone mad too—?

Her panicked thoughts dissolved in utter confusion.

'Good boy, Scaff.' Achel raised his voice on the far side of the door. 'Kemeti, come out of there at once!'

A feeble flicker of indignation countered the wretchedness overwhelming her. He presumed to command her?

18

Kemeti bit her lip and concentrated on holding the door closed. The river-cur growled angrily, scrabbling harder, faster. As it snuffled at the base of the door, she could feel its breath hot and moist on her bare feet. She screwed her eyes shut, fighting the choking terror rising in her throat once again.

'Come out,' Achel snapped. 'Or you'll be punished all the more.'

Outraged, Kemeti's eyes snapped open. Only her father and mother could order her punished. And she hadn't done anything wrong. He was the intruder here, him and his horrid cur.

One of her father's big hounds would defend her from this horrid river boy, she thought with desperate fury. She wasn't afraid of the robust hunting dogs and they liked her. They wouldn't tolerate this cur in their castle. Introducing them to Jastro's new whelp had taken all the kennelmen's guile, to save the pup from being torn to pieces.

A questioning whine made her yelp with fright. Spinning around, she pressed her back against the door. There was a shape in the room with her, a shadow beneath the window. Only it was made from moonlight rather than shade. How could that be?

She realised she could make out the outline of a sizeable hunting hound. Long muzzled, its head cocked to one side, floppy ears pricked with curiosity. Its ruff of thick white fur was fluffed up, curled tail held high over its muscular rump.

Only it wasn't real. Kemeti could see right through it. But as it whined again, expectant, she realised she couldn't see the upright of the lamp stand through its flank any more. Somehow it was getting more real.

On the other side of the door, the river-cur barked furiously. The hound's silent snarl drew its black lips back from perfect ivory fangs but it didn't move, still looking keenly at Kemeti. Now she could see the darker grey inside its ears, under its belly, inside the curl of its wagging tail. It made as if to take a step forward but paced on the spot instead, as the best-trained hounds did until a command released them.

'Come here, boy.' She bent to offer her hand. The hound thrust a solid wet nose into her palm, its warm tongue licking her icy fingers. She stroked it, feeling thick softness beneath the harsher upper coat. It hadn't been here a moment ago but it was undoubtedly real.

The river cur was barking hysterically now. The hound kept its eyes fixed on Kemeti's face as it growled low, deep in its chest. She felt its hackles rising beneath her hand. It was real and it was an ally. Wrenching the door open, she urged the hound on with hand and voice. 'See him off, boy!'

The white hound sprang on the river cur. Taller but lighter-boned, the other dog was unable to resist the solid impact. Snarling, the hound crouched astride the cur as it whimpered, bowled over, pale belly exposed. Moonlight shone on the hound's gnashing teeth then they fastened in the river-dog's throat. Gurgling, the cur drew up its hind legs to rake at the hound's belly but the heavier dog shook it like a rat, breaking its neck with an audible snap.

Kemeti stood, staring, mouth open, shivering with cold and fright. Achel swore an oath the stable boys used. She looked up, startled, to see him running away though the moonbeams and shadow dappling the corridor. Where was he going? Who else might he hurt? Jastro?

'Chase, boy!' She surprised herself by shouting to the white hound. 'Bring him down!'

Obediently abandoning its kill, the dog pursued Achel, its eager barks echoing back from the stone walls.

Steeling herself, Kemeti edged past the slaughtered river cur. Her toes cringed at the thought of sticky blood on the carpet. But as she strained her eyes to try and see any stains in the gloom, all she could make out was the pattern of inter-laced leaves.

Kemeti blinked and there was no river cur. It was only an illusion wrought by the weaver's design meeting the moonshine's deceit. Like one of those pictures in Perisen's book, where a beautiful girl in a sumptuous gown became a hook-nosed old woman swathed in a wrap if you looked at her the right way. A cloud slid over the edge of the moon.

When Kemeti looked again, she saw the hapless beast curled motionless in its death agony.

Tears stung her eyes. She hadn't meant to bring an innocent animal here to die in such pain, whatever that horrid Achel might say. If she had truly done something to cause this, she didn't know how and she really hadn't meant to. She blinked, wiping her nose on her sleeve, struggling not to cry in earnest.

But this wasn't over. She could hear the white hound baying triumphantly and Achel shouting foul curses at it. It must have him trapped. There must be someone she could find, a guard who could throw him into a dungeon. If this really was all somehow her fault, she must try to put things right, mustn't she?

Trembling with apprehension, she screwed up her courage and opened her eyes. As she looked, she saw the dead cur fading away. Just as moonlight had shaped the white hound, now the river-dog was dissolving into the shadows before her very eyes. She thrust a hesitant toe forward only to feel the soft dry wool of the carpet. The dog wasn't real. It had never been real.

You imagined me.

Achel's words echoed in her head.

She had. She had imagined him, and his dog. Because just about every trader's boat had a cur or two pacing its decks, splashing after the boys when they swam ashore, walking circumspectly behind the elders when a river clan anchored to pay formal visits on the city's merchants. But it hadn't been a real dog. Just the idea of a dog.

Kemeti groped for understanding but that was beyond her. She settled for concentrating on what was in front of her. Nothing. The dog had been nothing, not really. So Achel was nothing. Not real. And she'd tell him so. Not stopping to risk her new boldness foundering on some further inconvenient thought, she hurried towards the barking and shouting.

The white hound had Achel cornered. The river youth was pressed into a door recess where a side passage ended in a narrow window. He was cursing, vile as a trooper and Kemeti saw him kick at the dog. The hound's gleaming teeth missed his tanned foot by a hair's breadth and he hastily thought better of it.

As he saw Kemeti at the corner of the corridor he yelled at her, enraged. 'Call it off or I'll make you sorry!'

She could hear fear undercutting his wrath but wouldn't let satisfaction distract her. 'You can't do anything to me,' she said stoutly. 'You're not real.'

'I'm real enough to slap you senseless, you little bitch!' Achel tried to take a step forward but the hound snapped at him.

'No, you're not.' Kemeti couldn't help the tremor in her voice. She swallowed and pressed on. 'You're just someone I made up when I was thinking about river boys.' She pictured all the youths she'd seen, on walks with her maids, riding in the castle grounds. There had been so many glimpses of different boats, on journeys through the city or up and down the highroad that followed the great river's winding course across the vast plains of the kingdom. None of them was Achel. They were all different to him.

'I am—' He gasped and fell back, the door resounding with a hollow thud. 'Hah,' he spat. 'Hear that?' He hammered a clenched fist backwards to bang the door again.

But Kemeti saw the weakness in his legs. His face had blurred into uncertainty, a shiver of moonlight running through his body. 'You're not real,' she insisted. 'You're just—'

As she hesitated, Achel stood upright again, stronger, bolder. 'You know nothing,' he said with contempt.

'I just wanted a friend,' she shouted with sudden anger. 'I was lonely. I wanted someone to share things with, to play games, making up stories, like I used to do with Rasun—' Anguish choked her as she recalled all the times she'd been missing Rasun so badly, she'd pretended she had someone there to replace him. That's how all this had started. None of it was real.

Gritting her teeth, she forced herself to continue. 'You're

not real. I made you up. You're not even right. If you were a real river boy come ashore, you'd have boots on.' She was yelling at the top of her voice now, infuriated. 'They only have bare feet on board their boats.'

Images ran through her mind, of all the shirtless, shoeless youths she'd ever seen. They were real. This one was not. As she thought this, she realised she could see the outline of the doorframe through Achel's shirt.

'And you'd have brought a cloak,' she added scornfully. 'It's a cold night and you're dressed for high summer.'

Insubstantial as smoke, Achel opened his mouth but could make no sound. Kemeti could see the moonlight through him now.

'Go away.' Her conviction was firm now, hard as iron. 'And never come back.'

Abrupt shafts of light pierced him, shining through the empty hollows of his eyes and mouth, and he vanished.

Sarese's vice-like hand restrained Leshina. The younger woman blinked away her own tears, her vision flickering back to the lantern-lit warmth of the real corridor. Somewhere overhead, she could hear a maid or a manservant's soft footsteps. The castle never entirely slept.

With an effort, she focused on the empty darkness again, where Kemeti stood alone with the white hound gazing obediently at her.

'I'm sorry.' The little girl scrubbed at her tear-stained face with the cuffs of her nightgown. 'I know you came to help me but you're not real either. Please go away.' Her voice broke on a sob. 'I want to go back to bed and wake up and this all to be a dream.'

Leshina held her breath, tense.

The white dog dutifully lay down, its nose on its forepaws, and dissolved into nothingness.

'Good girl,' Sarese murmured with satisfaction. 'Her magic's strong. She'll do well.'

The two women stepped backwards as Kemeti came running towards them, unseeing, still lost in the deserted unreality of the castle confining her imagination. They followed her back to her room where the maid Feia dozed in the antechamber, thanks to the powdered oblivion Sarese had dosed her supper with.

Entering the bedchamber, Leshina saw Kemeti scramble into bed, pulling the covers over her head to muffle her weeping.

Sarese was looking around and Leshina knew she was seeing the real and the unreal side by side. 'Don't break the necklace tree,' the old woman decided. 'But smash that dish in the hearth. She'll need something to convince her it was no dream.'

Leshina nodded, not trusting herself to speak.

Sarese's thoughts were already moving on. 'I'll let the others know in the morning, as much as is necessary. Make sure you're at hand to answer her questions.' She chuckled. 'You had better empty that vase she peed in. But ask her what she knows about it, if you think she needs a prompt. Right, let's get back to our own beds.'

Satisfied, Sarese walked briskly from the room without a backward glance.

Kemeti's sobs were slowly subsiding beneath the quilt. Leshina slowly closed the window and the shutters, her heart wrung with pity and guilt. Then she closed the shutters on the unreal window too, and lit the thought of a candle besides, in case Kemeti woke in that terrifying darkness again.

She set the dish in the hearth and broke it with a savage stamp of her foot. Never mind Sarese's instructions. She'd wait out the night here in case Kemeti woke up before daybreak brought her securely back to reality. She could guide her home.

She was not going to see the little girl abandoned like Rasun. She owed him that. Since she owed her very existence to his fertile imagination, his adolescent longing shaping her seductive curves, her alluring blondness. But she had been

24

too bemused to help Rasun. Well, now she understood. Now she could repay him by being Kemeti's friend.

Noble Deceit

I'd always known the call could come. I'd never worried
about it. Knowing they were there was nothing I need fear.
I shared their secret. If I couldn't tell anyone else, that simply
made the secret more precious, something to hug to myself
when other children called me names.

Not that I suffered any more passing spite than other artisan quarter boys. No one knew I was special apart from Madam Sima. I wondered about that as I grew older. Had one of
my brothers said something? We were all learning our letters
at her school around the time we realised I was the only one
who could spin substance out of shadows. To make a ball to
play with when the long summer evenings sneaked through
the bedroom shutters our father had bolted. To make a
lumpy frog spring out of the chamberpot, when Seppin went
to pee, first as always.

He had yelled and fell backwards and pissed his night-
shirt. But he didn't tell on me, not even when our mother
slapped him, calling him a dirty barge boy. We stuck together, the four of us with barely three years between our birth-
days first and last. Besides, we didn't think much of it. Seppin
could add up numbers in his head. Rachik could whistle like
a willow finch. I could make frogs out of shadows and Marlil
could roll his tongue into a tube. He was only five, so that was
worth praising.

Then one day Madam Sima tapped my shoulder as we
sprang up from our benches when the noon bells called us
home for lunch.

'Thian, I have something for your mother.'

I thought nothing of it. She would hardly trust whatever
it was to Marlil, and Seppin had been first out of the door,
followed by Rachik.

All of us lads were eager for the afternoon's work around
our fathers' looms and lathes. Most were already counting
the new moons until their tenth birthday when they'd leave
the school Madam Sima had made of her dead husband's

weaving shed. I enjoyed my lessons more than most but like my brothers, assumed I'd take up the joinery trade.

So I dutifully followed Madam Sima across the yard and into her kitchen. She surprised me by leading me into the parlour.

'Sit down, dear. I want to show you something.'

I was expecting a book. She had a whole shelf full and she trusted a few of us to read quietly when she drilled the rest in their letters. I can picture her still, standing by the alphabet wall-hanging, straight-backed despite her years, her dress and lace-trimmed cap always mourning grey.

Sitting opposite, she spread her wrinkled fingers on the table's embroidered cloth. I sat uncertain as she stared at the empty linen. Then I caught my breath.

Something was taking shape. Like the bridge tower's turrets coming into view as the sun burned through spring mists. Madam Sima was drawing something out of nothing into a patch of sunlight.

A cat. Not a real cat, one barely as long as her forefinger. Ginger and white with different coloured eyes? I gasped with delight. It was Basu!

'Make Lagan,' I begged, 'and the black heron.'

That was my favourite tale about the wily cat and the yard-hound and the curious things the river brought them.

Madam Sima stroked tiny Basu's head. It stropped itself around her finger just like a real cat. 'Why?'

That flummoxed me. 'Why not?'

'What would I do with a pocket-sized dog and a bird the size of a clothes pin?'

Her voice was kind. She never asked questions like Havas, our father's journeyman, heavy with sarcasm to show you were a fool.

'I could have them?' I suggested hopefully.

'How would you explain that to your mother?' Her blue eyes twinkled. 'Or your brothers? What about Kettle-cat?'

Our mother's cat, named for his habit of sleeping among

the pans, had a reputation as a rat-killer the length of our street.

'I could keep them in a box,' I said uncertainly.

The tiny cat rolled on its back and Madam Sima gently tickled its belly. 'Wouldn't that be cruel?'

'It's just a toy.' I was itching to stroke the marvellous creature myself.

She sat back. 'Is it?'

The tiny Basu sprang up, just like Kettle-cat. I stretched out one finger. It pushed at my fingernail with its little nose. I stroked its silky fur, warm from the sun.

It flopped down and rolled over. Tentative, I touched its belly. Wrapping its forepaws around my finger, it bit, hind legs raking. Father played this game with Kettle-cat. None of us did, convinced we'd lose a hand.

'Ow!' I laughed but little Basu's teeth and claws were sharp as pinpricks.

'It's quite real,' Madam Sima said. 'Now I've made it, I must care for it until it fades. It's my responsibility.'

I had no notion where the frog had gone, I realised guiltily.

'There aren't many of us who can make things like this.' She gently unhooked the tiny cat, scooping it up in her palm. 'We must take care.'

I looked at her, wretched. 'There was a frog—'

'I know,' she nodded, untroubled. 'It'll have faded by now, most likely, and being a frog, I don't suppose it thought much about anything. But this one.' She smiled as the little Basu jumped down from her hand to explore the table top. 'I'll need eyes in the back of my head for a few days.'

'What will happen?' I wondered.

'It'll go to sleep and then it won't be here any more. As long as no one else sees it, to make it more real.' Madam Sima curbed the tiny cat's attempt to climb down the table cloth. 'It would fade sooner if I didn't feed it but that would be cruel.'

'Why did you make it?' I blurted out.

'To show what you can do.' She looked at me. 'So you real-ise what you mustn't.'

'I won't,' I promised fervently. If the notion of making tiny animals thrilled me, the thought of them dying mere days later was horrid.

'You might, by accident.' Her eyes were ice-bright. 'You could wake in the night and find the marsh bear you've been dreaming about. Or a mud serpent under the bed might strike at your foot one morning.'

I was only seven years old. Suddenly this was terrifying.

'I'll teach you how to make sure that doesn't happen,' Madam Sima reassured me. 'But this must be our secret.'

'Why?' I demanded.

'Why do you think?' she chided.

I bit my lip. 'Seppin wouldn't leave me be if he knew.'

'True.' She laughed. 'That's not the most important rea-son.'

'No?' Seeing her unconcern sparked faint hope in me.

She gathered up the tiny cat. 'When needs must, Thian, if danger threatens, you and I and others like us will defend the city.'

I gasped. 'How?'

'By shaping things to terrify the enemy, to drive them away, to block their path.'

'But—'

She understood my incoherent protest.

'I know the paramount kings have ruled in peace since before your grandsire's day but that could change. Then, if some enemy knew our city's defences relied on the likes of me and you, they'd kill us first, wouldn't they?'

I was struck dumb with fear.

'Provided no one knows who we are or what we can do, we're safe.' She stroked the tiny cat curled up asleep in her palm. 'So tell no one and all will be well.'

I nodded. If Madam Sima said so, this was how it must be.

She smiled. 'Now, run home with some pickled cherries.'

I can't recall how I found my way home, or if my mother was pleased with the cherries. But I can still picture that tiny cat and recall the hollow in my stomach when I found its basket empty three days later.

Summer turned to autumn and the dank days of winter. I stayed in school for half a chime each day after the others left. Madam Sima told my parents I was clever enough to apply to the Horned God's school. She would prepare me for the priestly tutors' examination.

She told me not one in a thousand can draw imagination into reality. First she challenged me to make everyday things like bricks and chairs. I was a biddable child and did as she asked. So she challenged me to create a blooming rose. I never thought I would master that but eventually I did. Gradually I became proficient at making creatures, mostly birds which no one would remark on if they escaped.

Thankfully I never woke up to find some nightmare become reality by my bed. Madam Sima taught me meditations to clear my mind before sleeping.

I proved particularly good at unmaking things. Perhaps because the more skilfully I shaped birds, the less I liked doing so. I would unmake them as soon as the sheen on their feathers stilled, before they could look at me.

Once I mastered the challenges of this strange power, its thrill receded. Madam Sima was adamant I tell no one and I dared not disobey her. Besides, I knew children made outsiders of people they thought too different, too strange. I didn't want to find myself friendless. As I grew older, I saw adults had their own fears and prejudices and I didn't want to end up chained in the madhouse.

Madam Sima told me time and again I must do my duty if I was ever called upon. I never questioned that but daydreams of saving the city from some peril I took care not to imagine too precisely faded after a while.

I had scant time for such fancies because Madam Sima was serious about presenting me to the priests. She taught me history and mathematics and natural philosophy and I was enthralled. The tutors at the Horned God's school recognised my enthusiasm when my father took me to face their questions. So when Seppin and Rachik took up their chisels, I was learning geometry and metallurgy. By the time Marlil joined the workshop, I was apprenticed to a master builder whose magnificent many-windowed house overlooked the Golden Goddess's own temple.

I saw Madam Sima occasionally on visits home. Once, I brought a girl to meet my mother. Falling into conversation with us, Madam Sima drew me aside to warn against plucking trinkets out of the air to impress my sweetheart. She need not have worried. It had honestly never occurred to me.

The next time I went home Mother told me Madam Sima had died in her sleep. I grieved for her and life went on.

The call came on a summer's day. Having long since left masonry and mortar for the lofty heights of the drawing house, I was calculating the width of beams for the new ropemakers' hall. Hearing boots on the stairs, I looked up. Instead of some guild messenger, I saw a youth barely old enough to shave but wearing fur-trimmed velvets.

'Thian Hindrie?'

'Good day.' I rose from my stool and bowed. He could only have come from one of my master's richest clients.

'Madam Sima told you your duty.' The young man stretched out his hand and an azure butterfly coalesced out of nothing. 'We need you.'

I watched the butterfly soar up to the attic's skylights. 'The city's threatened?'

My master was alert to every whisper carried up and down the great rivers. I'd heard nothing.

'In a manner of speaking.' The youth's face gave nothing away. 'Come with me.'

He was ordering, not inviting me.

My throat tightened. 'My master—'

'Will be thrilled that you're summoned to the palace.' His smile wasn't reassuring. 'Appalled if you demur.'

He was noble, he spoke with Madam Sima's authority and he was right. My master would insist I go. So I followed the youth down the stairs and we crossed the cobbled square in front of the Golden Goddess's temple.

'Who are you?'

'Eion.' He slid me a sideways glance. 'The Margrave of Jedfal's third son but that's not important.'

I wondered about that, as we walked along the broad avenue to the pleasure gardens beyond the palace. He headed for a distant summer house, shuttered up and draped with tarpaulins.

'Thian, good day.' As my companion unlocked a side door and ushered me in, a man turned from examining a mouldering fresco. Grizzled and weather-beaten, his shirt was creased and he smelled of stables.

'Good day.' I glanced at my companion.

Eion was locking the door. 'This is Alace, the queen's groom.'

I swallowed. 'How may I serve?'

Alace thrust his hands into the pockets of his stained leather breeches. 'By shaping a facsimile of the paramount king.'

'Treason!' I spat.

'I'm glad that's your first thought.' He smiled without humour. 'But no, we are all loyal.'

Eion spoke up. 'The king has been stabbed.'

'Silence.' Alace scowled at him.

'Forgive me.' The youth ducked his head, meek as milk. When his rank entitled him to have the groom horse-whipped for such impertinence.

'Madam Sima told you we defend the city.' Alace challenged me with a penetrating stare. 'These days our enemies don't send armies. They send spies and assassins and one has left the king for dead.'

'Who will stand as regent for Queen Giseri?' I was aghast. 'Prince Perisen is so young.'

Would Eion's father stand behind the throne? The other margraves wouldn't like that.

'There will be no regency because the king will recover, the goddess be praised,' Alace said firmly.

'Barely ten people know of the attack,' Eion added.

Alace nodded. 'The queen and the royal children have been sent away—'

'Princess Kemeti has toad-pox.' I remembered one of my fellow draughtsmen mentioning it a few days since, prompting us all to reminiscences of the tiresome childhood ailment.

'Quite so,' agreed Alace. 'As far as the world and his wife are concerned, the king has also succumbed. Unfortunate but no cause for alarm.'

I was confused. 'Then why—'

'Whoever wants the king dead will spread the word he's been stabbed.' Alace looked murderous. 'To kill that rumour, he must be seen. Thankfully, being seen at a distance will suffice.' His eyes strayed towards the main palace. 'His doctor will permit him to appear on the eastern balcony to greet the midsummer sun. Alone, naturally, to avoid an epidemic laying the whole court low. Then he'll join his family to convalesce in peace.'

That made sense. Toad-pox is virulently contagious and while not life-threatening, adult sufferers were left exhausted. Whenever the king returned, no one would wonder if he looked thin and weary. Provided he survived his wound.

'Who did this?' My mouth was dry.

'That's not your concern,' Eion snapped.

Alace looked at me, unblinking. 'Shape us a kingly puppet to walk from his majesty's apartments to the balcony, to smile and wave at his subjects and depart in a closed carriage.'

'At the queen's command?' I was still struggling to believe all this.

'Succeed, and you will be hired to rebuild this pavilion.' Eion waved a hand at the crumbling plaster. 'The first of many such commissions. This time next year, you'll have the coin to set up your own business and to wed in fine style.'

So he knew about Meriah. We had hopes of marriage within five years if I prospered.

'What if I can't?' I asked hoarsely.

'You can.' Alace was unyielding.

'In three days?' I shook my head.

'You're saying you won't?' Eion raised his brows. 'Then your promising career will founder on such a scandal—'

'Enough.' Alace's hand cut him short. 'We only ask that you try. I'm confident you'll succeed, given what Sima told me. If you cannot—' he shrugged. 'You cannot.'

'If you cannot, every margrave in the sixteen cities will fasten on rumours that the king is dying. Half will start calculating their chances of ascending to paramount rule,' Eion said savagely. 'We needn't fear upland horsemen or raiders from the marshes if we start fighting amongst ourselves.'

Civil war had ravaged the peace of the realm during the last regency and I had to keep faith with Madam Sima.

'I can try,' I said hesitantly.

'Good.' Alace momentarily betrayed his relief. 'Eion will see you have all that you need.'

'What?' I didn't understand.

'You'll stay here till it's over.' The groom walked to the door.

As I stood like a sun-addled fool, he left, locking the door behind him.

I looked at Eion. He had a key.

'Don't be a fool.' He twitched back his scarlet cloak to show his sword. 'Do this and you'll be well rewarded. Turn stubborn and we'll ruin you.'

I rubbed my face. 'I can't stay here. I'll be missed.'

'I've left word that you and I are surveying a project on my father's estates.'

Abruptly I realised Alace hadn't answered my question. 'Are we doing the queen's bidding?'

Eion shook his head. 'No one knows about this but you, me, Alace, the king's physician and his majesty's valet.'

Was it treason? I could only hope not. Would they reward me? Perhaps. Eion was certainly sincere in his threats to ruin me. So I tried. What else could I do?

That first day I made and unmade four hopeless puppets that sagged and collapsed.

Eion wasn't impressed. 'I thought you were an architect.'

'If it's so easy, do it yourself,' I snapped.

But his words prompted a thought as I unmade the fifth shapeless manikin sprawled on the dusty tiles. 'Get me paper and charcoal.'

He left me locked in. I examined the shuttered windows while he was gone. I could have smashed my way free. But Alace had known Madam Sima and she'd said this call would come. Besides, the challenge was beginning to intrigue me.

Eion returned with parchment, pen and ink. I searched my memory for everything the Horned God's priests had taught me of anatomy. Medicine was merely one of the mysteries they safeguarded in his name.

A maidservant brought us food and a lamp. There were tables and chairs upstairs. Later she returned with blankets and pillows. I don't know what Alace told her and I didn't ask. I was too busy thinking.

Only a fool builds a house without foundations, without load-bearing walls, rafters and trusses to support the roof. By the time the light faded, I knew what to try next.

When Eion opened his eyes in the morning, he yelled and scrambled to his feet, shirt flapping around his bare backside. I laughed, remembering Seppin and the frog.

'What's that?' He dragged on his breeches.

'Scaffolding.'

More precisely, it was an approximation of a skeleton. I hunkered down to contemplate the manikin's feet. Remaking those to my satisfaction, I shaped its knees and hips and worked my way upwards.

The next puzzle was making the thing move. Levers and pulleys. Mechanical advantage. I used such things without thinking on a building project.

'Eion, take off your shirt and your breeches.'

Thankfully he was well-enough muscled for me to see what I needed. Though I don't know what the maid thought when she brought us our lunch.

Drawing pale substance out of the air, shaping it with my fingers like clay, I spent the rest of the day carefully crafting a bloodless semblance of flesh.

'It looks like a flayed carcass.' Eion shivered as the manikin finally lurched across the room. 'And moves like a drunken whore.'

'Madam Sima said function follows form.'

Maybe Eion didn't know that, if he could only make butterflies. Whenever I'd made a bird well enough, it had always known how to fly. I could only hope this simulacrum would walk like a man when I'd finished it.

I yawned. A day hauling stone on a building site couldn't have tired me more. 'I don't suppose it'll try to leave in the night but you had better keep watch.'

My bed was all the cosier, knowing he was sitting vigil in the dark with my uncanny creation.

Alace came to see our progress. The manikin was smooth as a waxen image once I had laid a skin over the underlying workings.

'Well done,' he approved.

'I don't know what the king looks like close to,' I warned.

'What about clothes?' Eion asked.

Alace nodded. 'I'll see to it.'

He came back the following morning with brocade doublet and breeches, silk stockings and shoes.

'Do we dress it?' Eion was becoming ever more nervous around the manikin.

'Let's try.' His unease perversely calmed my own misgivings.

It proved disturbingly easy. As I lifted its hand, the creation held itself ready. I slid on a sleeve and it lowered its arm without needing my touch. When I knelt and raised its foot, it kept its balance as I rolled on the stockings.

'What about the face?' Eion demanded harshly.

'Here.' Alace produced a miniature portrait, oils on an ivory oval.

I hesitated. I'd never tried shaping something to a specific resemblance. 'How is the king?'

'Holding his own.' Alace looked grim. 'Rumour's running rife. He must be seen by the populace tomorrow.'

'I'll do my best.' It was all I could say.

As I summoned up hair to clothe the smooth head, I concentrated on the rich chestnut of the portrait, just as I had imagined the purple-shot black of a gable crow's wing. Smoothing colour into the face, I shaped the king's angular nose with my mind as much as my hands. Deft strokes of my fingers drew his brows and his beard.

It took me the rest of the day, with any number of false starts. Eion and Alace examined my efforts from all angles, interrupting to object or correct me. Initially I couldn't amend any mistake, forced to return to that pallid blankness. Gradually I learned how to make changes, crudely at first, then with growing subtlety. The last of the summer twilight was fading when Alace finally pronounced himself satisfied.

'No,' Eion said suddenly. 'It's not right.'

Trembling with fatigue, I rounded on him. 'If you think—'

He stepped back, hands raised. 'He's supposed to have toad-pox.'

It took me a moment to understand. I struggled to recall the pustules my brothers and I had scratched, twenty and more years ago. Slowly, I raised them on the manikin's face.

'Good.' Alace approved

'Goddess!' Eion knocked over a chair

As I touched the creature's cheek it opened its eyes. Brown, just like the king's.

The breath froze in my throat. I hadn't done that. Blood pounded in my head and I stumbled backwards, dizzy.

Alace guided me to the chair as Eion retrieved it. The creature's vacant gaze followed me.

'Close your eyes!' My voice broke on the command as my knees buckled. 'Face the wall!'

To my relief, it turned around.

'Goddess,' Eion breathed.

'I'll be glad when tomorrow's over.' Even Alace's composure was shaken. 'Right, get some sleep. We must get it to his majesty's apartments before the dawn chimes.'

He left me and Eion looking numbly at each other.

'Stay awake till midnight and then rouse me,' he said abruptly.

I nodded. There was no way I'd sleep without someone keeping watch over the creature either.

Alace appeared at first light with the yawning maidservant bringing hot water. She fetched bread and meat and warm spiced ale while Eion and I washed and shaved. Alace produced clean clothes for us; maroon liveries like the one he wore.

'Has it moved?' He studied the creature as we dressed.

'Not yet.'

As I spoke, it stirred.

Alace threw me a hooded cloak. 'Hide its face.'

Steeling myself, I draped the heavy cloth around its shoulders. As it looked at me, I saw its eyes were no longer so vacant. Was there was comprehension behind that gaze now?

I hid my unease with a curt order. 'Follow me.'

I followed Alace and it followed me. Eion brought up the rear.

Alace led us quickly to the palace and in through a servants' entrance. Back stairs and uncarpeted passageways took us to a plain door where a stern-faced man in doctor's robes waited. Silent, he unlocked the door and ushered us into an antechamber hung with ornate portraits. We must be in the king's apartments.

'Remove the cloak,' Alace ordered.

I stepped forward but the creature was already throwing back the hood. As it untied the cloak, it looked faintly puzzled.

Function follows form. It looked like a man. Could it begin to think like one? How quickly?

Alace took the cloak and looked the creature in the eye. 'Go with this man.' He pointed to the doctor.

The creature looked at me, like a hound unsure of its master's wishes when another voice gives it commands.

I cleared my throat. 'Go on.'

The doctor led the manikin out into a richly carpeted hallway. Alace disappeared though a side door.

'Come on.' Eion ducked his head, hands folded, every measure the humble lackey.

I followed his example and when the doctor and the creature halted, we both hurried to throw open the double doors ahead. I saw a wide window open from floor to ceiling on the far side of the room.

The doctor didn't seem to find the manikin disconcerting. He led it out onto the balcony. 'Stand and wave and smile.'

It nodded, walking through the lace curtains fluttering in the breeze. A great cheer went up from the crowds gathered on the parade ground below. I had often stood there, at midsummer and midwinter, when the nobles left their upstream estates to mingle with artisans and merchants and all the countless lesser folk who thronged the alleys and crowded tenements of the dockside quarters. The whole city celebrated the peace secured by the benevolent rule of the paramount kings.

Sooner than I had imagined but not so quickly as to prompt discontent below, the doctor urged the creature back inside.

'Where will the carriage—'

As I turned to Eion, a man rushed into the room. He wore the same maroon livery as us. Then I saw the flash of steel. I lunged for him but Eion tripped me. I scrambled up, torn between punching Eion or seizing this newcomer. Too late. The assassin plunged his knife into the manikin's chest.

It staggered and recovered its balance. Puzzled, it tilted its head, frowning. Dumbfounded, the attacker stabbed again. The blow was equally ineffective. Ripping his blade free he looked incredulously at the shining steel, unstained by blood.

Eion moved, twisting the assassin's hand so viciously he dropped the dagger. Wrenching the man's arm behind his back, he forced him face down to the floor.

'Get him on his back.' The doctor dug in a pocket.

'Help me!' Eion glared at me as the assassin struggled.

I kicked the knife out of reach and we rolled the writhing man over. Eion pinned his arms and I leaned on his legs.

'Do you recognise him?' The king stood in the doorway.

At his side Alace gripped a sword. 'No, majesty.'

The king didn't look like a man who'd been stabbed. Though the toad-pox story was true, judging by the scars on his drawn face.

Looking from the king to the manikin, the assassin gaped, astonished.

The doctor seized his chance to thrust something into his mouth. The assassin would have spat it out but the doctor's strong hands held his jaw shut, long fingers pinching his nostrils closed for good measure.

The man struggled in vain. A few moments later, he lay

limp. Eion stood up.

I did the same. 'Is he dead?'

'He'll wake,' the doctor assured me. 'Ready to tell all he knows.'

The king entered the room and walked slowly around his counterfeit. The creature regarded him with amiable interest.

'Astonishing,' he marvelled. 'You made this?'

'Only to serve,' I mumbled, bowing low.

The king nodded before turning to Alace. 'See this vermin is carried below and questioned. I shall join the queen and tell her all is well.' He favoured us all with a charming smile and departed.

The doctor followed, pausing on the threshold. 'Clear up. No one must know.'

As the door closed, I looked at the unconscious assassin. 'He knows about the creature.'

Eion laughed callously. 'You think he'll tell anyone?'

Alace retrieved the fallen dagger from beneath a chair. 'A gallows in the cellars will silence him once he's given up his paymasters.'

I didn't want to think about that. 'You said the king had been stabbed.'

'That was their plan.' Alace tossed the dagger into the air and caught it. 'We needed to know if you knew anything of it before we brought you into this masquerade.'

'You suspected me?' I was horrified.

'No.' Eion shrugged. 'We don't take any chances though.'

'We've let the rumour spread through a few selected courtiers.' Alace closed the windows to the balcony. 'We're watching to see who's insufficiently surprised.'

Eion nodded. 'And for anyone expecting some calamity today.'

'Of those few who knew the king would be making this unannounced appearance.' Alace smiled coldly.

I saw the manikin was looking from one to the other as they spoke.

'You had to lure the assassin,' I realised, 'but you couldn't put the king at risk.'

'Thank you for your service.' Alace smiled. 'You'll be well rewarded. Now, unmake it, quickly.'

'What?' Incredibly, I hadn't thought beyond making the creature. The intensity of the task had consumed me.

'You must unmake it,' Eion insisted.

How could I have been so foolish? 'Of course.'

'No.'

In that single utterance I heard the creature's confusion, its fear and defiance. Growing intelligence shone in its eyes.

'Unmake it!' Alace snapped.

The creature shot him an angry look. Its glance took in his sword and the door beyond.

I closed my eyes and tried to imagine the creature pale and featureless. But when I looked once again, it was still there, unchanged.

'No,' it said defiantly. Lifting a hand to its cheek, it wiped away the pox marks I had raised there.

'Kill it.' Alace threw me the assassin's dagger.

I caught it instinctively before protesting. 'No.'

'You're the only one who can.' Eion was barring its way to the window, a dagger I hadn't known he carried in his hand. 'It can't attack its maker.'

'Not yet,' warned Alace. 'It'll soon break free of you.'

A bird loose amid the flocks that roosted in the city's towers and bridges was one thing. A man wearing the king's face, something that wasn't even a real man wandering the streets? That couldn't be permitted.

Besides, the creature was frightening me now. I wanted to get rid of it, to have all evidence of what I had done obliterated.

'Stand still.'

I walked slowly forward. The creature struggled to raise its hands. I saw it couldn't ward me off.

'A single blow suffices, provided you truly intend to kill it.' Eion moved to stand behind me.

'Go on!' Alace's shout spurred me to action.

I thrust the assassin's knife into its belly. It gasped just like a man of true flesh and blood. Tears brimmed in its brown eyes.

'I beg you—'

Before it could plead further, it vanished, gone as though it had never existed.

I collapsed to the floor, dizzy and nauseous and darkness claimed me.

I came to my senses tucked in a bed. Evening sun slipped through the narrow window. From the slope of the ceiling I guessed this was some servant's garret. Trying to move, I found I was as weak as a man after ten days of fever.

'Thank the goddess.'

I rolled my head on the pillow to see Eion sitting on a stool by the door.

'How—?' My mouth tasted stale.

'Three days.' Eion shrugged. 'As long as you took to make it.'

'You knew,' I accused him weakly. 'That's why you didn't do it.'

'Would you have tried, if you'd known?' I hadn't seen Alace, slumped in a chair beyond the foot of the bed. He rose and came over. 'Well done, Thian. You even passed the final test, the hardest one of all.'

'What—?' What else had Madam Sima not told me?

'You killed it, thankfully.' Eion rose to his feet. 'If you couldn't bring yourself to do it, I'd have had to kill you.'

The door closed behind him.

'Well done,' Alace repeated, looking down at me. 'Now

you're truly one of us.'

They cosseted me for six days as I gradually recovered my strength. I took the king's commission to rebuild the summer house back to my master, along with assurances of work for the Margrave of Jedfal that were promptly honoured. I was certified as a master by the masons' guild by midwinter and married Meriah on the first day of spring.

Every morning, my first thought is still terror: that this will be the day the call comes again.

JULIET E. MCKENNA

Remembrance

I had just turned seventeen. This was my first midwinter in the capital not staying in my parents' house, my days filled by their obligations to entertain, with those parties where my father learned of the latest political intrigues while my mother assessed aristocratic marriages likely to blossom in the spring.

Before I left our country estate, my elder brothers hinted at riper entertainments open to men of rank and fortune. Negotiation houses would offer their prettiest, freshest girls in tantalizing gossamer. Multifaceted spinning tops would whirl across the gaming tables, fortunes won or lost as they toppled this way or that. Our name would secure my admittance to private cellars stocking the finest wines, where noble decorum was left at the door along with sword and dagger. Where nevertheless, my brothers promised, unobtrusive men with faces like weathered oak would ensure no harm came to Eion of Jedfal, third son of so influential a Margrave.

Yet I was sitting in this icy gatehouse without even a candle to lighten the darkness. The meagre brazier offered only a sullen red glow and with the door standing wide, it did little to raise the temperature. All it did was strengthen the stable stink of my companion's battered boots and his filthy breeches.

'Not what you were expecting, laddie?' He chuckled, huddling deeper into his heavy quilted coat. 'Never fear. You'll prove more valuable to the king than either of your brothers, even if no one ever knows it.'

Would that prove some consolation? While they were honoured in turn as Jedfal's heir and as our family's representative among the kingdom's cavalry officers? While I remained the dreamer, the reader, my expectations modest?

'Must we stay here all night?' I looked through the open door, past the crescent moon crowning the statue of the Horned God. The real moon, gibbous and golden, crept across the cloudless sky.

'That all depends.'

The first fireflowers bloomed above the rooftops. I went outside to get a better look. Southwards across the river, over in the heart of the city, the great square in front of the palace would be thronged with crowds gasping and cheering at the alchemists' artistry.

Prudent men and women loudly proclaimed their loyalty. The king celebrated more than mere midwinter, even if no one spoke of it. It was under cover of these festivities that his grandsire had overthrown a treacherous regency to reclaim his birthright, saving the realm from civil war.

Here though, all was dark and silence. Whoever lived in these mean houses around the burial ground had gone to celebrate the turn of the year with more favoured friends and family. Only the Horned God's statue kept us company, keeping his secrets as close as ever.

I shivered, and not just from the frost. We all hear whispers about the mysteries the masked priests guard. I had never imagined the truth so recently revealed to me.

'Alace—' I began.

He laid a bony hand on my fur-clad arm. 'See there?'

I squinted into the shadows, still dazzled by the fireflowers.

'There!' The groom pointed, insistent.

I saw a translucent shape drifting between stone pillars marking graves.

'Will it—?' Apprehension choked me.

'That all depends,' Alace sounded grim. 'Come on!'

I stumbled on reluctant feet. But I couldn't let him face this horror alone. Though I was more callow youth than mighty warrior, he was half a head shorter than me and as slightly built as the race-rider he had once been, proudly wearing the queen's sash. I gripped my blade's hilt and felt better for it.

We took a fork in the cinder path. I nearly lost my footing on a patch of black ice. In these districts to the north of the rivers, the ground slopes so abruptly that even the dead rest at odd angles.

Alace grabbed my elbow to save me from a fall. Even through thick fur, his grip was brutal. He might be wiry but he could still curb a bolting horse.

'Thank you.' I rubbed the bruise.

'No need to whisper, lad. It can't hear us. Not yet anyway.' He peered through the shadows as we skirted a family plot.

Ahead, the misty shape stepped onto a moonlit path. For an instant, I could see the clutch of pillars behind it, clear as day. As my next breath shimmered in the air, the phantasm turned opaque.

Now it was a man. No greybeard, nor even some fellow still vigorous though his children were grown. He didn't look that much older than me.

'A young husband, or courting his bride to be.' Alace spoke more softly. 'See its footprints?'

My gaze followed his finger. Where the phantasm had reached the path, the frosted cinders lay undisturbed. Now footsteps appeared and I could hear the slow crunch of its boots.

I nodded hesitant understanding. 'It's a fetch?'

No longer some mere phantasm but a creature of solid heft and purpose; intent on finding whoever's inconsolable bereavement had brought it into being.

I frowned. 'It looks—'

I had heard the tales, as everyone does. Like anyone else with the least common sense, I dismissed stories of decaying corpses walking through burial grounds as fables for the witless.

'Whoever mourns him never saw him dead.' Alace was distantly sympathetic. 'This is how he's remembered.'

I swallowed hard. 'What must we do?'

'We can't let him leave.' Alace was gesturing me towards a different path so we would intercept the creature before it reached the gate. 'It would be good to learn his name though.'

I understood. If we knew who this man had once been, then we could discover whose grief had summoned the fetch. Even overwhelming anguish cannot spawn such a thing without some spark of magic to give it life.

'And then?' I had to ask.

Alace took a moment to answer. 'Most likely there'll only be a trace of magic deep within whoever mourns him. All we need do is soothe such festering sorrow to see an end of it.'

Who would offer such consolation? One of the nameless associates that Alace had hinted at several times? This magicians' cabal was intent on finding anyone with the talent to strike a magic spark, humble or high-born.

If that person's magic proved more than feeble instinct? They would be told, as I had been, that this unlooked-for talent compelled them to serve their king. That they must obey whoever came to train them, whatever their disparity of age or status. Just as I now obeyed this no-account groom, scrambling through a burial ground in the dead of night.

I had not been told what penalties I would face if I refused to do Alace's bidding. But it had been mentioned in passing that no magicians were tolerated outside the king's loyal cabal.

Alace shook my shoulder. 'Challenge the thing!'

I threw off my hesitation and stepped forward. Flinging back my fur cape revealed my sword.

'Halt and name yourself!'

I had ten generations of wealth and privilege to stiffen my backbone, even if my knees felt weak as water.

The fetch stopped and looked at me, bemused.

I laid a hand on my blade hilt. 'Give me your name, groundling!'

That was an undeserved insult. Moonlight picked out the detail of the man's velvet breeches and his polished boots. His long grey coat hung open over an embroidered waistcoat and a shirt with lace at the neck. A prosperous tradesman at very least, to be buried in such finery. Had he been wed in it?

The fetch slowly breathed a single word. 'Home.'

'Name yourself,' I demanded.

The fetch stared at me, uncomprehending. 'Home.'

'Where is your home?' I asked instead, my voice was tight with apprehension. 'Who do you seek? What is your name?'

'Who...?' The creature paused, seemingly lost in thought.

'Kill it,' Alace ordered abruptly. 'Before it gets any stronger. Before it begins to recall.'

A single thrust, fluid with a lifetime's training, drove my blade through its heart.

The fetch looked down at the shining steel piercing its chest. It seemed puzzled. Then it reached out and seized my hand, crushing my fingers so hard I feared the bones would crack.

I sank to my knees, gasping at the pain. Before I could think how to break its grip, the creature shoved me away. My sword slid free of its chest, unbloodied. How foolish to think a blade could kill it, when it wasn't even alive. But how was I supposed to stop it?

Sheathing my sword, I hurried to stand in its path. 'No. You may not leave here.'

'Home!' A glint of hostility in the fetch's eyes drove out its initial bemusement.

'You are dead.' I shook my head. 'To see you would terrify your loved ones beyond reason. You cannot wish for that.'

'You can't reason with the thing,' Alace snapped. 'It has no wits to understand you!'

As he spoke, the thing pushed me aside, as effortless as a child rejecting a toy.

'You have to stop it,' Alace warned.

Now I realised this was a test. What sanctions would I face if I failed?

My mouth dry, I hurried after the fetch as it strode down the slope towards the gate.

If it was dead, or indeed, had never truly lived, then no code of honour applied to our contest. Without a word of warning, I grasped its shoulders with both hands. Thrusting my booted foot between its legs, I tried my best approximation of a wrestling move that my soldier brother had taught me.

Taken unawares, the creature toppled to the ground, falling awkwardly and making no effort to save itself. For a moment it lay still, as if stunned.

I looked back up towards Alace, half hidden in a shadow. 'How do I—?'

The fetch grabbed my ankle. It pulled my foot out from under me. Arms flailing in a futile protest, I fell on top of it. Close as lovers, my cheek brushed against its own. The thing was as cold as the wintry earth but now I saw burning anger in its eyes.

I set my hands on the path to push myself up. It seized my wrists, quick as thought. The fetch threw me sideways, rolling over to crush me beneath its weight. It was no longer content to discard me.

That realisation terrified me. I was pinned, cinders digging into my back even through my thick fur cape. Whoever this man had been, he had been taller and more muscled than me.

I recalled my brothers saying all men have the same weaknesses, whatever their strengths. I couldn't have driven a knee into its groin if my life depended on it but I could still smash my forehead into its nose. I did so, with all my might. Only there was no crack of bone, no gush of blood. Its flesh was unyielding as wax.

If the fetch didn't recoil in pain, at least it was startled by this attack. In the instant I felt its surprise, I wrenched one hand free of the creature's grip and drove my fist into its ear.

We rolled down the slope, punching and kicking. My efforts were as ineffectual as a scrapping schoolboy's but every blow that the fetch landed on me raised a vicious bruise. A clout split my lip, the next blacked my eye. With sharp agonies in my chest I just prayed that my ribs were still whole.

I didn't dare let up. If I did, the thing would either kill me, or toss me aside to escape into the city, leaving me to face Alace's wrath. I couldn't say which prospect terrified me more.

But all my resolve couldn't outweigh the fetch's single-minded purpose. Its punches set my head ringing with pain, sent vomit surging up my gorge to burn my throat. My retaliation grew more feeble. Clotting blood closed my eyes.

It landed one last blow with a feral growl and then I heard the fetch get to its feet, its boots crunching on the cinders. The sound faded as I lay limp as a soiled rag.

'On your feet, laddie.'

I expected Alace's fury. I truly feared he would leave me to succumb to the cold. A tragedy soon to be forgotten, as befitted a minor nobleman foolish enough to fall prey to footpads.

'It fought me,' I protested stupidly.

'You attacked it.' Alace's tone fell somewhere between sympathy and amusement. 'It only did what came naturally.'

That fired my resentment. I struggled to rise, getting as far as sitting up. 'You said I had to kill it.' I spat blood and phlegm. 'So how do I do that?'

Alace hauled me up, surprising me with his strength. 'For a start, you don't help it become more real.'

I resisted his efforts to go down the path, turning to glare at him instead. 'What?'

He stared back at me, unblinking. 'What did your uncle tell you?'

'Precious little,' I snarled.

What he had told me, I mostly ignored. Who paid any heed to the Margrave of Jedfal's notoriously drunken brother? A fifth son? When his noble parents so hoped for a daughter to adorn their house till she could be married to best advantage. The Sun Goddess be thanked the Jedfal estates were rich enough to withstand such a misfortune.

I had heard all these whispers as an unobtrusive child.

51

I had wondered if this was to be my fate. Now I knew we shared a very different destiny.

'What did he tell you?' Alace recalled my wandering wits from this reverie.

'He said—' I fumbled a kerchief from my breeches' pocket and wiped blood out of my eyes.

He'd said he knew I wasn't lying, when I woke the house with my screams. When I swore the Marsh Pirate King had been standing at the foot of my bed, as vivid as he had been in my dreams. I had evaded everyone's attention to spend that long rainy day playing with the maps and figurines in my father's library, even though they were only supposed to be used to train my brothers in the arts of battle.

Best not to tell anyone else though, Uncle Pafor had said, when he slipped into my room with a comforting bowl of sweetmeats, after I heard the half-hearted protests of the maidservant guarding my door dissolve into giggles. I had been wide awake, lying face down to ease the pain in my strap-thrashed buttocks.

Best to keep it our secret not to worry my mother. When the time came, Uncle Pafor promised, he would take me to people who understood such things, who would explain why this was best not spoken of. Meantime, if it happened again—

'He said I must disbelieve my own eyes,' I said through gritted teeth. 'I must learn to distinguish between what can and what cannot be. Then what cannot be will disappear.'

Thankfully he was proved right, on those few occasions when I had seen half-imagined shapes sneaking through the shadows.

'Quite so.' Alace still sounded sympathetic, provoking me all the more. 'Only you treated the fetch as though it were flesh and blood. You engaged it in conversation. You tried to spill its blood. Then you tried to beat it into submission. But every blow you landed, everything you've suffered at its hands has simply made it stronger.'

I realised the extent of my folly. I had done better as a

terrified child, hiding under the blankets to deny what I had glimpsed out of the window.

'All bristling like a fighting cock.' Alace chuckled. 'So proud, so bold, one of the kingdom's secret defenders. You forgot everything I've been telling you.'

'We can discuss my failings later.' I took a deep breath of the cold night air and was relieved to feel bruises rather than breaks to my ribs. 'We still have to catch the thing.'

Because if we didn't, I couldn't imagine Alace's mysterious cabal would give me a moment's more thought, beyond doing whatever they must to make certain I couldn't betray them.

'Good lad,' Alace approved.

I forced myself to walk faster. As long as I was moving, my bruised limbs couldn't stiffen. We soon reached the gates to the burial ground, where my newfound determination faltered.

'Which way did the creature go?'

'There.'

I didn't waste time asking how Alace knew. He could show me that trick later, once I redeemed myself. We headed down the street and cut through a narrow alley, the frost subduing its stink.

Now our path followed a cross-cut lane. This time, as Alace indicated another alley, I saw a dark figure striding out ahead.

'That's him.' I bit my tongue. 'I mean, that's the fetch.'

My apprehension rose along with the sounds of revelry growing louder. Alace broke into a run, forcing me to jog beside him. Despite all our efforts, we couldn't catch up before the fetch turned out of the alley's far end though.

I halted, appalled. 'Where is it?'

This broad thoroughfare was thronged with people. Now I recalled Alace's earlier tutelage. Every glance that saw the fetch, from every passer-by who believed it was flesh and blood, would strengthen the creature's presence in this realm. Now it would be all the harder to send the thing back to the realm of imagination that spawned such monsters.

'Look for the unreal,' Alace commanded.

I closed my eyes, trembling, with apprehension, with exhaustion and the Moon God only knew what confused emotions.

Opening my eyes, I concentrated on the street. The inert, the unthinking, the buildings with their bright windows and fire-baskets warming their thresholds, all those remained. The crowds had melted away.

Everything truly living vanished once one mastered looking into the imagined realm. One only saw the unreal creatures. Alace had been training me in the stable yard where he tolerated a few harmless creatures drawn into reality by someone's unconscious intent. I had idly wondered who dreamed up the cat-faced gargoyle hunting corn-finches round the dung heap.

This fetch was far more perilous than some tiny gargoyle. I had to find it.

'Don't get distracted,' Alace warned at my shoulder.

'Don't worry,' I said curtly.

In truth, that was a timely caution. I could see faint shapes like wisps of rising river mists. Where my gaze lingered, they swirled and coalesced. A maiden? A child? I felt their longing to understand what had drawn them here, hovering on the edge of consciousness. I hastily looked away, searching for the ominous bulk of the fetch.

'There it is!' Stepping forward, I immediately collided with a solid stevedore, enjoying his holiday from dockside labours.

'Watch your step!' He shoved me away, affronted.

'Sorry, friend, the boy can't hold his liquor.' A coin glinted between Alace's fingers before he clasped the stevedore's hands in a gesture of goodwill. 'You drink the next one while I get him sobered up.'

'Good luck to you.' Laughing, the man went on his way.

'Always look back into reality before you take a step,' Alace advised.

I licked the oozing split in my lip. 'Indeed.'

That was easier said than done. Alace could switch between seeing the real and the unreal with the blink of an eye. I found altering my perceptions as dizzying as standing on top of one of the mighty bridge towers.

I swallowed my nausea. Now I knew what I was looking for, I could pick out the fetch striding through the crowd.

'Come on.' Now Alace's slight build was more help than hindrance as he slid between the merrymakers.

I followed, almost treading on his heels, before the gaps he found in the crowd closed behind him.

Sooner than I thought possible, the fetch was only a few strides ahead of us.

'Hey, friend!' Alace clapped a hand on its shoulder.

'Wha—'

As it turned with a half-formed question, Alace threw himself at its chest.

'Into the alley!'

I flung myself at the creature. Taking it unawares, our weight together was just enough to force it back into a narrow entry between two tall houses.

'You!' The fetch lunged at me, fury and loathing in its eyes.

'No you don't.' Alace slapped its face.

I expected the fetch to swat him aside like a horsefly. Instead, I saw his hand pass clean through its chin.

The thing recoiled, flinging up an arm to hide its face. Alace pursued it with open-handed blows, slapping its hands, its shoulders. Every time his thin fingers raked deep into the creature's substance. Every blow dragged its outline askew.

'Come on!' he shouted exasperated, 'or this will take all night.'

Now I saw him tearing handfuls of shadow out of the

fetch. As he tossed them into the darkness, they dissolved into nothingness. After all, it wasn't real, was it?

I ran up to begin punching holes in the thing myself. Satisfaction warmed me. This was some small payback for the beating I had suffered. But in the instant I thought that, my swollen knuckles jarred against the fetch's chest.

Its gaze locked with mine. 'Home,' it pleaded, despairing.

'Don't listen,' Alace warned, menacing.

I hardened my heart. This insubstantial shadow before me was mere fog and delusion. It had no more voice than the breezes wailing round these alleys. Scatter this fetch to the four winds and that would be an end of all the night's confusion and humiliation.

Sooner than I imagined, the creature was gone.

Alace grinned at me, breathing hard. 'Well done.'

'Truly?' I could hardly believe it.

'Barely.' Alace was already walking back to the busy street. 'It must have been getting very close to its maker this time.'

'This time?' Now I grabbed his arm in a vice-like grip as we stepped into the light cast by a hanging lantern.

'It's walked before.' He looked at me unrepentant. 'We always keep watch at Midwinter, for that one and a number of other such fetches. Midwinter's a time for remembrance as well as celebration and it's the anniversary of a good many deaths. Where one mourner's summer loss might raise a phantasm to vanish with the sunrise, at this season such a thing can draw strength from all the grief in the air.' He glanced back down the alleyway. 'As far as we can tell, our dead friend fell in the battles for the regency. But we've yet to find out who lost him, lover or husband or brother. So we can do nothing to lay the fetch to rest.'

'So long ago and still mourned so fiercely?' I shook my head, disbelieving. 'And most likely a traitor, living on this side of the river!'

But Alace was shaking his head. 'We should all be so lucky to be loved thus, to be remembered with such passion.' He sighed. 'Every year we wonder if it will walk again. Whoever grieves for him surely cannot be much longer for this world.'

'You've never let it walk all the way home?' I could have bitten my tongue but the question was out so I persisted. 'You'd find out who summoned it up soon enough that way.'

Alace shook his head. 'If that person laid eyes on it, we'd never be rid of the thing. What price our secrets then, once folk start asking how the dead can come back from the grave?'

I had no answer to that, so asked a question of my own. 'What now?'

Alace grinned ominously. 'First we'll clean you up so no one starts asking awkward questions. Then we'll find a tavern and empty our purses on its finest liquors. I'll see you dead drunk before you sleep tonight, laddie. I want to be certain that fetch won't find some way back here through your dreams, to strangle you in your bed.'

That was a truly terrifying prospect. Thankfully, Alace was as good as his word. I remember nothing more of that Midwinter beyond the miseries of the morning after.

Truth, Lies and Consequences

Which falsehood should we tell? Two masked and black-cloaked priests sworn to serve the Horned God, the keeper of secrets.

Everyone was watching Josan, on one knee to examine the pitiful corpse. A balding man lay with skinny arms and legs sprawled. Blood soaked his tidy jerkin, shirt and breeches.

Josan wore the silvered visage of the Lord of Night, guardian of the dead. He would be trusted without question by this small crowd gawping at the corpse in the alley. My novice's mask was merely carved wood.

'His killer used a knife,' he said heavily.

Ragged wounds would have made our task much easier. We could have blamed the city's feral dogs. They could hardly protest.

'He was murdered!'

I searched the crowd but couldn't see who had spoken.

'Not necessarily.' Josan rose and turned quickly. Men and women shrank from the dark swirl of his cloak. 'Who knows his name? What manner of man was he?'

A plausible tale of quarrels over money or bitter rivalry in trade or love could suggest manslaughter in the heat of a moment. That would be an unhelpful complication. While we had no intention of telling the truth, we couldn't allow an innocent to be accused of this crime.

One of the Justiciar's constables cleared his throat. The oldest man of the trio who had stumbled across the body and sent word to the Moon God's temple. Broken veins threaded his face after years of patrolling these streets from winter's freezing depths to summer's scorching height. 'We don't know him.'

'No reason why you should!'

'He's a good man!'

His words prompted a torrent of replies.

'He's Ornas Rechel.'

'A tailor. He lives on Ward Street.'

'Holy Mother,' a woman wailed. 'Who will tell his wife?'

Josan clapped his gloved hands for silence. He nodded at the constables. 'Take him to the Crescent Moon Gate.'

The youngest sacrificed his cloak for a shroud and he and his partner lifted the corpse. The grey haired constable led them away. The crowd watched, wordless.

'We will tell the sisters at the local shrine,' Josan announced. 'They will break such dire news.'

The crowd nodded, reassured. The Sun Goddess's priestesses care for the living through every joy and sorrow.

Meantime, we must discover what killed the tailor. Josan led me swiftly through the streets. Some of the crowd trailed after us. More went about their business now that both temples and the Justiciary had taken charge.

In the heart of this city confined within twin rivers, the neighbourhood shrine was as cramped for space as the workshops surrounding it. Every building, sacred and secular, rose four storeys high with living quarters above business premises.

The circular shrine's door stood wide. The Sun Goddess's bronze statue on the right cradled a sheaf of wheat in her arms. We bowed to the Golden Mother whose sun is the source of all life and everything that sustains it. Josan tugged on the bell pull. Other folk could cross this threshold as they wished. We must wait for an invitation.

A novice priestess sat sewing in the entrance hall. Leaving her needlework on her stool, she came to the threshold.

'We wish to see Mother Aksarre.'

The girl bit her lip. 'She is very busy. Could Sister Risva help?'

'No.' Josan offered no more.

The novice squared her shoulders and went to knock on an inner door. A voice invited her within.

Scant moments later, a serenely mature woman appeared, sunburst pendant bright gold against her unbleached linen robe. Shooing the girl back to her sewing, she beckoned.

With the inner room's door closed behind us, Josan told her Master Rechel was dead. As we sat on visitors' stools and removed our masks, he gestured. 'This is Ulias, sworn to the Horned God half a year ago.'

Then he asked our most urgent question. 'Was there ever some hint that Rechel had magic? Could he have brought this on himself?'

'No.' Mother Aksarre resumed her seat behind the desk piled high with ledgers.

'What about quarrels?' Josan persisted. 'Some unjustified hatred against him?'

She shook her head. 'He was even-tempered and fair-dealing, in his business and with his family.'

Josan and I exchanged a glance. There's no gainsaying a local shrine's Mother. The priestesses have their fingers on every pulse within the city, from the midwives who deliver babies through the sisters who bank every household and business's coin to those who care for the indigent and aged. The Sun Goddess's daughters go everywhere and see everything.

Everything that exists in this realm and this reality, I mentally corrected myself. As with the Moon God's servants, few priestesses know that magic exists. There's rarely more than one such initiate with such dangerous knowledge in any neighbourhood shrine. I am still learning their names as I shadow Josan around the city.

Like him, like Mother Aksarre, I would combine my sacred duties with responsibilities secret from all but a few. The few whose magical talent had been discovered and whom the hidden guardians of these perilous mysteries judged suitable for conscripting into their ranks.

'Have you any idea what killed him?' She looked from Josan to me and back.

He shook his head. 'We had to say that his killer used a blade. Everyone will be flinching from shadows, imagining lurking cutthroats.'

Mother Aksarre grimaced and surprised me with a shrug. 'At least we won't see packs of nightmare hounds roaming the streets.'

Whatever my face betrayed, she saw it.

'You're still struggling with the paradoxes? You think we should tell everyone about the unseen realm? You think they would ignore it once they knew? That would ensure no one with a talent for magic would inadvertently draw imagined creatures into tangible reality?'

I held my unpainted mask tight on my cloaked knees. 'I'm trying to understand, Mother.'

She cocked her head, crowned with silvered braids. 'Before you joined the temple, were you ever asked not to take undue notice of someone's ridiculously large nose?'

'Forgive me, I don't follow—'

'Try to *not* think about something,' she invited. 'Try to *not* think about my novice's breasts when she escorts you out.'

'Mother—' I protested.

Josan laughed. 'She's right. Oh, I understand.' He turned serious. 'We all wonder, sooner or later, if bringing magic out of the darkness and into the sunlight wouldn't be the better path. But that bell could never be unrung.'

He looked down into the empty eyeholes of his own silvered mask. 'What then? Wouldn't everyone want to know if they had magical talent? Wouldn't everybody try to see into the unseen realm? What would happen to the unwary who succeeded, glimpsing the horrors lurking alongside the wonders? When those horrors saw them?'

I nodded. I still remembered the terror of seeing some fearful creature in the corner of my eye. Learning such phantasms weren't figments of my imagination was more frightening still.

'What would the foolish or malicious do?' Mother Aksarre asked tartly. 'Who learned that their talent for magic was strong enough to deliberately draw a monster from the unseen realm into tangible reality?'

'We have enough to do,' sighed Josan, 'dealing with manifestations from nightmares and dreams born of unconscious longings and hatreds. We'd face hundreds more such creatures.'

He looked at Mother Aksarre. 'If Master Rechel had no magic within him to create whatever killed him, where did it come from? If he had no enemies with an unsuspected talent and hatred fierce enough to spawn a monster? Who in this neighbourhood could summon something from the unseen realm strong enough, for long enough, to kill innocents?'

'I will make enquiries—'

A frantic hand hammered on the door. 'Mother!'

'Enter!'

It was the shapely novice. In an instant I realised I was looking at her breasts. I hastily donned my mask to hide my chagrined blush.

She dipped a swift curtsey. 'There's a constable — another dead man.'

'By your leave.' Masked once again, Josan didn't wait for Aksarre's dismissal, striding past the novice and out of the shrine.

The weathered constable stood beside the Sun Goddess's statue. 'Brother—'

'Show us.'

I followed, silent. This corpse lay some distance from the alley where Rechel had died. A younger man, slightly built, wearing an artisan's smock now stained with his life blood.'

'Do you know him?' Josan asked the constable.

There was no crowd, just a few onlookers aghast in the windows of nearby buildings. The other constables talked quietly to a man in a doorway.

One gory death offered guilty entertainment. Two murders hinted at danger for all the locals. Traders and workshops would be closing up early, everyone going home to lock their doors.

'No, but would his own mother recognise him?' The constable gestured at the man's brutally disfigured face.

'Ulias?' Josan looked over his shoulder. 'What do you see?'

The constable couldn't know what he meant. I drew a steadying breath and expanded my vision from the everyday world into the unseen realm.

The houses and cobbles were unchanged. Lifeless things exist in all realms. A few phantasms flickered and vanished; half-imagined creatures insubstantial even in this intangible world. The minimal talent creating them could safely be ignored.

I glanced at the open windows and doors. There were no witnesses in this unseen world. None of these onlookers had sufficient innate magic to make them manifest here, even unconsciously.

The dead man's presence proved this was no mundane slaying. If so, there'd be nothing to see. But death at the hands of some magical being drew him across the veil between the realms of existence. His murder was as gruesome and as tragic here as it was in the Golden Mother's sunlight.

I looked up and down the street and saw a shadow where an alley cut between two houses. Realising I had seen it, the creature stepped into the street. Mother Aksarre had mentioned nightmare hounds. Someone hereabouts must be truly terrified of dogs for their unspoken dread to create this beast.

It stood as tall at the shoulder as me, black hackles bristling with malice. Paws bigger than my outspread hand supported thick legs and a muscular body. Its head hung low, snarling jowls drawn back from white teeth as long as my thumb. Drooling, it had caught the scent of blood.

Not our killer but it could still be lethal. I summoned my magic. Mist swirled in front of the hound. As I focused, the pale vapour solidified. A bird hovered, twice as big as any fish eagle, with talons and a hooked beak ten times more vicious. Red flickered at its heart. In the next breath rich colour suffused it, paling to gold at its wingtips.

The hound snarled, rearing up. The bird bated angry wings and tore at its muzzle with razor sharp claws. The black beast wasn't deterred, leaping, jaws snapping. The bird pecked at its eyes. The hound recoiled but barely for an instant.

I gritted my teeth. The phoenix burst into flames. That sent the hound scrambling backwards, down its alley to disappear. I fought the temptation to send the phoenix to kill it once and for all.

No. The longer the bird endured, the greater the risk of it becoming a presence in the unseen realm which I couldn't dispel. It was already strong enough to soar into the sky, wheeling and screeching in triumph. I had used it too often as my familiar.

I focused my magic and searing flames consumed it. A drift of ash blew away on the wind.

'Are you all right?' Josan appeared, his hand on my forearm.

I blinked to shift my vision from magical sight to the tangible world. 'Yes, forgive me.'

'So much blood in a single day.' Josan looked ruefully at the constable.

The grey haired man nodded. 'It takes a while to get used to it.'

Josan beckoned to the younger constables. 'You can take him away.'

We waited until they departed.

'What did you see?' Josan asked in low tones.

I told him. 'What did I miss?'

I hadn't heard a word of their conversation while I focused on the unseen realm. I wouldn't have noticed someone in the tangible world coming up to cut my throat. Magic's hazards are many and varied.

'The tailor was killed late last night.' Josan retraced our steps. 'This silversmith was attacked on his way to work this morning.'

So dawn hadn't been enough to dispel the creature. 'How can we find it before dusk?'

If whatever emotion had spawned it sustained the unknown killer through another night, its ability to encroach on the tangible world would be significantly strengthened.

'We need to find out where their paths crossed.' I caught the flash of Josan's eyes behind his mask. 'The tailor and the silversmith.'

We tramped the streets for the rest of the day, visiting both bereaved households and then both men's places of work. We asked who each one had dealings with, daily, monthly or yearly.

We returned to Mother Aksarre. Had any of these men or women come to her notice in some way that hinted at magical talent? Where there was the faintest suspicion, we made further discreet enquiries.

Everyone dutifully answered us. Everyone always does when masked and black-cloaked priests come calling. Nothing we learned offered us anything helpful.

With dusk encroaching, the streets filled with weary men and women heading home. We contemplated a street corner tavern. The Harvest Moon's sign offered a pious nod to the Sun Goddess and the Lord of Night alike. More importantly we had discovered both murdered men quenched their working day's thirst here.

'In there.' Josan nodded and we slipped into an alley's shadows. Shedding our masks, we folded our cloaks into the cunning pockets sewn within them. Now our priestly garb became workaday bags such as an ordinary man might carry his lunch in instead of a sacred mask. Enough passersby wore black breeches and tawny jerkins for us to walk into the tavern barely meriting an incurious glance.

'Ale.' Josan handed me some coppers before heading for a vacant corner table. I paid for a foaming flagon and two leathern cups at the counter. We settled in to watch and to listen, drinking as little as we could without irritating the tavern keeper.

By mid-evening, we had an answer of sorts, though I wasn't quite sure what it meant. The man we were interested in stood up to offer a newcomer his hand.

'I'm Berid Gilemar. Join us,' he invited with an expansive gesture.

His circle of friends obligingly shifted tables and stools to make room. They occupied a good third of the taproom. As Master Gilemar raised his voice to share further words of wisdom, everyone else was obliged to listen.

'No one knows who holds the River People's allegiance,' he observed. 'Who do they worship? Have you ever seen one of them, shoeless and feckless, in your local shrine or temple.

His cronies nodded and frowned.

'We see them prowling back alleys. How often do they scale a fence or crack a window to steal whatever's easily snatched? How often do they cozen our daughters with lies and leave them ruined with a swelling belly?'

How often did a priestess's truth-telling magic prove some city lad was a liar, I wondered, when he blamed some yellow-haired, dark-eyed stranger for the child he had fathered?

Berid Gilemar continued. 'Where do they go, upstream or down, once their barges pass beyond sight of the Paramount King's garrisons? They have no settled homes, no lands that we know of. Who takes a share of the coin they've made at our expense, tying up at our wharves without offering a silver mark for their upkeep?'

Ignoring his malice, I focused on the unseen realm. In the blink of an eye the taproom was silent and empty but for a few fleeting shadows. Except for Master Gilemar, gesturing and posturing like a marionette. So he had sufficient magic to manifest but not enough to make himself heard.

Barely enough magic to manifest here. His phantasm came and went like a shadow as clouds race across the sun. For a moment, he seemed as solid as Josan beside me. Then he was so insubstantial I could see the tavern counter through the wave of his misty arm.

Was something being drawn to his magic, inconsistent though it was? Yes! I saw a shadow peer through a window. More than a shadow. The semblance of a man. A pale-haired man with dark eyes. One of the River People.

I blinked to restore my vision of the crowded taproom and stood up. 'Time to shake the dew off the lily.'

Josan rose from his own stool. 'I hear you.'

In truth, I was in dire need of a trip to the easing house. There was no one else in the back yard shack as we unbuttoned and helped fill the vats of piss that traders in the city pay good money for, from the Paramount King's gunpowder mills down.

Josan tucked himself away. 'Come on.'

I nodded as I rebuttoned.

We edged around the building, picking our way carefully through the refuse-cluttered alley. As we reached the tavern's corner, a glimpse into the unseen realm showed us the lurking shadow more clearly.

A River Man of a true bigot's imagining. Hulking, ungainly, with hair like matted straw and coarse features twisted in a brutal sneer. Clutching a long knife in one rope-scarred hand, the creature paced back and forth, its bare feet filthy and with toe nails as long as talons.

I looked at Josan, questioning. He shook his head. We were to wait.

The night dragged on. Every few moments one of us snatched a glance at the prowling phantasm, praying it wouldn't look our way. I hated to think what might happen if it saw us keeping watch.

But all its attention was on the man who'd created it, all unawares. So far, so predictable. But what enabled it to break free of that tie, to kill innocent men with no part in its making?

Eventually the tavern disgorged its patrons. Men and women wandered into the darkness, more or less steadily. The phantasm tossed its knife from hand to hand, gaze fixed on the door where its quarry would appear.

'What now?' I breathed.

If the creature manifested solidly enough to attack Gilemar, all and sundry would see it. There would be no dispelling the thing with a crowd convinced of its existence.

Josan answered just as quietly. 'We save him from a footpad.'

Gilemar left the tavern. The creature sprang, knife raised. I blinked to view the tangible world, expecting to see its menacing presence tear through the veil. But Gilemar sauntered onwards, oblivious.

I looked into the unseen realm. The monster hacked at him with its vicious knife, throwing punches with its other hand. Blade and fist alike passed through Gilemar's shadowy shape like a stick through smoke.

I turned to Josan, mouth open. He silenced me with a finger to his lips, before urging me on with a hand at my elbow.

We followed Gilemar all the way to what must be his home. A substantial town house with tree-filled gardens behind a high wall. An obsequious lackey guarded the gate.

Gilemar entered but the creature couldn't pursue him. I halted to watch the killer howl with frustration in the unseen realm.

'Why can't it touch him?'

Josan appeared beside me.

'Because he doesn't truly fear it. He hates the River People but he doesn't think they can harm him. He's armoured by his faith in the protection that his wealth and connections offer. What gives him a thrill—' Josan's voice thickened with contempt '—is making other people afraid.'

He broke off as the phantasm lurched away from the gate. It broke into a loping run.

I followed, at Josan's side. 'What's its new quarry?'

'My guess? Whoever Gilemar frightened most in the tavern this evening,' he said grimly.

We ran faster. I was soon stumbling, dizzy from snatching glimpses into the unseen realm to keep track of the creature at the same time as hurrying through these tangible streets. Every second step, I had to blink and check I wasn't about to collide with some hapless passer-by. Thank the Horned God this prosperous neighbourhood's folk were mostly at their own firesides at this time of night.

'There!' Josan pointed.

The creature cut down a side street, intent on whatever scent of terror lured it.

Josan sprinted ahead of me. 'Keep watch!'

I skidded to a halt. I had a lot to learn before I could dispel creatures that weren't of my own making. Ridding the tangible world of a creature that could already manifest so strongly that it could kill would be a challenge for the most experienced priests.

Heart thudding in my chest, I looked for any sign that some anxious householder had sent a servant scurrying to summon the Watch, for fear of drunks and ruffians running through their respectable streets.

I couldn't hear any suggestion of constables approaching with blazing torches and bruising ash staves. So I blinked for a view of the unseen realm and saw Josan wrestling with the monstrous River Man. They stood, face to face, each with a solid grip on the other's shoulders. Knees bent and feet scrabbling for purchase on the cobbles, each fought to throw the other off balance.

My money was on Josan. The Moon Temple's priests are trained in unarmed combat, whether or not they have magic. Since Gilemar wasn't the sort who fought his own battles, his inadvertent creation was relying on brute strength. More than that, Gilemar's prejudice clearly relied on second-hand reports. The monster's feet kept slipping. He'd never noticed that River People do wear shoes when they leave their barges for the city's paved thoroughfares. They only go barefoot on their clean-swept decks.

Josan's booted feet found solid purchase. A head shorter than the phantasm, he crouched lower still, so the creature overbalanced as it lunged to punch him. Josan side-stepped and twisted to stand chest to chest with the thing for an instant. He used one hand to force the creature's punching arm down. His other cupped its rearmost elbow from underneath, shoving upwards.

Caught unawares and thrown off balance, the creature went flying to land with a crash on the cobbles. Josan was on it, pummelling with merciless fists. Even as it fought back, the creature grew fainter as every blow landed.

I tore my gaze away to check the tangible streets. I couldn't think how I might explain this scene to anyone coming upon us unawares. As the night stayed dark and empty I breathed silent thanks to the Horned God.

Sooner than I expected, I saw Josan resting on his hands and knees, head hanging in exhaustion. A glimpse into the unseen realm proved the creature was gone. I went to help Josan to his feet.

'That's done.' He licked blood from a split lip. Battles on the cusp between tangible and unreal had very real perils.

'For the moment.' I hated myself for saying so. 'How long before Gilemar's spite creates another phantasm? How long before it finds the strength to manifest in this reality?'

Josan ran cautious hands over his ribs and winced. 'We can delay that for a good long while if we give him something more immediate to worry about. Something to discredit him in his cronies' eyes.'

I was intrigued. 'Such as?'

Josan began walking, stiffly. 'First thing in the morning, we'll ask Mother Asksarre to call down a Sun Temple audit on him.'

'An audit?' I shuddered even though I'd left my father's pottery long before I was co-opted into the priesthood.

Father always said no business's accounts, however honest

or diligent, were proof against Sun Temple scrutiny. The priestesses assessing taxes owed to the Paramount King could always find some anomaly.

'That'll keep him far too busy to spend his evenings spewing spite in taverns.' Josan unpacked his cloak. I did the same.

He grinned before donning his mask. 'Take note of this lesson, Ulias. We don't always fight magic with magic.'

A Warning Shiver

We may thank the Sun Goddess for her blessing that day, for ensuring I was the sister on duty in the entrance hall. It was not long before noon when I heard Sijan stamping her feet outside to shed the snow from her boots before she entered the shrine.

'What have you got there?' I nodded at the battered basket she set down on the floor. It clinked as the contents settled. Not charitable gifts for us to distribute, I was sure of that. It looked like something she'd plucked from a midden.

'Curses, sister.' Her mouth twisted unhappily as she unwound the scarf around her head. 'Thrown under a jetty towards the upper end of the Tane wharves.'

'You put yourself at risk retrieving such nonsense?' I set my sewing down in my lap and looked sternly at her. 'What if you fell into the river? The water's cold enough to be the death of you!'

'I was careful.' Sijan unbuttoned her sturdy woollen cape and hung it on a peg. 'Besides, the ice around the wharves is thick enough to take a man's weight now.' She sat on the bench to unlace her heavy-soled boots. 'Do you think the rivers really will freeze over? All the way from bank to bank?'

'Perhaps.' I have seen a handful of these iron-hard winters in my long life, so I had already considered this possibility. I was alert to the consequences that could then follow for those of us who guard this city from worse than cold or hunger.

'The boatmen were laying bets with each other, whether the Tane or the Dore will freeze first.' Sijan stood up, smoothing her plain wool robe as she slipped on indoor shoes.

'Not enough work to keep them out of mischief?' I enquired tartly. 'I take it you did your errands before you were distracted by such nonsense?'

She had been sent down to the wharves to plead for

scraps of wood, the tail-ends of rope and sacks of swept-up wood-shavings. Even an ordinary winter slows the kingdom's trade and barges and river-boats tie up to make repairs at their leisure. This year with lesser waterways already choked with ice, the city's docks were lined with vessels two and three deep.

'I did my duty well enough, sister.' She squared her shoulders and met my eyes with a hint of defiance. 'We will have fuel for the needy.'

'Go and tell Mother and then warm yourself in the kitchen,' I approved. 'You've earned a respite before we start serving the day's soup.'

She looked down at the dirty basket. 'What should I do with those?'

'I will see to what's necessary,' I assured her.

Sijan hesitated then shrugged and went on her way through the door that leads to the Golden Mother's sanctuary and thence to the rooms beyond reserved for those of us who serve the Goddess here.

As soon as the door closed behind her, I hurried across to the frayed basket as quickly as my stiff joints allowed. Potsherds, as I'd suspected. Wrapping the woven cane tight, I thrust the bundle deep into my sewing bag and returned to my stool.

I continued with my needlework, by the brazier that strove to hold off the chill. A voluminous cloak donated by some rich household upstream was making sturdy trousers and skirts for the penniless children of the spear-point of land where the city's rivers meet and the poor huddle in crowded tenements.

Soon, as the noon bell rang, I heard voices outside as the district's indigent lined up at our kitchen door. A hot bowlful would stave off their cold and hunger for a little while.

'Sister Jounay.' Sister Marrel entered from the sanctuary, carrying her own sewing basket. 'Would you like to get some food? I can sit here.'

'Thank you.' I secured my needle and thread and rose to

my feet, careful of my back. 'You've had precious few callers this morning.'

She had been on duty in the ledger room, ready to disburse the coin banked here under the Goddess's protection, released to those whose claim is confirmed by our records and the Golden Mother's magic.

Marrel sighed. 'The wealthy aren't venturing out to spend their coin in this cold weather and the rest are hoarding whatever they have saved against the winter turning worse. If we don't see a thaw soon this city will grind to a halt.'

I nodded. 'Goddess grant the waters will continue to flow.'

'I hate to think what will happen if the Tane and the Dore do freeze.' Marrel settled on the stool, stripping off her fingerless gloves to warm her hands at the brazier's charcoal glow. Not even such subdued embers can be permitted in the ledger room.

I entered the sanctuary at the heart of the shrine and curtseyed to the Sun Goddess's statue. The potsherds in my bag clinked. I looked up at the Mother. 'I know my duty, never doubt it.'

Instead of passing through to the kitchen, I knocked the Shrine Mother's door. Hearing her summons, I entered her office and Mother Dela looked up from a pile of letters.

'Sister? How can I serve you?' She fiddled nervously with her pen.

'May I be excused from kitchen duties? Sister Sijan found a heap of curses by the river and I would like to see what I can glean from them.'

'Of course,' she said quickly. 'Let me know what needs to be done.'

'Thank you, Mother.' I curtseyed and turned away before she realised I had seen her blushing.

I don't know what disconcerts her more; that I call her 'mother' when I am old enough for her to be my own daughter and one offering the promise of grandchildren besides. Or that she was privately told, when she was sent to guide this shrine, that my age and experience means I answer first and foremost to the Golden Mother's great temple at the heart of the city. Not that she has the least notion what my special duty actually entails.

No matter. I had her permission to investigate these curses and that would satisfy my sisters' curiosity. I crossed the Sanctuary to enter our common room. Fetching a sheet too ragged and threadbare to give to even the destitute, I spread it on the table. Setting my sewing carefully aside, I dumped the potsherds on the stained linen and threw the frayed basket into the hearth. The fire blazed for a moment, consuming the cane as I fetched paper and pen.

The potsherds were a fine assortment; from the crude earthenware of warehouse storage jars to fine ceramics with coloured glazes that had come to grief on some wealthy household's flagstones. Some of the curses were easily legible where pen and ink had been used on a porous surface. These people wanted to be certain that the Icicle Witch would get their message. Others were harder to decipher, either written by an unpractised hand or clumsily scratched onto the potsherd with whatever sharp point was to hand. Those ill-wishers trusted that this token was sufficient to draw the Coldheart's attention to their malicious desires.

I began to make notes. Kreyn the butcher was resting his thumb on the scales again if the many vehement complaints could be trusted. I was inclined to think so. Why would so many tell the same lie? Well, that was a matter for the Justiciary, so I would alert the local constable.

Tasiac the rope-maker's name was on more than a few pieces, though without specific accusations. What lay behind such incoherent expressions of hate? I would refer that question to our masked brothers in the Moon God's service. His priests are as good at uncovering secrets as they are at keeping them.

Angry voices outside the window distracted me until I got the gist of the quarrel. Someone whom we knew full well could afford to feed his family had brought them here to claim our charity regardless. There are always some who think we'll be easily cozened. Those who need to be remind-

ed that tending women from childbed to deathbed takes us
into every household. We see who holds the purse strings
and whether they're miser or spendthrift. Add our role as
guardians of the wealth which the Sun Goddess bestows and
the sisters of every shrine know precisely who needs our
help.

I returned to the potsherds, trying to decipher the
scratches and scribbles fuelled by envy, anger or some incoherent tangle of emotions. It was a hopeless task with many
but eventually I had a scatter of spite and resentment to assess. I knew some of the men and women whom anonymous
ill-wishers longed to see punished for sins real or imagined.
Turning over my sheet of paper, I sketched a map marked
with their homes and workplaces.

'What are you doing?' Sijan was the first to return from
doling out soup to the needy.

'Could you throw some more wood on the fire please?'

As she went to find the largest chunk in the log basket,
I turned my paper over so she could see my notes but not
the map. 'I'm seeing if I can identify those offered up to the
Icicle Witch's claws. I have Mother's permission.'

She came over to the table to gaze at the broken pottery.
'You don't think—'

'The Icicle Witch does not exist, little sister.' I kept my
voice calm and kindly though I resisted the temptation to
clasp my sunburst pendant. 'It is merely an ancient myth. It's
only ever resurrected when folk are forced into unwanted
idleness by an unduly harsh winter. When they cannot earn
the coin to replace what they must spend to keep themselves
fed and warm.'

I swept the potsherds together. 'Cooped up at home,
people have the leisure to dwell on their grievances, whether or not such ill-feeling is justified. They see smoke from a
neighbour's chimney and cannot believe that someone they
already dislike came by that firewood honestly when deserv-
ing folk such as themselves have nothing to burn. They see
someone stride well-shod through the snow and hate them
simply because the holes in their own shoes mean their feet

are freezing. They lie in bed with empty bellies beneath threadbare blankets and brood on supposed slights because they cannot get to sleep. When people are miserable and fearful, any careless word can seem like a calculated insult. Never mind that relentless bad weather makes the most even-tempered spit ill-considered remarks.'

'Indeed, sister.' Sijan was abashed.

'You have done the Goddess valuable service, all the same.' I tapped my notes for the Judiciary and for our brother priests. 'There's cause for concern in some of these pleas which we must not ignore. Will you carry some messages for me before the daylight fades?'

'Of course, sister.' Her expression brightened.

I knotted the potsherds inside the sheet. 'Could you dump this in the midden for me, while I write my letters?'

'Of course, sister.' She seized the bundle and hurried off.

Sijan is always pleased to be of service. If she finds more pleasure in errands that take her out into the city rather than in washing pots or sorting clothes, there is no harm in that. Some of the most prosperous districts in the city give us clothes so soiled that we tie herb-scented rags around our faces before we handle them.

As she left the room, I turned to the icon above the fireplace. I grasped my sunburst pendant tight and appealed to the Golden Mother. 'Goddess, be my witness, tell me the Icicle Witch does not exist.'

My heart pounded in my chest and my mouth was dry as old bone. Then I felt the welcome warmth of her blessing in my pendant. The radiant gold glowed brighter and brighter between my fingers and I heaved a sigh of relief. This evil was not yet upon us.

Of course there was no saying how much time I had left. When a myth is so widespread and so long established as the Icicle Witch, once her name is being whispered in corners by those who nurse a grudge, sooner or later she will manifest. Where and when would this ancient evil cross into the tangible world? Well, that knowledge was in the Goddess's gift and

I must be patient.

So I wrote my letters and gave them to Sijan to deliver to the district's House of Restraint and to the nearest Crescent Gate. I invited Sister Marrel to stay in the entrance hall by the brazier and spent a solitary hour in the ledger room, undisturbed. When a succession of boatmen arrived with the fuel they had promised Sijan, I helped my sisters to tie up bundles that would burn bright and hot.

After that Sister Castia and I replenished our stock of the basketwork cribs we keep ready for new mothers, packed with all they might need. Babies come when they will, regardless of the bitter weather. As the sun sank behind the rooftops, I spent a companionable hour in the common room with my sisters as we hemmed swaddling to wrap such vulnerable newborns in the Golden Goddess's love.

In between times, when I found myself alone, I clasped my pendant and sought the Blessed Mother's confirmation that the Icicle Witch hadn't stirred. Time and again, the ornate gold glowed with reassurance. Then, some while after supper, as we built up the fires against the encroaching night's chill, the sunburst stayed dull within my fingers as I paused in the wood store.

There may be less than one in a thousand born with the arcane gift that enables us to see the unreal world. Of those with such magic in their blood and bone, barely one in a thousand has talent enough to be trained as I had been. The rest are left to their own devices, by and large, never suspecting that their idle daydreams or nightmares can call creatures into being in the intangible realm. In a city this size however, when enough of those with some small capacity for magic are thinking about the same thing? That can be enough to create monsters.

I went to Mother Dela. 'Excuse me, but I must leave the shrine to address some Temple business.'

'Of course.' She looked apprehensive all the same. 'But take care. The cobbles will be treacherous. The streets will be empty and if you were to slip and fall—'

'I will take a staff,' I assured her. She need not know what other uses I could make of that prop.

'The Goddess go with you.' Her hand strayed to her own sunburst pendant.

'Always.' I smiled as I left her room.

In the entrance hall where I had my pick of the winter capes and boots by the door. My favourite staff was at the back of the rack where I always tucked it.

'Do you expect to be out long, sister?' Onati was taking the first of the night's shifts, ready to help any who came to our door.

'I cannot say,' I answered honestly.

'Where are you going?' She wanted to know where to send folk to search, if I failed to return because I was lying somewhere with a shattered hip. Well, accidents do happen.

'The Lotebourne district, somewhere about Mabbot Lane.' There was no harm in her knowing that much.

'Goddess bless your work.' She broke off as a frantic hand rattled the shrine's knocker.

Opening the door, I went quickly on my way as a man hurried past, incoherent with distress.

The night was crystal clear and bitterly cold. Too cold for more snow which was a blessing of sorts. The paths already trodden through the drifts and between swept-aside heaps remained clear enough. Dark smears showed where thoughtful householders had spread ashes to foil ice underfoot.

Few had hung lanterns on their doorposts. Why bother when anyone with a scrap of sense would be safely by their own fireside instead of roaming the streets? No matter. The full moon's silver radiance showed me my way. I breathed silent thanks to the Horned God.

The frigid air burned my throat. Pausing at a crossroads, I pulled a fold of my scarf over my mouth and nose. I glanced ahead and then to either side. Then I looked again, this time choosing to use the magic the Goddess has blessed me with to see into the unreal world.

I cannot recall when I last saw so little difference between the tangible and intangible realms. There is always much that's familiar, of course. The houses and streets and everything else that's without a spark of life remains the same in both. Usually though, the contrast is striking between the bustle of reality and the sparse inhabitants of the unseen world. Not now this cold weather was keeping the city's mortal inhabitants within doors as well as keeping their thoughts were focused on the brutal weather and what further trials it might yet bring. No idle imaginings were drawing creatures into fleeting life in the intangible world.

I looked again, wary for any sign of movement. The Icicle Witch would be no insubstantial phantasm. Her presence in so many stories through so many generations had made her an enduring presence in the unseen realm. Now so many curses gathered together had drawn her into this tangible world. The Goddess had told me so, when my pendant refused to confirm that she didn't exist.

Now I must banish the Witch to the darkness that had spawned her. I stamped my chilled feet to get the blood flowing. Swapping my staff from gloved hand to gloved hand, I tucked the other inside my cape to keep warm, turn by turn as I hurried on.

Walking this city's highways and byways for so many years, I can find my way anywhere by the quickest route. It didn't take me long to reach the silent streets which I sought. The Lotebourne crossed Mabbot Lane in the midst of the spread of houses where those so savagely cursed were living.

So where was the Icicle Witch? I began to quarter the district, street by street and alley by alley. I held my staff ready in both hands, partly to save myself if I slipped and partly in case I encountered some housebreaker or cutpurse more desperate than the rest.

Pausing at every corner, I surveyed the cobbles ahead. Time and again, there was no sign of life in the tangible world or the unseen realm. Even cats and rats must be huddled in some warm refuge. Every house was closely shuttered and one by one, chimneys ceased to smoke as fires were banked with ash to sleep through the night.

Time wore on and still I saw no trace of the Witch. I began to doubt myself. Was I searching in the wrong place entirely? Had this evil manifested by the riverside, drawn to the jetty where those curses had been tossed onto the ice? If so, how long before she was seen by some unsuspecting boatman heading back to his bunk from a tavern? Then she would have a firm foothold in this reality.

I heard a noise behind me. I spun around, nearly losing my balance on the frost-slick cobbles. The Icicle Witch was there. Tall and bone thin, she was swathed in a long cloak as ominously black as water beneath broken ice. Her long white tresses bristled with hoar frost.

She was as solidly present in this world as she was in the intangible realm. I brandished my staff to warn her off, as I used my mind's eye to confirm that. She stiffened, hands raised as my use of such magic meant she saw my presence in the unseen world, as well as standing here before her. Did she realise that meant I was blessed with the power to challenge her? How much does a phantasm remember, from one manifestation to the next?

It was hard to read her expression. Her face shifted and blurred, like something seen through fog. I stood firm. If she wasn't yet wholly fixed in a form, I need not take to my heels in search of reinforcements. Not yet, anyway.

I still needed to be wary. Her face might be indistinct but I could see her hands clearly. Her outspread fingers were tipped with talons of ice as clear and as sharp as shattered glass. Cold as the night was, those claws were colder still, trailing ribbons of vapour in the moonlight.

As soon as she found someone those curses called her to punish, a lacerating thrust of those claws could very well kill them. Even if her victim survived, they would be scarred for life. Scars would prompt questions and answers. Even if ninety-nine in every hundred who heard scoffed when that victim blamed the Icicle Witch, some would believe it. That was how she endured.

She stepped closer, hissing, her breath like smoke. I stepped back, still warding her off with my staff. I must learn all that I could about the emotions that summoned her.

Silver combs swept back her white hair, glittering as though they were studded with diamonds. Rings and bracelets weighed down her outspread hands. Her swirling cloak was as weighty as the warmest, most costly velvet. Beadwork patterns like frost on a window pane shimmered around its hem. Only the city's wealthiest women could afford such adornment. So this manifestation of malice was also fuelled by the common folk's envy of the rich whose money could insulate them from winter's privations.

I must report this to my superiors. Not the elders of the Sun temple set in authority over the Goddess's shrines. I also answer to those who govern the secret cabals trained to use this perilous magic. They have the king's ear. They would advise his majesty to blunt such dangerous resentment with royal distributions of bread and fuel until a thaw arrived.

That distraction was nearly the death of me. The Witch's face snapped into clarity, gaunt as famine yet painted like a courtesan. Her eyes burned with cold, blue fire and her rictus grin widened with cruel anticipation.

I tried to unfasten my cape but my gloved hand fumbled the buttons. She took a step closer, flexing those fearsome talons. I seized the cursed glove's fingertips in my teeth and ripped it from my hand. I had the neck of the cape undone in an instant but the Witch was so close that her grasping hands stretched out for my throat. Cold vapour burned my skin.

'You defy me?' Her voice was the insidious whisper of snow sliding from a roof to crush some innocent below.

I recoiled, swinging my staff in circles between us. She snatched at the weapon, swift as lightning. She gripped it, ignoring a blow that would have shattered a strong man's bones. I let go before she could drag me towards her. Her fist tightened around the wood and it shattered into splinters.

'By the Sun Goddess's blessing.' I pulled my golden pendant clear of my cape. The metal glowed to soothe the aching numbness in my fingers and face.

The radiance strengthened, bright as day. The Witch shrank back. Now I was the one stepping closer. Her phantom jewellery vanished like ice at noon. As I thrust the sunburst towards her, she flung up her hands to ward off the light. Now her face looked like a skull newly dug from a grave. Her painted features melted like wax and her hair fell away in lank clumps.

She staggered backwards. I still pursued her. Now that velvet cloak weighed her down, sodden and clinging, with that costly beadwork melted into smears of muck. Even stiff with cold as I was, and so far from my youth, she couldn't outrun me.

The Witch sank to the paving. She buried her face in her hands. Now she was growing transparent. I could see the solid reality of a house's steps behind her. She grew still more indistinct. I couldn't tell where the sweep of her cloak ended and the house's shadow began. The remnants of her hair faded into a moonbeam cutting between two rooftops to strike the flagstones. Within a few more moments, all I could see was a slick of filth staining the snow.

That's all I could see in the tangible world. I glanced into the unseen realm and recoiled. In my mind's eye, the Icicle Witch was as fearsome as before. Talons glittering in the moonlight, she flexed her fingers with unmistakeable threat. She would kill me if she could reach me without the light of my pendant touching her. The only thing that could save me was the Goddess shielding me from her malice.

I shuddered and returned my gaze to the mortal world. The street was empty. I found my discarded glove, stooping painfully to retrieve it. At least I could keep both hands inside my cape now, once again buttoned tight.

My walk home was chilled and weary. I shivered as I paused at every crossroads and not just from the cold. Was the Icicle Witch pursuing me? Could the lingering power of those curses give her the strength to manifest here again? Could I win another confrontation in the tangible world?

I didn't dare glance into the unreal world. As soon as I did that, I would become manifest in the intangible realm. The

Witch would be able to attack and she would be far stronger than me.

At long last, I reached the shrine. Onati welcomed me back with loving concern. 'You look half-frozen!'

She ushered me to the stool by the brazier and fetched me a bowl of hot soup. While I relished its savoury warmth, she collected one of the bricks which we keep heated in the kitchen range at this season. Wrapped in flannel, it took the chill off my sheets in my dormitory bed. I pressed my cold feet against the reassuring solidity and settled down to sleep. Now I was secure in the Goddess's shrine, the Witch couldn't possibly reach me. Better yet, before weariness claimed me, I had an idea how to foil her further.

The following day dawned bright and cloudless, still bitterly cold. It was market day, in theory at least. Precious few stall-holders would be setting out their wares with so few people looking to buy more than immediate necessities before scurrying back home.

Those without coin to buy such essentials and with nothing left to sell to raise it came to our door at noon. The crowd grew larger every time. As always, we offered them warm clothing, what blankets we had been given, one per household, and the bundles of scrap wood gleaned from the wharves, tied tight with discarded rope.

First though, Mother Dela addressed them, as I had asked her earlier, after making very certain that my night's work hadn't been undone.

She stood on the steps outside the shrine door beside the Goddess's bronze statue. 'Good people, may I have your attention? I have heard some distressing news.'

Since her unhappiness was plain for all to see, the crowd quickly stilled, concerned faces turned towards her.

'It seems that some in this district have recalled the legends of the Icicle Witch. Worse, they relish the thought of her spite. They have called on her to send curses to strike their neighbours. Suffering in the midst of this winter's privations, some are determined to see everyone else made just as wretched.'

Anger sharpened her words. As I had realised the night before, Mother Dela took this outpouring of malice to be a personal affront. She worked so hard to see everyone treated fairly, their needs met as best we could.

'Do not yield to superstition. Do not become so mean-spirited. Such ill-will will fester and poison you as surely as an untreated wound beneath a hasty bandage. If you have justified grievances, bring them to us. By the Goddess's grace, we will see the truth brought into the daylight. If you're uncertain where blame might rightly lie, take your complaints to our masked brothers who serve the Moon God at the Crescent Gate. You can trust them to fathom all falsehoods and to protect those secrets which need to be kept.'

She wasn't pleading with the crowd so much as ordering them. I kept my face impassive as I searched the onlookers' varying expressions. Some were visibly abashed merely because a priestess rebuked them. Here and there though, I saw a gaze averted, a shoulder half-turned, heard the shuffle of guilty feet. I made note of those I recognised. Not in order to punish them. Where shrine resources could help those families, that would help keep them from the unhappiness that had drawn them to the Icicle Witch. Visiting their houses would also enable me to watch for any magical talent among them.

Mother Dela swept the crowd with a commanding glance as she concluded in ringing tones.

'As the Golden Mother is my witness, as I stand before you in her blessed sunlight, I swear to you by all that is sacred, the Icicle Witch does not exist!'

She held her golden pendant high. It glowed as bright as fire. More than that, the sunburst hung around the Goddess's statue's neck shone with equal fervour. The crowd gasped and exclaimed, awestruck. There could be no doubting the power of the Golden Mother's magic. It confirmed their Shrine Mother spoke the truth. There couldn't possibly be any such creature as the Icicle Witch.

A WARNING SHIVER

As long as so many of them were so utterly convinced, she would remain banished from this world. Now I just had to avoid her in the unseen realm.

JULIET E. MCKENNA

Do You Want to Believe in Magic?

Gold is the Sun Goddess's gift. It's the colour of her bounty ensuring we all thrive. Grain from the southern wheat fields, reaching to the horizon. North of the great rivers' union, dairy women make golden butter and cheese from the creamy milk of tan cows roaming the hill country. All this and more brings in the gold coin that's made our city more prosperous than any town upriver or down. Such wealth signifies the Goddess's favour as she guards and guides us all, from the Paramount King on his throne down to the humblest urchin.

Silver is the Moon God's metal. Keeper of secrets, he hides it mingled with lead and other ores. Only those with the patience to study learn the secrets of extracting it from the darkness of the mines. Even so, hidden hazards still trip the arrogant or unwary. But those with the relevant knowledge can cure deadly maladies with those poisons bound to silver. Silver is the physician's metal in so many ways. As his priests in their schools and hospitals often remark; every coin has two sides.

So the poets and pious say, Ruvon reflected. But the men at this table had no time for such fancies. Gold or silver, all coin was for spending.

'My purse is as empty as a marsh trader's promises,' Scop groused. 'Anyone got a proposition to fill it?'

A proposition. No one would say it outright, not even among friends. The truth was, if Scop wanted coin to spend, he'd have to steal it, or steal goods that could be sold quick and without questions. He wasn't alone in that. Ruvon reckoned the men and women who did an honest day's work for a fair day's pay could be counted on the fingers of one hand in this crowded and noisy tavern.

He wasn't one. Ruvon didn't lie to himself, whatever false-

hoods he told the constables prowling these wharfs whenever some merchant went bleating to the Justiciary about
cargo pilfered from some barge or a warehouse where it was
stowed.

At least he'd had no choice. He'd been born to this life, in
this narrow spear-point of land where the great river Tane
tumbled down from the hills to join the mighty flood of the
Dore winding its way across the plains. Where the perpet-
ual flow could wash away the blood and stink of tanneries,
slaughter houses and dye works, so all those upstream could
enjoy sweet water and fresh air.

'I have a notion.' Alinar paused. Of course. He wouldn't
share his scheme without sufficient entreaty.

Alinar had a choice. Ruvon studied him over the rim
of his tankard as he drank. Alinar hadn't been born to a
rag-picker; scavenging for linen to sell to paper makers.
Ruvon had been sent to steal shirts and chemises as soon as
he was big enough to climb garden walls in the fine broad
streets upstream. He'd done so willingly, once he'd realised
the alternative was his mother bringing barge-hands back to
their meagre home, to do whatever they wanted with her, as
long as they left coin to pay the rent.

Scop rubbed filthy hands together with gleeful anticipation. 'This'll be worth hearing, lads.'

'You've not steered us wrong yet,' Haspel agreed, obsequious.

As every other man nodded, Ruvon forced himself to
bend his neck in a show of assent. Haspel was right. Alinar
was clever and he'd learned all manner of things from the
Moon God's priests, at one of their schools for the sons and
daughters of those houses Ruvon stole from. Alinar could
name all the towns upstream and down within the Paramount King's rule and list all the nobles who swore him
fealty.

Ruvon had learned his numbers and letters from a man
once crushed between a laden barge and a wharf's wooden
pilings, never to walk again but still with children to feed.
Those lessons had ended as soon as he could write his own

name and read a notice posted by the constables, in case the description of a man sought might match him.

Ruvon only needed enough reckoning to be sure of his fair share from a night's thieving. So his father had said, reclaiming him from his mother once he grew too big to escape with a thrashing for stealing clothes. Like the priests said, every coin has two sides. That meant Ruvon was old and strong enough to join his father's gang. Until the constables caught Erzet and the Justiciar hanged him.

Why hadn't Alinar joined his father's business? Ruvon longed to ask. The man bred and sold horses and that was a lucrative trade with the Paramount King's cavalry and garrisons always needing new mounts. Why had Alinar abandoned his comfortable life to play cock of the dunghill among the Spearhead's depraved and desperate?

He didn't ask. He never did. Besides, Alinar was now sufficiently flattered to share his new scheme with the table.

'The new moon rises to shine on the last month before midsummer. Everyone wants their books balanced before the Goddess's shrines update their ledgers and the Golden Temple sends out writs for the King's taxes—'

'Everyone knows that.' Ruvon was tired of Alinar treating them all like halfwits.

Alinar slid him a narrow-eyed look before continuing as though no one had spoken. 'That's just as true for the money-changers. They'll be sending plateau coin upriver and marsh coin downstream to their partners who trade in the towns that lie beyond the Paramount King's suzerainty.'

Ruvon watched everyone nodding sagely, even though they had no more idea than he did, what holding outlandish coin would mean when the Goddess's auditors assessed a man's taxes. No one hereabouts ever banked coin with a shrine, not with the King's head stamped on it or the heraldic beasts that signified towns beyond his majesty's reach.

'A goodly number of strong boxes will be loaded on barges these next few nights,' Alinar went on.

'Aye, and locked up tight in the holds with guards armed

with bows and hand-cannons up top,' Ruvon objected.

Alinar glared at him. 'So we hit them before they reach the wharfs, in the streets after they've left the money-changers.'

'With an escort of constables?' Ruvon challenged. 'We've all seen them shepherding such chests.'

But Alinar shook his head. 'Not those who don't want any Justiciar's men seeing how much coin they're shifting, in case some whisper finds a priestess's ear. Especially not Pallot Usenain.'

Ruvon didn't have an answer for that. Though everyone looked much less eager at the thought of robbing Pallot. Money-lender as well as money-changer, he paid brutal men to deter undue interest in his affairs.

Not even Alinar's honeyed tongue would persuade them to risk crossing Pallot, Ruvon thought with sour satisfaction.

Then Scop cleared his throat. 'Just supposing — we did snatch such a strongbox, what do we do then?'

'Take the coin to a money-changer?' Ruvon scoffed. 'You don't think they talk to each other, to fix their rates and swap news from plateau towns and the marsh?'

Alinar smiled, smug. 'We take the strongbox to a tinsmith I know. He'll melt every last penny down, for a tenth share of the weight,' he allowed. 'We sell our share to craftsmen making brooches and rings for the nobility.'

'When they ask where you got this gold and silver?' Ruvon demanded stubbornly.

Alinar waved him away. 'Once coin is melted and cast into ingots, no one will ever be able to say where such bullion came from.'

'A priestess will, or a priest.' Ruvon spoke before he could stop himself.

Alinar crowed with laughter. 'Bless the boy! You truly believe your grandmother's stories of their magical powers?'

Ruvon ground his teeth. 'You try telling lies to a priestess, to convince her you're entitled to withdraw money from your mother's deposits at her shrine. See how far that gets you.'

Alinar stared at him with ostentatious wonder. 'You do! You honestly believe those tales! That the Golden Mother can really see into a man's heart and judge his honesty? That the Moon God truly tells his priests when a man's burdened by dark secrets?'

Such open derision for the divinities prompted shivers of unease round the table. Alinar spoke quickly before he lost them. 'I'll grant priests and priestesses alike can read the faintest hints in a man's expression. They pick up all manner of news from folk visiting their shrines and sanctuaries. True, only a fool would try to deceive them, but we won't be doing any such thing.'

He laughed and the rest laughed with him. Only Ruvon sat stony-faced.

'Do you want to believe in magic?' Alinar challenged 'To give you an excuse for not playing your part? So no one can call you a coward?'

'I'm no craven,' spat Ruvon.

'Good, then you're in.' Alinar leaned forward, elbows on the sticky table. 'Now, here's the plan...'

It was a good plan, much as it galled Ruvon to admit it. He scouted ahead down the narrow alley, cudgel in hand and Beasel at his shoulder. Pausing at the far end, he glanced back.

Scop and Pinse lugged a strongbox between them and Cheffe and Narrias followed with another. Alinar brought up the rear with Vulse and Toka, armed with daggers and clubs in case Pallot's men recovered from their beating to follow.

'All clear,' Ruvon murmured to Beasel. They stepped out to guard the alley mouth as the men carrying the strongboxes emerged. They crossed the street together to duck down another dark entry. No one knew the Spearhead's shortcuts better than Ruvon.

This one opened into a cobbled yard overlooked by

crowded tenements. Beasel looked up warily but Ruvon knew these folk wouldn't open a shutter whatever they heard out back.

He skidded to a halt all the same, seeing movement in the gloom ahead. 'Clear out,' he growled, 'if you know what's good for you!'

Something growled back. The bestial snarl sent a shiver down his spine. Ruvon readied his cudgel. Heavy and copper-banded, it was barely the legal handspan shorter than a constable's iron-shod ash stave.

'Ruv?' Beasel quavered. 'What's that?'

As the man tugged at his sleeve, Ruvon realised he wasn't looking at the snarling thing. Beasel had seen a long, sinuous shape in the muck to their right.

'What is it?' Alinar demanded.

'Not sure,' Ruvon shot back before he realised no one was talking to him.

'It's getting closer!' Vulse's voice cracked with apprehension.

Before Ruvon could ask what was going on, Scop and Pinse barged into him and Beasel. With Alinar and the others following, they all staggered into the cobbled yard, strongboxes scraping on the ground.

'Watch—' Ruvon's rebuke died on his lips as the growling thing stepped into the starlight. It was akin to a giant cat though walking on its hind legs as steadily as any man. Its long-haired pelt was edged with eerie golden light.

Ruvon gripped his cudgel in both hands. The creature's ruby red eyes fixed on him and it spread forepaws tipped with ebony talons.

'Ruv!' Beasel pressed close.

Ruvon snatched a frantic glance and saw a snake as thick as a man's thigh. Sickly, silvery light outlined every lurid green scale. As it opened its mouth and hissed, its fangs were as long as his forefinger.

'That's a gryphon.' As Alinar spoke, Ruvon heard a hunting bird's cry behind them and the rattle of bating wings.

He wanted to turn, not to see what a gryphon was, but to seize Alinar and shake loose some answers. Where had these creatures come from and what did they want? But that would mean turning his back and that giant cat was edging closer.

As he kept his gaze fixed on the creature, rainbow mist shimmered beside it. Another nightmare solidified, with a rooster's head and scaled, spurred feet. Only it stood as tall as Ruvon's waist and he'd never heard of any fowl so large. Besides, its body was scaled like the snake and it flapped bat wings, lashing a serpent's tail.

Beasel yelped. 'What's that?'

If there was truly no such thing as magic, what was this madness?

'What do we do?' rasped Scop.

'They tell tales of gryphons in plateau towns,' Alinar remarked, 'and that's a cockatrice. They're a Nilgeh Marsh myth, I believe.'

Ruvon couldn't help looking round. He found himself staring at Alinar. The fool had turned to see what he and Beasel faced. The man might have been scoring casual points in tavern conversation, proving he was the best-educated as well as the quickest-witted.

Not tonight, he wasn't. Ruvon watched, disbelieving, as the fool turned back to face the advancing gryphon. The beast was as big as a dray horse, though it had paws rather than hooves at the rear and a long tufted tail besides. More incredible, it had the head and wings of a bird of prey, and taloned fore-feet as massive as the rest. How could such a creature exist except through magic?

Vulse and Toka shrank away from Alinar. Scop and the rest huddled closer to the strong boxes, seeking the reassurance of standing shoulder to shoulder over their loot.

Ruvon snatched a glance at the cat-man. The creature was standing still, its glowing red eyes fixed on the gryphon. The cockatrice stood beside it, leathery wings folded, while the snake slithered back and forth behind them.

'This is just some dream.' Alinar waved a scornful hand at the gryphon.

The beast's head darted forward and bit clean through his wrist. Alinar's scream echoed back from the buildings as the gryphon tossed back its head to drop the morsel down its gullet.

Ruvon was deafened as chaos erupted all around. Alinar fell to his knees, screeching and clutching his spurting stump. The gryphon sprang at Scop and the others who yelled defiance and terror alike.

Their flailing blows didn't leave a mark on the beast but its quick beak and claws inflicted ghastly wounds. Narrias reeled away, pressing bloody hands to his ruined face. 'I'm blind! I'm blind!'

Vulse darted forward, dagger drawn, to stab the beast in the flank. His blade barely grazed its hide before a clawed hind foot raked his belly. His entrails spilled onto the cobbles.

Beasel yelled as the giant snake slid between his feet, intent on Toka or Cheffe. The cockatrice took flight, flapping high enough to rake Beasel's face with his claws. He smashed at it with his cudgel. The creature pecked viciously at his weapon hand. As it tore at his scalp, hair and skin tangled around its feet.

Ruvon wasn't fighting. He locked gazes with the red-eyed cat-man. The creature stood poised for him to make the first move.

'I won't fight you.' Ruvon extended his hand, cudgel loose in his fingertips. 'Not unless you fight me. Then I'll do my best to kill you, the Horned God is my witness. But leave me be and I'll let this fall and walk away, leaving every penny in those boxes.'

The cat-man retreated, lowering its taloned hands, still eyeing him intently.

Ruvon took a step away from the mêlée and dropped his weapon. None of the beasts paid any heed. If any of the gang condemned him for a coward, Ruvon didn't hear their voices in the uproar.

He walked across the courtyard and went on his way without a backward glance.

The gang's survivors soon scattered, leaving Vulse and Cheffe dead on the cobbles. The cockatrice capered on the blood-spattered strongboxes while the giant snake's maw gaped to swallow Cheffe's booted feet.

'No,' a woman chided, emerging from a doorway. 'It's back to the Unseen Realm for you.'

She wore a hooded cloak and the gleam of a sunburst amulet illuminated the lower half of her face. The snake retreated in a sullen coil. As she gestured, it vanished in a sparkling mist.

A tall man in black followed the priestess. Starlight shone on his silver mask. He turned to the gryphon. 'Thank you.'

The beast preened for a moment and sprang into the air. By the time it reached the rooftops it had faded to transparency. With the next beat of its wings, it disappeared. The cockatrice and the lion rampant had already returned to wherever they dwelled.

The priest contemplated the strong boxes. 'What will Pallot Usenain say when we return his property?'

The priestess snorted. 'How will he explain such discrepancies in his ledgers?'

The priest looked towards the alley Ruvon had taken. 'Why do you suppose he was so desperate to believe in magic?'

The priestess shrugged. 'Just be grateful that he was. It drew the creatures to him. We'd never have got wind of this plot otherwise.'

The priest cocked his masked head. 'You know him?'

'I knew his mother.' The priestess hesitated. 'Can you see to this?'

As the priest nodded, she ran after Ruvon, light-footed in her billowing cloak.

He didn't know where to go or what to do. He couldn't say how long he wandered through the dark streets. After the night's shocks, it was hardly a surprise when he saw a spark of light ahead blossom into a white dove. He halted as the bird hovered in front of his face.

A woman's kindly voice whispered in his ears. 'Break free. Seek a new home and a fresh start. Go, tonight.'

Ruvon couldn't see who was speaking. He didn't look. He simply watched the bird circle upwards and fly away. Then he turned to head for the wharfs. He'd take the first barge to hire him, whether it was heading upstream or down. He'd go as far as he could, way beyond the Paramount King's rule.

He'd often longed to leave his sordid life and the Spearhead behind. He'd never dared to try. But after everything he had seen tonight?

Now Ruvon knew he could believe in magic. Now anything was possible.

JULIET E. MCKENNA

The Legend of the Eagle

'... and the brass eagle stood proud on the highest pinnacle of the castle gate, overlooking the town grown up around the margrave's walls. Flying high on our flags, it was the token of our luck and so the eagle itself was carried into battle against the River Kingdom's army...'

Nedirin ducked his head to hide a yawn. He'd had a tiring day, herding obstinate goats in these gullies and thickets between the river and the uplands. Now that the herds were penned for the night with the dogs on watch, he wanted to wrap himself in his blankets and yield to his weariness. He'd heard old Thulle's stories so often that he could recite them in his sleep.

They all could, from the dog boys younger than Nedi to the grey-bearded herd masters as old as his grandsire. Their town had yielded to the men of the River Kingdom when Thulle was still a babe in arms.

If someone other than Thulle was telling the tale, the brass eagle had been cast into a charnel pit with the battlefield dead, or fallen into the river, or been stolen by the Paramount King's men to be thrown in their furnaces far away to the south, in their capital city where the ruddy brown Tane flowing from the high plateau met the pale silty waters of the mighty Dore which cut through grasslands bounded only by the horizon to east and west and by mighty forests to the south. That was what folk said but no one from Hatalys had ever travelled so far to seek their fortune and returned to confirm such stories of woodlands without end.

Still, listening to old Thulle was the price which Nedi must pay for a seat by the fire pit and the weather was growing colder as the hazel and ash trees turned to autumn gold. So he hid his boredom and edged closer to the embers.

'If the eagle ever returns,' Thulle continued, 'Hatalys will be free.'

That was the one thing which all the tales agreed on, though Nedi had wondered since he was small, how that could happen if the bird had been melted down and turned into door knobs or buttons for fancy waistcoats.

'Give it up, for pity's sake,' growled Uderil from the far side of the stone-lined pit.

Some of the men who had already forsaken the fireside for their bedrolls murmured agreement. Nedi's mother's youngest brother and his father's next elder were among them. They had promised to watch over him as he tended his family's goats while his father's broken ankle mended. They couldn't afford to abandon this last trip into the hills to fatten the billy goats born in the spring and now destined for salting and smoking after autumn's slaughters.

Uderil was still speaking. 'I'll take the River Kingdom's grain and fine horses and black powder weapons to keep moor dogs from killing my goats over foraging for nuts and fruit and hunting hill elk with bow and arrow.'

Seeing Thulle's eyes widen with outrage, Nedi gazed mute into the flames, keeping his face as expressionless as a freshly wiped slate. Antagonizing the spiteful old man was never a good idea. Nedi would wager his best gloves that Uderil's most highly prized goats would lose their bells and stray over the next few days or fall victim to stinking flux. Not that any-one ever caught Thulle wreaking such revenge.

'It's worth it, is it?' A new voice spoke up from the shadows on the far side of the fire. 'Paying for black powder and lead shot carried a hundred leagues upstream? Paying tithes in coin and in kind to the Paramount King to feed and clothe the garrison who watch over us? Bending our necks to the justice of strangers?'

'Getting our necks stretched, more like,' Plore said quietly.

Nedi remembered his father and mother talking in low tones, sitting either side of the stove at home, the evening after Plore's cousin had been hanged. They hadn't realised Nedi was listening, sat behind the curtain hiding the stair to the loft where he and his brothers and sisters slept, four to a bed. Nedi had got too used to sleeping alone in his blankets now that he was old enough to go herding goats with their father through the summer, only returning to the town each market day.

Plore's cousin had been a violent fool. His parents agreed on that. But did he deserve to hang for being the only man caught by the troopers after a drunken brawl where another bully had died? Any one of twenty men could have struck the fatal blow. Even the dead man's brothers and wife had said so.

Father recalled the old margrave's lesser sentences. A man got a chance to mend his ways if he was punished with a flogging or a spell in the stocks or the pillory. But the new margrave had gone south and the castellan handing down judgements stamped with the Paramount King's seal only ever sent men to the gallows.

Nedi's mother was more distressed to hear that the hanged man's body had been given to the Horned God's temple, for the masked priests' secret rites before he was buried. Plore's family would have laid him out in a funerary gully, she wept, to be unmade by the beasts and birds of hill and valley to release his soul.

Nedi had crept silently back to the crowded bed, privately vowing to never fall foul of the Paramount King's garrison.

'Granted, there's bitter to go with the sweet.' Uderil glanced at Plore, apologetic. 'But we must live each day as best we can.'

'Must we?' the voice challenged. 'Can't we make our own choices?'

'How?' Zanner, his mother's brother, sat up.

Nedi was startled to hear the hope in his young uncle's words.

'We look to our own lore,' Thulle said robustly. 'We all know that the eagle flew away when the Horned God's priests conjured monsters to break down the castle's gates. The king of the skies went to rally the beasts and birds to fight with our forefathers. Before he could bring them salvation though, the fools had surrendered for lack of faith!'

Along with everyone else, Nedi looked at Thulle. Only the crackle of burning wood broke the silence around the campfire.

Did the old man truly believe that the Horned God's priests had summoned up ogres to smash the city's defences? That griffins had soared up to the ramparts, rending the brave defenders with deadly beaks and talons?

'The eagle could win back our freedom, together with our own courage and resolve.' The stranger walked into the soft orange light, carrying a heavy sacking-swathed bundle.

Uderil shuffled aside and the man knelt to begin unwrapping whatever it was. He was dressed much the same as everyone else; buff leather breeches and high-topped boots to foil the thorn thickets, a leather jerkin over woollen shirts layered to keep out the cold. He had sturdy gloves tucked through his belt and a knitted cap warming his head. His complexion was weather-worn, his brows and stubble dark and his eyes brown, like everyone Nedi had known all his life.

Everyone gasped as the last fold of sacking fell away. A statue shone golden in the firelight. It was an eagle rearing upright with mighty wings outspread and its head turned to one side. Flowing lines marked every detail of its feathers while carved facets gave the eye turned towards Nedi a piercing glint.

'The king of the skies has returned!' Thulle was so ecstatic that he almost fell into the fire pit as he scrambled to his feet. As it was, he brushed so close to the flames that Nedi smelled leather scorching. Tears glistening on his wrinkled cheeks, the old man dropped to his knees before the brass statue.

It was a sizeable thing, at least a cubit tall, with the bird perched on a square pedestal which had four stubby feet. Thulle stretched out a trembling hand only to snatch it back before his fingertips touched the gleaming metal.

'Where did you find that?' Uderil wondered aloud.

'How is that effigy going to restore our liberties?' Uncle Zanner demanded. 'Who are you?'

'My name is Sincai,' the newcomer told him, 'and I believe this statue can help Hatalys regain its freedoms if you men are brave enough to follow me to the town.'

'We will follow you anywhere!' Thulle still gazed at the statue, rapt.

'Speak for yourself,' Uderil snapped.

'Hear me out before you make any decision.' The new-comer surveyed the assembled men. Even those who'd already fallen asleep were tossing aside their blankets, wide-eyed and open-mouthed.

'The River Kingdom has over-reached itself.' Sincai rose and tugged a long stick from the firewood piled close to the pit. He scraped swift lines in the dirt.

'Here is the Tane coming down from the high plateau and here is Hatalys. Here is the Dore, cutting the grassland from sunset to sunrise.'

Then, to Nedi's surprise, he drew a second river joining the Dore far to the west.

'This is the Fasil and the town of Gotesh.' Sincai dug a little hole in the ground where the two rivers met. 'That has been a River Kingdom town for five generations but Hedvin and Bastrys—' he marked two more towns some distance further upstream on each river '—they drove the Paramount King's armies away in their grandfathers' day and the plains-men have never returned.'

He swept the stick across to the other side of his dirt map and scraped four rivers fanning out eastward from the River Dore. 'You've heard tell of the Nalgeh Marsh? It's bounded by three cities, Scefet, Julach and Avelsir. They have never fallen to the plainsmen. The most westerly River Kingdom town is here—' he stabbed the dirt a good way short of the sprawling marsh. '—Usenas.'

'What has this to do with us?' Zanner asked impatiently.

Sincai drew a slow circle around his map. Nedi saw the stick's tip pass through the marks signifying Gostesh in the east and Usenas in the west. It cut through the writhing line of the Tane to the south and east of Hatalys. The triangle of land between the Tane and the Dore where the capital city ruled over the bridges and all river trade up and down stream was at the centre.

'Here's where the River Motar joins the Tane.' Sincai drew a second line coming down from the north. It met the Tane just where the circle crossed the river. 'Where the plainsmen hold Mithess.'

Nedi longed to visit Mithess. The town was only four days travel down river by barge. Three days, so Uncle Zanner said, when the spring swelled the Tane with snowmelt from the mountains far beyond the high plateau. When he was older, his father said. If his mother agreed.

'Wait.' Nedi's Uncle Isom walked forward to study the scrawled map. 'We're the only town outside that circle which is under the River Kingdom's heel?'

Sincai nodded. 'Anything beyond is too far from the Kingdom's heart, as the folk of Hedvin and Bastrys showed and so did the men and women of Scefet and the Nilgeh Mire. When their people rebelled, the Paramount King's cavalry couldn't arrive soon enough. Not before the townsfolk drove out all those sworn to the Paramount King.'

Sincai raised a warning finger as the men murmured surprised approval.

'They let them leave with food for themselves and their horses. They didn't put the River Kingdom castellan or garrison to the sword or drag them to the gallows. They didn't ravage the Horned God's temple or tear down the Sun Goddess's statues. They simply restored their old rites alongside the new.'

He raised his voice over Thulle's muttered outrage.

'They chose trustworthy men to serve as constables to keep order in every district and to make up a jury for an assize at every third full moon, with a judge chosen by drawing lots among them. Merchants honoured their agreements with traders up and downstream. They proved that they did not need the Paramount King's rule to secure peace and prosperity so he had no excuse to send his cavalry against them.'

'Good for them,' one of the old men sneered.

'We could do the same,' Sincai assured him. 'Winter is nearly here. Drive out the castellan and his men and even if one of them sends a pigeon flying with the news, the Paramount King's army won't get here before the first snows fall.'

'The castellan in Mithess could send his cavalry to join forces with the men we've thrown out,' Uderil countered.

'As long as Hatalys men hold the walls and gates, all they can do is sit outside and battle the frosts,' Sincai insisted.

'While they wonder if Mithess' people are contemplating their own rebellion,' Isom mused, 'while their garrison's elsewhere.'

'Quite so.' Sincai grinned.

'The harvests are all in,' someone beyond the fire observed. 'Even if we couldn't go hunting for fear of the Paramount King's men, we wouldn't starve within the town.'

'The storehouses will only stay full until the castellan starts sending barges downstream,' Zanner said abruptly.

Nedi saw the men stiffen and glanced at each other, grim-faced. Nedi remembered the hungry days at the end of last winter when the snows and the river ice had endured for a full half-moon longer than usual.

Even the thriftiest bakers had run out of flour so there was no bread and the men couldn't hunt or fish to ease their wives' struggles to eke out their pantries' dwindling supplies. Old Mistress Tigad who ran the dame-school where Nedi had learned his letters and numbers had been found dead and cold in her bed.

'Who are you?' The question was out before he realised he had spoken aloud.

Sincai smiled. 'I'm the man who's spent these past eight years sneaking out beyond the walls to search every nook and gully for the place where the eagle must be buried, after hearing my grandfather's tale of his father carrying it away for safekeeping.'

He looked at the rest of the men. 'My family name is Dorsin. We're leather workers and we live around the Aspen Gate.'

'I've sold hides to a Rever Dorsin,' Uderil said thoughtful-ly.

'The eagle wasn't carried off. It flew away.' Thulle was still gazing, entranced, at the statue.

No one paid him any heed. Uncle Isom looked at Plore and Nedi saw something pass unspoken between them.

'What do you have in mind?' Isom asked cautiously.

'Men were hanged for talking treason in the old mar-grave's day.' Plore tossed another log into the firepit sending up a shower of sparks.

Sincai nodded. 'We cannot debate and discuss our plans in the streets and taverns. Word will get back to the garrison and the castellan will send ten men to seize each one of us. We need to strike as unexpected as lightning and in as many places as we can. Let the garrison try stamping out ten differ-ent fires when twenty more have sprung up before the first is quelled.'

'Fires?' Thulle looked around with unnerving eagerness.

'No one will be lighting fires, you old fool,' Uderil said scornfully.

'Just kindling a lust for freedom in people's hearts.' Chal-lenge shone bright in Sincai's eyes.

'Fine words,' Uderil observed. 'What do you actually want us to do?'

'Raise a cry for Hatalys and the eagle,' Sincai said prompt-ly. 'Rouse everyone to come to the castle and see it for them-selves. Then we'll tell the castellan and his men that they're no longer welcome. If they come out to confront us, they'll be outnumbered and we can drive them to the gates. If they hide behind the castle's walls, we bar the gates to keep them inside until they've emptied their store rooms. Then the price of food and drink will be leaving the town.'

'Why should we be the ones to start this landslide?' Zan-ner demanded.

'Who goes around the town more unnoticed than goat herders and their wives?' Sincai grinned.

104

He was right, Nedi realised. Day in and day out, men too old to endure these hills drove freshly purchased beasts to each district's butchers, from the tender and sweet-fleshed kids to the aged nannies destined for the stewpot. The women sold milk and cheeses from door to door each morning, leaving the dogs and younger children watching over the milking flocks grazing around the town walls.

'The townsfolk will laugh in our faces,' one of the grey beards prophesied.

To Nedi's surprise, Sincai shrugged. 'Then what have you lost? What have you risked? Calling folk to come and see a marvel isn't treason. You won't even look foolish when the mockers learn that the eagle is there for all to see.'

Uncle Isom raised a hand. 'How do you propose to get something that size back up onto the gatehouse pinnacle?'

'We need someone who can climb.' Sincai looked around the fire. 'That's my other reason for coming out here.'

Muted laughter eased the tension a little. Goat men were well known for their surefootedness. They had to be as nimble as their charges, given the beasts' perverse ambition to scale the steepest crags in search of forage. Come the winter, when the snows penned everyone up within the town, Nedi's father and uncles mended leaking roofs and rebuilt unsteady chimneys.

Abruptly he realised that everyone was looking at him. Despite the heat from the fire, Nedi was chilled to the bone.

'The lad's the best climber here.' Thulle's unblinking gaze was profoundly unnerving.

Nedi silently cursed his own readiness to help the old man rescue a cragfast goat the day before last.

'The garrison would just think some lads were larking about,' Uderil observed slowly.

'I couldn't!' Nedi's voice rose embarrassingly and he swallowed hard. 'Not without my father's say-so.'

'Your father would agree in a heartbeat.' Plore looked steadily at him and Isom nodded.

Zanner grinned. 'You'll be up there, back down and away before any River Kingdom man can find a foothold.'

'If we're to do this, let's do it sooner than later.' Plore rose to his feet.

Half the other men joined him, their faces eager in the firelight. Did that mean it was agreed? Was there to be no show of hands? No further discussion? Nedi wanted to ask but the words froze in his throat.

'If we leave now, we can be at the gates by daybreak,' Sincai said swiftly. 'You can go and wake your wives and all spread the word.'

'We'll tell your father and mother,' Isom assured Nedi.

'If they forbid it, we'll come at once to call you down,' Zanner promised.

'We'll keep the goats penned until you come back,' one of the greybeards announced. 'The dog boys can cut fodder and shovel shit for a few days.'

Nedi saw the other men were already rolling up their blankets and securing their few possessions in the bags which each herder carried. He rubbed a shaking hand across his face and felt the prickle of bristles. So much for his pride in those. At the moment, he'd give anything to still be a smooth-faced dog boy.

'Come on, young hero.' Sincai was at his side. 'Don't you want to be the man who restores the eagle to Hatalys?'

Nedi supposed that would be something, since it seemed he had no choice. He gazed at the statue. Thulle was wrapping it in the sacking again, as gentle as a man swaddling a baby. 'Who's to tote that weight back to the town?'

'I will,' Sincai assured him.

Nedi looked up at him. 'Where did you find it?'

Sincai grinned. 'In the last place I looked.'

Before Nedi could press the stranger, Isom came over. 'Your father will be proud of you.'

And that was that. The rest of the night passed more quickly than Nedi could have imagined. The men all knew the path and then the familiar road and the air was cold enough to turn muddy ruts solid enough for them all to find sure footing. The moon rode high in the sky, round and full, to light their way.

By the time the sky paled, the town's walls cut a jag-toothed line of darkness across the horizon. Nedi was stumbling with exhaustion but he still kept pace with his uncles at the head of the straggling column. Fear of falling behind and being lost on the road faded, replaced with dread at what was to come.

Someone cried out from the rearguard, chagrined 'The gates won't unlock till dawn!'

'They'll open to me.' Sincai shouted over his shoulder.

Nedi caught a glimpse of his face in the strengthening light. The stranger had carried the eagle's great weight all this way yet his pace was unflagging, his certainty undimmed. Nedi began to wonder if this madcap plan might actually succeed.

Reaching the gatehouse, Sincai knocked with a brisk triple rap on the porter's door cut into the great double oak gates.

Like every boy, Nedi knew that opening the gate was completely forbidden between the dusk and dawn horn calls from the castle. Get locked out, their mothers warned, and you'll be cold and hungry all night, if the moor dogs don't get you.

But the porter's door opened up and a man greeted Sincai with a fervent smile. He ushered them all through the portal before locking it securely again.

The goat herders quickly dispersed, each man heading for home. Zanner clapped Nedi on the shoulder. 'We'll meet you at the castle. You need not climb if your parents forbid it.'

Before Nedi could answer, Zanner hurried away to catch up with Isom.

'What's the matter?' Sincai murmured.

Nedi turned to see the gatekeeper drawing Sincai close to say something in urgent low tones. Nedi couldn't make any of it out.

'Let me take that.' Thulle had been following Sincai so closely that he'd been all but treading in the younger man's footsteps. Now he reached out to slip the rope sling supporting the sack-swathed eagle from Sincai's shoulders.

'I'll take the boy to the castle. No one will look twice at an old fool like me.'

Sincai let the old man take possession of the bird before looking intently at Nedi. 'There's something I must attend to. Can you see this through without me?'

He's asking me, Nedi realised with nervous pride. Not old Thulle. He nodded jerkily, his mouth dry and not just from the long night's journey.

'Come on.' Cradling the eagle in his arms, Thulle forced the boy onwards like a grizzled dog herding a young billy goat.

Nedi didn't need any old man chivvying him. He knew the quickest routes to the castle through the town's back alleys, up the sloping streets to the highest point of the wall-girt hill. More than once, he glanced over his shoulder to see Thulle labouring under the eagle's weight and had to slow to let him catch up.

All the while, the daylight was strengthening. Nedi saw the first signs of households waking; threads of smoke from chimneys and upper shutters unlatched as chamber pots were emptied into the gutters below.

The castle's gates were still firmly bolted when they arrived in the cobbled square in front of the ancient stronghold. Twin towers, as round as a drum, stood on either side of the peaked arch of the gate. Above the iron-bound oak, the wall linking the towers stretched upwards high, as sheer as any cliff. Rising like steps on either side, the stonework rose to a pinnacle above the wall-walk which circled the castle's battlements. The highest point was the plinth where the eagle had once stood.

How was he supposed to get up there? One slip and he would plummet to his death. Nedi turned to Thulle. 'I can't—'

He gasped as Thulle's knife prodded his belly. The old man had set his burden down and drawn the long, square-ended blade that every goat man carried to hack a path through brush or to cut fodder.

'You will,' Thulle assured him.

'Or you'll gut me?' Nedi cried, incredulous. 'Who will carry the eagle up then?'

'I'll say a cavalryman killed you.' Mad cunning lit the old man's eyes. 'While the townsfolk raise a hue and cry, I'll slip inside and go up the stairs.'

He was, Nedi realised, quite crazy enough to imagine he could succeed.

'So climb,' Thulle snarled, 'before your fool of a father arrives or your uncles.'

Could he yell for help, Nedi wondered, if the castle gates opened? Not before the old lunatic killed him.

Trembling, he studied the angle between the curve of the closest tower and the wall spanning the gateway. The stonework had been coarse when it was first built and long years of rain and frost had crumbled the mortar away. Moss outlined useful ledges and tufts of yellow grass were seeded here and there. Nedi and his friends had climbed just such weathered stretches of the town wall when they'd been supposedly herding milch goats in the pastures.

'Take it up!' Thulle jabbed his arm with the blade.

Nedi felt a sting like a wasp. Had the lunatic drawn blood? 'All right! All right!'

He grabbed the loop of rope and slung it over his shoulder. The eagle wasn't as heavy as he had feared but it was still a substantial burden. He worked his other arm through the second loop to pull the lump of sacking tight between his shoulder blades.

'Let me look for the best route,' Nedi snapped as Thulle advanced his menacing blade again.

He contemplated the round towers. They were only

two storeys high, albeit high-ceilinged within. If he could get as far as the top, he could climb up the stepped side of the stonework rising behind the wall-walk easily enough. It wasn't so far. Not as far as he had climbed before up in the hills, at least a few times.

Nedi reached up for a handhold on the gatehouse wall and found another on the side of the tower. As he pulled himself up, he wedged his toes into convenient cracks. He was grateful for his sturdy boots, though he knew his mother would scold him for scarring the leather.

More handholds presented themselves. Nedi climbed as quickly as he dared to get beyond Thulle's reach, pressing himself close to the masonry.

'You have two hands and two feet. Keep three of the four firmly planted all the time.' He recalled his father's words when he'd first been sent up a crag to chivvy a young goat who saw no need to be penned for the night.

Moving more slowly as he climbed higher, the cold stones numbed Nedi's hands. Perversely though, his fingertips felt scoured raw. He should have put on his gloves.

As he stopped for a moment, his foot slipped on sodden moss. The eagle on his back swung sideways, nearly dragging him to his doom. The ropes cut deep into his shoulders, agonizing. Heart pounding, Nedi scrabbled desperately at the masonry. Finally his boot caught on some foothold.

Breathlessly, he tested its strength. Would it bear his weight? He clung to the stones with one hand and forced his other toe deeper into its crevice. Snatching for the next handhold, he pulled himself upwards.

Someone exclaimed below in the square, only to be cut short by a warning murmur from a handful of people. Nedi could not look down. He wasn't even sure he could climb back down. He had no choice but to continue with this madness even though his arms and legs were trembling with effort and fear.

Nedi pressed his face against the cold stone and craned his neck, trying to see upwards without fatally unbalancing himself. He was heartened to see he was closer than he had imagined to the dubious safety of the tower's crenellations.

He could hear baffled voices within the tower. Narrow windows overlooked the approach to the gate and along the length of the castle wall to either side. Nedi guessed that more windows overlooked the courtyard within the gate. The garrison had woken up. What would happen when someone roused the castellan?

Was there someone already up on the tower keeping watch? Nedi couldn't see. Would he get to the top only for grasping hands to drag him onto the leaded roof, demanding to know what he was doing?

Then they would seize the eagle and he would have risked his life for nothing. Thulle would never forgive him. Whatever Sincai and the others might say, the old madman would cut his throat one dark night, Nedi was sure of that. Or the castellan's men would throw him off the tower to fall to his death, smashed and broken on the cobbles below.

He began climbing faster regardless. He must climb up onto the gatehouse pinnacle as soon as he possibly could. His only hope of safety was getting higher than bigger and heavier men dared to climb.

There was no one on top of the tower. Nedi hauled himself up and toppled forward between the upthrust masonry to land painfully hard on his numbed yet aching hands. The eagle's weight bore down mercilessly between his shoulders.

He scrambled across the tower roof. The stepped facade of the wall spanning the gateway seemed impossibly narrow. How could he possibly do this?

How could he turn back? Hearing shouts in the castle's courtyard, Nedi looked down to see men pointing upwards. He unslung the eagle from his back and looped his arms through the ropes again so that the ungainly bulk was held against his chest. He began climbing up the stepped stones rising behind the wall-walk on his hands and knees even though the wall itself was barely wide enough for that.

He kept his gaze fixed on the next step and then the step

after that. If he slipped, he would try to fall sideways towards the gatehouse's outer face. He might just land on the wall-walk. Capture and a broken arm or ankle would be a fair trade for his life.

Nedi reached the top, breathless and sweating despite the cold air. Agonisingly careful, he sat astride the last stone below the plinth and gripped the wall with his knees and ankles. The sacking-wrapped bundle sat safe within the circle of his arms as he clung onto the plinth for added reassurance.

Now he dared to look down. Outside the castle, he saw a crowd with their pale faces all turned upwards and hands pointing just like the garrison men. They had all come to see the eagle returned. So Nedi had better oblige them.

He began picking at the ropes with his sore, cold fingers. His breath came faster, harsher, as he broke his nails on the knots pulled tight by the eagle's weight. Finally the hemp yielded and Nedi could unwrap the coarse sacking to reveal the eagle's head.

Close to, it was crudely made. Rough edges on the cast metal hadn't been filed smooth. The incised lines marking its feathers were uneven and incomplete. Its head and beak looked more like a crow than an eagle and Nedi had never seen any real bird spread its wings in such ridiculously rounded fashion. Its legs were slightly different lengths with clawed feet seemingly melting into the square pedestal.

The crowd below began cheering nevertheless as the strengthening sunlight struck golden fire from the brass. So now Nedi had to secure the thing in its plinth. He could see the four holes where the brass pedestal's stubby feet would hold it secure. He held on tight with his knees and feet as he lifted the eagle up.

His arms burned, already so tired from climbing up here. Nedi was seized with terror. He wasn't going to be able to do this. At the last moment, with his last despairing effort, he lifted it a little higher and further. As his strength failed, the pedestal's brass feet slid into their sockets.

A triumphant cry rose up from the crowd below the gate.

Newcomers were swelling the tumult. Now pots and pans clashed loudly together, punctuating a rhythmic chant.

Rough music. Nedi had heard it a few times. When a man persisted in beating his wife. When a mother let her children go hungry and barefoot. When some adulterous couple dishonoured their vows and their spouses. When remonstration had failed. When help was rejected or abused. Then the clamour would start. It would last night after night until exhaustion wore away defiance and the guilty sneaked away with nothing but the clothes on their back.

Did the River Kingdom men understand? Did they realise that the Hatalys folk were telling them to leave? That they would brook no refusal? Nedi looked down into the castle's courtyard and shuddered so violently that he almost lost his balance. He clung to the stone, pressing his cheek against the eagle's plinth.

The garrison had drawn up in serried ranks. They were loading their hackbuts with black powder and lead shot. Nedi saw faint wisps of smoke rising from the coiled lengths of alchemist's twine which each man would clamp in his weapon's serpentine lock. Uncle Isom had shown him how a pull on the trigger snapped the curved lock down to ignite the priming powder in the flash pan. That prompted the black powder in the iron barrel to fire quicker than blinking.

Nedi was aghast. The cobbles would run red with blood. Why hadn't the older, wiser men foreseen the castellan would order his men to fire on the crowd? Was Uncle Isom going to be killed? Uncle Zanner? Where was his father? Was his mother among the women drumming on cookpots with their ladles?

Raucous shrieks closer at hand suddenly deafened him. Nedi was completely surrounded by fluttering wings and screeching birds of every size and colour. Had they been startled from their roosts by the noise?

As he ducked the countless scratching talons and piercing beaks, he froze, astonished. All his terror of being up here so high, all his fears for his family's fate vanished like morning dew. He could see the eagle despite the swirling cloud of birds. Only it wasn't the rough-hewn brass effigy which he had carried up here.

The golden metal bird was a thing of beauty, precise in every lifelike detail. It perched, wings raised and angled, as though it was ready to plunge from the sky to seize some unsuspecting prey. Its hooked beak gaped. Its eyes shone bright as diamonds. It turned its head to look at Nedi with a fierce hunter's gaze.

The birds swooped down to fill the castle courtyard. The garrison men shouted and cursed, flailing with their arms and hackbuts. It did no good. From hedge sparrows to crag crows, the birds clawed and pecked and shat all over the River Kingdom men and their weapons.

When the flock dispersed as suddenly as it had appeared, the courtyard was deserted. Nedi saw that the men had fled back into their barracks. Some had held onto their weapons but more had let the precious hackbuts fall to the ground. Powder was spilled over the cobbles along with lengths of alchemist's twine, all now soiled and useless.

Someone had opened the castle gate! He saw the townsfolk crowding into the courtyard. Soon the men were banging on the doors all around. The garrison emerged with their hands raised in surrender. A knot of richly clad River Kingdom men were swiftly surrounded by Hatalys's leading craftsmen and merchants. They broke into several earnest conversations.

Nedi looked down outside the castle again. The crowd was still growing there. More and more people were coming to see this marvel and to join in the triumphant cheering.

They were pointing up at the eagle. Now it looked just the same as it had done when it was first revealed. It didn't matter. From that distance no one could see it was ugly and crude.

Nedi contemplated the effigy. Had he imagined the living bronze's magical beauty? No, he hadn't. He could go to his deathbed as an old, old man, quite sure of that. Though he didn't think he would tell anyone. Not and be mocked for a fool like Thulle.

Firstly though, if he was to live to be a greybeard, he must get safely down from this perilous perch. Nedi considered his options and decided to climb slowly and carefully down to the battlements and wait there until someone came to show him the proper route through the castle.

It wasn't until he was safely there on the wall walk that a profoundly unnerving thought struck him. If the eagle's magic had summoned the birds to overwhelm the garrison, did that mean the rest of Thulle's tales were true? Could the Horned God's priests truly conjure up monsters?

Nedi looked up at the eagle and a golden shimmer blinded him. For an instant he thought he saw the bird transformed once again. As he blinked he fervently hoped that was a promise of the eagle's aid, if the River Kingdom's masked priests could really call on such sorcery and try to reclaim Hatalys for the Paramount King.

The Ties That Bind

Chapter One

This is the story of how my life changed. How my life changed for the second time. But I chose my own course that first time. I wished for a better future and I set out to find it. This time I was wholly overtaken by events, at first at least. Now I have no idea what the days ahead will bring, for better or for worse. I only know that my life has changed beyond all recognition. Beyond any hope of going back.

I had no reason to imagine that calamity was soon to overwhelm me on this fine clear day in late spring. With the morning half passed, the sun was warm enough to forego a cloak so I wrapped a flower-embroidered shawl over my duck-egg blue dress. Picking up my basket, I planned my walk to the butcher's shop and the local market where I would find fresh milk and eggs, leafy greens and moist roots.

No other city enjoys so much bounty brought by the barges trading with the farms and gardens up and down-stream, as the River Tane cuts southward from the high plateau to meet the River Dore carving its broad path from west to east through the boundless grasslands. No wonder Hurat has prospered so mightily.

Though we lived in a modest neighbourhood, my husband and I. These row houses sheltered many of the clerks who worked for the merchants' brokerages. They spent their days in counting houses overshadowed by the lofty warehouses overlooking the riverside wharves. Journeyman craftsmen left each morning to carve and polish and cut and stitch for their masters. All were saving for the day when they could set up their own workshops.

Clarks and artisans alike returned home each evening to their loving families. Some of those growing households were hard pressed for space. Front doors opened onto a single room with the kitchen behind, two bedrooms above and only a garret above that. Resolute women found ways to cope. Renting a larger house for the same coin would mean moving closer to the city's point. Mothers would see their children sleep three or four to a bed before contemplating such an upheaval.

They already lived far enough down this wedge of land thrust between the Tane and the Dore. Everyone knew that the closer one went towards the rivers' meeting, the streets grew dirtier and more dangerous, the houses more ramshackle and the people less and less honest.

I knew the truth of such stories, and of the falsehoods that swirled alongside them, better than my neighbours. I doubted that any of them had ever set foot in the alleys cutting between those crowded tenements. No one they knew toiled in the tanneries and slaughter houses relying on the fast flowing rivers to carry their stench and filth away. No one I spoke to hereabouts ever mentioned how the Tane's waters, dark as sodden autumn leaves, eddied and battled with the Dore's flood, pale green as spring wheat out on the plains. I never mentioned that strange beauty amid the ugliness and desperation of the Spearhead. Not and have someone ask what business could possibly have taken me there.

Closing our house's red-painted door, I locked it securely behind me. The brass knocker which I polished daily sparkled in the sunlight. I rubbed the heron's head affectionately and wondered how soon Teutel would announce his return with a brisk double tap. Then we would share love and laughter in the soft warmth of our featherbed.

We missed each other sorely when he travelled to the towns downstream towards the Nilgeh Mire. But he was buying dyestuffs and alum on his father's behalf. Master Menore sold them on to the weavers and fullers in the towns upstream on the Tane, where sheep and goats grazed the gentle hills. So we accepted such separation was the price we paid for our contented life in our comfortable house. Besides, as soon as the Sun Goddess was willing, I would have a baby to cherish whenever Teutel was away.

With my keys jingling merrily on their chain hanging from my waist, I made my way through the throng of women about their errands. Delivery boys and traders were intent on their own affairs. Hurat's thoroughfares were never empty, day or night. I visited the butcher and then the daily market's stalls close by the looming towers of the great bridge carrying the Paramount King's road southwards over the Dore.

My household needs met, I decided to pay my respects to the Golden Mother. In the outer courtyard encircling the little, local shrine, children played cheerfully beneath her benevolent statue's gaze while their parents sought counsel inside. I touched the polished bronze of the Goddess's foot with a brief prayer that I would soon be seeking her mid-wife-priestesses' care while Teutel visited their sterner sisters to bank his share of this latest trip's profits.

I considered going within to ask to see the ledger record-ing all my husband's transactions between those who banked their coin here and in the Goddess's other shrines, across this city and far beyond. I had that right, like every wife, as keeper of our household purse. More than that, I loved to see those neatly inked and steadily increasing totals, reassur-ing me that the poverty which had blighted my childhood was safely in my past. When our family-to-come, Goddess willing, outgrew our little house, we would be able to move upstream, not down, to those leafy districts where the city spread itself ever wider between the converging rivers.

As I turned, I saw a travel-worn priestess coming down the street. She escorted a gaggle of exhausted and blank-eyed families clutching meagre bundles. I hastily found a few coppers in my skirt pocket. As one of the shrine's priestesses hurried to open the gate, I detained her briefly with a hand on her forearm.

'For the destitute.' I pressed the coin into her hand.

Where should the desperate come but to our great and glorious city? Once it had merely been the wealthiest of the towns dotted up and downstream thanks to the twin bridges which brought the roads to meet the merging rivers. Now Hurat ruled over all those lesser towns, their barons and no-bles pledging fealty to the Paramount King in return for his cavalry's protection.

'Bless you, my daughter.' The priestess spared me a brief smile.

I slipped through the gate as she opened it and went on my way. Those men, women and children needed the Golden Mother's care and attention far more urgently than me. Eight days ago the market had been buzzing with news of a fearsome whirlwind. The talon cloud had clawed at villages between the towns of Rarcul and Eldil four or five days ride southwards into the wheat fields. Homes, livelihoods and loved ones had all been destroyed.

Even as my heart went out to those suffering, I had no notion that disaster was to strike me just as suddenly out of this clear blue sky.

Not that I went on my way with any great cheer. Duty led me towards my parents-by-marriage's house, not affection. No, that's not quite true. I had no quarrel with my husband's father and he seemed fond enough of me for all his misgivings about my origins.

My mother-by-marriage? That was a very different tale. Her plans for her beloved only son had never included him wedding the daughter of a feckless artist born in her mother's deathbed. It made no difference to her that I had cared loyally for my father until his occasional solace of a bottle of liquor became a daily indulgence and, all too soon after that, proved the death of him.

By then I earned my own keep as a daily maid-of-all-work in a respectable travellers' hostel. With the housekeeper's help and her generous testimonial, I secured a live-in maid's post in a leather merchant's house. His son had been schooled by the Horned God's priests alongside Teutel. That's how we had first met and whatever his mother might say, I had never sought to snare her son. Teutel was the first one struck by the Goddess's smile when our paths crossed in his friend's hallway.

As I turned into the broad street where his parents' home stood amid well-tended and fruitful gardens, I reminded myself of Teutel's own words. His mother might have been content if he'd married Princess Giseri. No lesser bride than

119

the woman who would one day follow her father to rule from the Paramount Throne could ever hope to win Mistress Menore's approval.

'Mistress Deyris.' The gatekeeper admitted me with a warm smile. He took his lead from the master of the house.

'Are there any letters today?' I asked hopefully. Master Menore had business at any number of places around the city on any given day so messengers always brought correspondence here, returning to collect their replies the following day. Teutel said that even though his father rose at dawn and worked beyond sunset, he would often still be writing beyond midnight to keep faith with his business partners up and down the Tane and the Dore.

Mistress Menore insisted that any letter for me, even one addressed in her own son's handwriting, must remain inside the courier's bag until her husband returned to authorise a lackey to carry it to me.

Teutel and his father had remonstrated with her more than once and she always promised to despatch such letters promptly. She never did, always claiming she had forgotten this setting aside of her own beloved father's customs, when he had been master of this business.

'Not this morning,' Okem said, regretful. 'There's more than half the day to go though,' he added, encouraging.

'True enough.' As I smiled, I saw movement behind one of the windows. I stifled a sigh.

I couldn't count on that being just a maidservant busy about her duties. If my mother-by-marriage saw me leave her gate without seeking to pay my respects, Teutel wouldn't hear the last of it before midwinter. 'Is Mistress Menore at home?'

'I couldn't say,' Okem replied, guarded.

So she was within but in such an uncertain temper that he didn't know if she would receive me. So I had to knock and ask, to avoid giving her that stick to beat me with.

'I can leave my compliments with her maid.' I smiled at Okem and walked up the path.

The house steward opened the door so quickly he must have been lurking in the hallway. 'Good day, Mistress Teutel.'

He had entered this house as a barely-whiskered lackey in his mistress's father's day and took his lead from her in disapproving of me.

'Good day.' I smiled sunnily. 'Is Mistress Menore at home.'

He looked me up and down for a long moment before replying. 'This way, if you please.'

I followed, my basket in the crook of my arm and my shawl decorously draped around my shoulders.

'Deyris? What a pleasant surprise.' Mistress Menore was reading in her sunlit parlour. As she glanced up her sour expression blatantly contradicted her words.

I wondered how two people who looked so alike could be so different in character. She shared my husband's chestnut hair and warm brown eyes, his height and slender build, though lending a hand aboard the river barges had broadened Teutel's shoulders and hardened his muscles. By contrast, age and indolence was softening my mother-by-marriage's fine features.

'Good day to you, Mother.' After nearly three years of marriage, I managed not to choke on the word. I would never choose to call her that but as long as I refused, she had complained to Teutel of my disrespect. What of her rudeness in never inviting me to use her given name?

She looked up further to meet my eyes. The first place she always looked was my waist, for any swelling to my belly. I couldn't tell if she was disappointed to see no such sign. She longed to cradle her son's own child but as long as I stayed slender, she could use that against me. I wondered how long it would be before she started hinting to Teutel that we should hand our marriage bracelets back to the Goddess, to dissolve our marriage on account of our barrenness. She would soon contrive introductions to far more suitable brides.

'Are you well?' I asked politely. Though there were three elegant chairs arranged on this side of the low table beside her sofa, I knew better than to sit down uninvited.

Her feathery-pelted black lap dog jumped down from its cushion beside her. It ran over to leap up at my basket and its untrimmed claws, unworn by exercise, snagged on my skirt.

'What have you got there?' she snapped.

'Bones for soup.' I challenged her to condemn me for frivolous extravagance with my husband away.

She sniffed. 'I'm glad to see you know your limitations as a cook.'

I ground my teeth. She was never going to let me forget the beef I had ruined when Teutel and I were first married. Since my father and I never ate such fine fare, I'd had no notion how to baste and turn roasting meat. One side had ended up charred while the other was still raw.

Still, as they say, rubbing can raise a shine instead of a sore. Teutel had expected his mother's sympathy and some advice for me in the kitchen. Her spiteful response then and thereafter, had convinced him that I didn't exaggerate her loathing of our marriage.

'I had better get home before the marrow spoils in the heat.' Curtseying, I managed, accidentally-on-purpose, to threaten the dog with my basket. The greedy little beast scurried away, not as foolish as it looked.

Mistress Menore's lips thinned but before she made some barbed reply, commotion erupted in the hall behind me.

'Where is he? I must see Master Menore!'

'You cannot—' The parlour door flew open to cut the steward's remonstrations short.

'Mistress Menore, where is your husband to be found today?' A barge captain, ashen-faced, stood on the threshold. Still grimy from his voyage, he must have hurried here as soon as his boat bumped against the wharf.

The feathery black lapdog jumped onto the velvet sofa, yapping. My mother-by-marriage sat upright, stiff with outrage. 'What do you think—'

'Mistress Teutel?' The barge captain rubbed a rope-

122

scarred hand over his bearded chin. To my growing alarm, his hazel eyes glistened with tears. 'I didn't think to find you here.'

'What—?' My mother-by-marriage broke off to silence her barking lap-dog with a slap.

'I have letters from the Castellan in Usenas.' Advancing, the captain reached inside his sturdy blue jerkin. 'For your husband and for the young master's wife.'

His hand was shaking so much that he could barely get the stiffly folded paper out of his inner pocket. I stared, speechless. Why would the Paramount King's representative write to me from the Kingdom's furthest town downstream on the Dore?

'Where is my son?' Mistress Menore was as pale as her creamy silk gown.

'He went ashore in the morning.' The barge captain offered me a letter. 'We never thought to worry, not till sunset had come and gone.'

The thrice-sealed paper raised a breeze like a fan. It wasn't only the cold draught raising goose-flesh on my arm as I snatched it from him.

The captain turned to plead with Mistress Menore. 'We made the Castellan send out search parties from the garrison.'

'I'll send a runner to fetch the master.' The steward turned so fast that he slipped and nearly fell on the polished wood-block floor.

'What are you saying, dolt?' Mistress Menore snapped. 'You have left my son behind? How is he supposed to get home?'

'He is— He is—' The grizzled captain couldn't continue, tears spilling down his weathered cheeks.

I snapped the Castellan's wax seals and unfolded the paper so fast that it tore.

'What does that say?' Mistress Menore demanded.

I ignored her, reading stark words in ink as black as fate.

'... I regret to inform you that the fifth day following, we recovered a body from the river. Captain Stryet identified the man's purse and rings as your husband's...'

I crushed the letter in my fist. 'What of his wedding bracelet?'

Wordless, the barge captain reached into his jerkin once again.

'What are you saying, you stupid girl!' Mistress Menore shrieked.

She sprang up from her sofa, grabbing at the paper. I let her take it. I had no use for the Castellan's sympathies.

Sometimes, as a child caught in a nightmare, I would realise that everything around me was an evil dream. Soon, I was able to will myself awake. Was this a dream? I felt numb from head to toe and Teutel's mother's cries swirled around me, meaningless. The rest of the room might just as well have faded into mist and all I could see was the burly, weeping barge-man. But I knew I wasn't sleeping. This wasn't some horror to be driven off by lighting a candle or opening shutters to the dawn.

'Any man might wear such rings as my son's. Any number might carry the same purse.' Mistress Menore threw the letter to the floor and advanced on the hapless captain. 'Did you see the body for yourself?'

He drew a deep shuddering breath. 'They said it would do no good. After those days with the river rats and turtles—'

Mistress Menore silenced him with a brutal slap across the face. 'Then you cannot say anything for certain!' she screamed, striking him a second time and a third. 'I will have you flogged for this, you villain. When my son comes home—'

'This is his wedding bracelet.' I took the silver circlet from the barge captain's unresisting hand.

Any number of men might buy similar rings. A leather worker might make ten purses with a pattern he liked. Every pair of wedding bracelets was unique as the match between two lovers. No craftsman would dishonour the Golden

124

Goddess, or worse still, risk the Horned God's displeasure by copying some earlier design.

I slid the silver ring onto my wrist. My hand was small enough that I had no need to open the clasp to unhinge it. Even tarnished, the pattern was plain for all to see. This bracelet was twin to the one I had worn since my wedding day.

'No. No.' Mistress Menore turned her fury on me.

I raised my hands to ward her off. She grabbed my braceleted wrist.

'You stupid girl. He must have been robbed. He fought back. That's how this villain fell into the river to drown!'

She was trying to force the discoloured bracelet back over my knuckles. I clenched my fist and pulled away. She would not take this remembrance from me.

'Where is Teutel then? What's become of him if the dead man is some unknown thief?'

Now I was screaming at her as the cursed lapdog yapped, dancing around us and jumping up.

Mistress Menore recoiled from my anguish. Tripping over the dog, she fell backwards onto the sofa. Collapsing onto the cushions, she wept hysterically.

I don't remember much more of that dreadful day. My father-by-marriage soon arrived, summoned by the steward's lackey. He drew the tear-stained barge captain aside to question him closely.

'I didn't see his body but they showed me his clothes,' Captain Stryet pleaded. 'His green coat with the brass buttons and his boots. He'd had them mended on the voyage. I could see where the stitching didn't match. I have all his gear on the barge.'

I watched as Master Menore aged ten years before my eyes. His shoulders slumped, his chin sank to his chest, sorrow deepening every crease on his face.

My husband's sisters began to gather, fetched by other servants. Vari and Tracha joined their mother in alternating between outbursts of weeping and wrathful denial, cursing everyone in Usenas from the Castellan down as liars and thieves. The three of them would assure each other that Teutel would soon return with a simple explanation for this foolish misunderstanding. Then they would all fall silent until one or other broke into noisy sobs.

Astrila and Lessane, eldest and youngest, stood silently beside their father, listening to Captain Stryet's halting explanations. I was too far away to hear him. I had retreated to a window seat overlooking the gardens. Teutel and I had loved to walk among the flowers and scented blossom trees. He had often spoken of his plans for a garden of our own.

Soon the neighbours noticed all this upheaval. Their servants approached the gate. I watched, dry-eyed, as Okem wiped away fresh tears every time he had to explain what was amiss.

I could not weep. I don't know why. I sat, numb in mind and spirit, staring out of the window until Astrila's soft voice startled me.

'Deyris?'

'I need to go home.' The words came unbidden to my tongue. As soon as I had spoken, I knew that nothing else would do. There was no place for me here. My only hope of solace was in the house which Teutel and I had shared.

'You cannot be alone.' Astrila was horrified. She was the best of my sisters-by-marriage even if there were ten years, her own marriage, her two sons and a year-old daughter between us, There were six years, two living sisters and two lost infant siblings between her and Teutel.

I rose to my feet. 'I am going home.' Somewhat surprised to find it close at hand, I picked up my basket and drew my shawl around my shoulders.

Whatever Astrila saw in my face convinced her that I would not be gainsaid. She hurried across the room to command the steward's attention with a discreet gesture and a low word. 'Gelar?'

He stood just inside the door, wretched with uncertainty

and anguish. What could he usefully do amid all this sorrow?

'Mistress Deyris wishes to go home. Summon the carriage and I will escort her.' Astrila glanced towards the sofa to see her mother and middle sisters overcome with grief once more. Her father, Captain Stryet and Lessane had dragged the three empty chairs to the far side of the room and sat with their heads together, hands joined in mutual consolation. I hadn't even noticed.

Steward Gelar hurried away. Astrila and I waited in the hallway, in silence, until the coachman knocked tentatively on the door. Seeing the shock and sorrow on his face, I looked away. I couldn't bear the burden of anyone else's grief.

'We'll see that all is well at your house.' Astrila ushered me down the steps, along the path and through the gate to the waiting carriage.

Much later, I realised that she never had any intention of allowing me to remain there. When we arrived, she told the coachman to wait. She used her own key to open my cheerful red door and took a few steps inside. 'Everything is just as you left it, surely?'

I was still standing on the step. My feet refused to carry me across my own threshold. I had to summon up all my resolve to force myself forward.

'Thank you for the use of the carriage. Don't let me keep you from your mother.'

As I walked past Astrila to take my market basket through to the kitchen, my own words sounded as though they came from some great distance.

'You cannot stay here alone,' Astrila protested, more forceful.

I stooped to throw a handful of kindling into the grate to reawaken the fire. Swinging the pot hook over the flames, I hung a sturdy pan ready for me to start cooking. As I picked up the water pail from the warming stone at the side of the hearth, I saw there was barely a cupful left. I hadn't gone to the well before I went out this morning but now I must.

'What are you doing?' Astrila tried to take the pail from me.

'Making soup.'

'There is no need—'

'Please!' I begged her. 'Leave me be. Comfort your mother and your father. Go and help your sisters.'

Whatever she saw in my face convinced her. She released the pail's handle, though she shook her head with misgiving. 'I will call on you later.'

'Very well.' I managed a meaningless smile as I followed her to the front door and waved from the steps. She departed, still looking anxiously at me through the carriage window.

Closing the door, I was overcome with dizziness. Fearful that I might faint, I made my way to the old-fashioned settle in front of our living room's modest fireplace.

Looking around the room as my light-headedness passed, I saw that Astrila was right. Nothing had changed here. My home was as clean and tidy as Mistress Menore could wish to see if she were ever to cross my threshold. Not that I swept and polished for her. All my endeavours were to welcome Teutel home. Surely I would hear his knock on the door at any moment?

For the first time in my life, I agreed with my mother-by-marriage. There must be some mistake. He could not be dead. I would hear his step outside on the street and he would knock on the door, home to explain this dreadful error.

As I clenched my fists, Teutel's marriage bracelet clinked against my own. I looked down to see it on my wrist. Pain seized me beneath my breastbone, as violent and as agonising as a knife to the heart. Now I wept and once my tears had started, there was no stopping them.

I don't know how long I grieved. I only know that I woke with the following dawn, stiff and chilled, awkwardly huddled on the settle with only my shawl to cover me. Thin sunlight fell through the unshuttered window, no warmer than the empty fireplace. My mouth was as dry as ashes. I remembered the scant water in the kitchen pail. That would have to suffice.

Easing my cramped limbs, I walked to the back of the house. As I did so, I smelled something faintly and remembered the marrow bones forgotten in my basket on the scrubbed table. Nausea seized me and I fumbled for my keys. Unlocking the back door, I emptied the basket's entire contents into the refuse pail.

At least that handful of kindling had burned out before the pan I had hung over the kitchen hearth could scorch. I reached over the dead fire to cup a handful of water from the pail. Stale as it was, it eased my parched throat like finest wine.

Rat-tat. The door-knocker's summons echoed through the silent house. I spun around, startled.

Rat-tat. Whoever it was knocked again.

Astrila? At this hour? How early was it? I couldn't recall hearing a shrine clock strike since I had woken.

Rat-tat.

She hadn't returned last night, I realised. Doubtless her mother's demands had made that impossible. After a wretched night between the household's sorrow and her own, she must have risen with the dawn and hurried here.

Rat-tat.

I didn't want to open the door to anyone but my beloved husband. As long as I stayed safe inside and alone, I could make believe that nothing had changed. That I was still waiting for him to return from his travels.

Rat-tat.

But Teutel always said that Astrila was his most determined sister. She would make a worthy successor when the day came for her to take over their father's business. She would also be wracked with guilt over failing to make good on her promise last night. I couldn't let her bear that burden along with her own grief today.

Slowly, still reluctant, I walked to the front door. As I reached for the keys hanging at my waist, I realised with a sudden shock that I hadn't locked up the day before. Furious at my own folly, I reached for the handle and wrenched the door open.

I screamed, shocked beyond all reason. Teutel stood on the doorstep. I pressed my hands to my face, digging my own nails into my cheeks. Was I still asleep? Was this some dream? Or had everything I'd endured the day before been some appalling nightmare?

For a moment, I had no notion what might be true and what might be falsehood. In the next instant, joy warmed me from head to toe. I threw myself into his embrace.

But he didn't catch me. As I flung my arms around my beloved husband's shoulders, his hands hung limply at his side. He stood still, stiff and unyielding.

'Darling?' I withdrew half a pace to look up into his face. 'What's wrong?'

'This is my home.' He pushed past me to enter the house.

'Yes.' I stared at him, utterly at a loss.

'This is my home.' He took a seat on a stool in front of the empty fireplace.

'Sweetheart?'

There was no sign that he'd heard me. His head didn't turn. I moved to stand where he could see me.

'Darling?'

'This is my home.' He sat staring blank-faced at the wall.

Had he been injured? Were his wits addled? Surely he must have been beaten unconscious for his marriage bracelet to be stolen. How soon would he recover?

I took a step closer. 'Teutel? What happened?'

'This is my home.'

He looked up and I recoiled. There was no spark of warmth in his dull eyes. No recognition, never mind any hint of love. I recalled tales of men injured in accidents on the wharves who never recovered their memories, who were left as incapable as infants. The delight I'd felt at seeing him evaporated like mist seared by the morning sun.

'Yes, of course this is your home.' I couldn't think what else to say.

'This is my home.' He stared straight ahead at the wall again.

So he remembered that much at least. Why couldn't he remember me? I couldn't make any sense of this. There was no visible wound to his head, no other injury. He looked just the same as he had done when he'd left on his journey.

I clenched a fistful of my skirt as a tremor of unease shook me. Teutel looked precisely the same as he had on the morning when he'd left on that fateful journey. He was wearing his green coat with the bright brass buttons. His linen shirt beneath his embroidered waistcoat was still as crisp as my hot iron had left it. His boots boasted the sheen from his diligent polishing the night before. He always sought to look his best when he was setting out to do business in his father's name.

Whenever he returned though, his linen would be creased and grimy. His buttons would be tarnished from the river mists and his boots dusty and scuffed. He would be weary from spending long days tense with determination not to let his father down, after nights disturbed by the other bargemen sharing the long cabin with its tiers of narrow bunks.

'Teutel!' I said sharply.

He looked up so abruptly he startled me. 'That is my name!' There was an unpleasant challenge in his harsh tone.

I took a step backwards, hastily placating. 'Of course it is your name.'

He nodded, looking back at the wall. 'That is my name. This is my home.'

I must send for an apothecary. I must send word to Master Menore. Someone must be able to explain my husband's unnerving behaviour.

As I retreated, my marriage bracelet snagged on my skirt where Mistress Menor's cursed lapdog had clawed at the cloth. As I freed it, I saw the blackened bracelet which Captain Stryet had brought home. It clinked softly against my own

He'd said that he had all Teutel's gear safe on his barge, I remembered. But when had Teutel ever returned from a voyage without his leather barge bag carried high on one shoulder, his other arm cradling oilcloth-wrapped packages full of gifts for me, his sisters and his mother?

I darted forward and seized his wrist. Pushing up his coat sleeve and shirt cuff, I sought his silver wedding bracelet. It was there, bright and shiny. How could this be? How could there be a second such bracelet? What silversmith would ever make a copy of such a thing? Why would Teutel have commissioned one?

'That is my name!' He seized my wrist so brutally that I yelped like his mother's lap dog.

'This is my home!' He flung me away so hard that I fell backwards onto the cold flagstones.

I cried out from the pain of landing awkwardly on the unyielding flagstones. He gave no sign of hearing me. Still staring at the blank wall in front of him, he spoke once again in that peculiar monotone.

'That is my name. This is my home.'

What had happened to my husband? How could he have forgotten me so completely? How could he leave me here on the floor, bruised and abused by his own hand?

Fresh tears filled my eyes. Not of sorrow but of bone-chilling fear.

Chapter Two

I can't say how long I sat there, snared between dread and utter confusion. Then the knocker rat-tatted again. The door swung open. Teutel hadn't latched it. Astrila stood on the step, a shawl shielding her head from the morning chill. A linen-draped basket hung in the crook of her elbow.

Seeing Teutel sat on the stool, she shrieked. He had his back to the doorway so she couldn't see his face. I did. I saw instant aggression twist his lips in a snarl. I saw the hands loose in his lap clench into menacing fists. Then a shudder ran through him. He blinked, swiftly, once, twice, thrice. His expression turned wary as he rose and turned towards Astrila.

She saw none of this, blinded by tears of joy. As she rushed across the room to throw herself onto his chest, her basket went flying. Carefully sliced and buttered bread and thick, sustaining soup spilled across the floor amid the shards of an earthenware basin.

I stared, still sprawled inelegantly on the flagstones. Teutel hadn't returned my embrace but slowly and awkwardly, he raised his hands to encircle his sister. Astrila sobbed, incoherent with emotion as she buried her face in his shoulder.

I saw his eyes narrow, still wary but now calculating as he stared towards the open door. There was still no hint of warmth or affection in his distant gaze. Nothing of my loving, beloved husband.

Cautiously, I got up. His head snapped around and his eyes fixed on me, cold and challenging. His abrupt movement interrupted Astrila's weeping. She took a step backwards, wiping away tears with the hem of her shawl.

'Oh, Deyris!' She turned to me before she could see Teutel's ugly expression and wrapped me in a crushing hug. 'Oh my dear girl.'

I held her tight and closed my eyes, wishing with all my heart that I would open them to see my husband just as he had been. But when I looked, that same stiff stranger was silently studying us in an eerily measuring manner.

'He – is not himself,' I said haltingly.

'Teutel?' Astrila spun around, concerned. 'What's the matter?'

'That's my name. This is my home.' A faint smile now curved his thin lips.

I had no notion why but I found that more chilling than his earlier blankness.

'Teutel? Don't you know me?' She took a step towards him, holding out her hands. 'It's me, Astrila, your sister!'

'Astrila,' he said slowly. 'My sister.'

But I could see that he hadn't recognised her in the least. But he reached for her, curling his fingers around her own.

'Deyris?' She turned to look at me, concerned. 'What's wrong?'

'I don't know,' I said helplessly. 'He's just arrived, but he's making no sense.'

'Deyris?' He echoed Astrila, looking at me.

I couldn't help a shudder. That wasn't my husband's loving greeting.

'Are you hurt?' Astrila raised a hand to brush the chestnut locks from his forehead.

He shied from her touch like a startled horse. Knocking over the stool, he whirled around and kicked it away, fists clenched.

Astrila retreated, taken aback. 'What's the matter with him?'

'I don't know,' I snapped, provoked.

Astrila pulled her shawl tight around her shoulders, biting her lip. Teutel stood motionless and stared back at her, unblinking. She twitched, startled, when he smiled that eerie smile.

'You're Astrila, my sister.' His cold eyes slid to me. 'You're Deyris.'

'That's right,' Astrila said eagerly. 'Deyris, your wife.'

'My wife,' he echoed.

He hadn't known that. The realisation sent shivers down my spine, swiftly followed by a still more chilling thought. Would this cold, violent stranger expect to share our marriage bed when night fell?

I turned to Astrila. 'He must see a doctor.'

Whatever was wrong with Teutel went far beyond an apothecary's skills at tending trivial injuries and everyday ailments. We needed the medical lore husbanded by the Horned God's acolytes. Golden Mother forgive me, I wanted him safely in the masked priests' care, not here in our home staring at me with those cold, dark eyes.

'Help me take him to the temple.' I was too afraid to try forcing this intruder wearing my husband's face to the Crescent Moon Gate without help.

Astrila hesitated. 'We'll send for my mother's personal physician.'

'What? No!' I protested.

Between the apothecaries and the priests, with their arcane knowledge and surgeries, physicians like Master Fyrid battened on women like Mistress Menore, prey to megrims and imagined maladies when all that truly ailed them was lack of occupation and exercise.

Astrila drew me aside towards the kitchen door. 'If we take him to the temple, think who will see us? Who knows what rumours will go swirling along the gutters with the other filth? Father has already gone out this morning to tell his most trusted partners that Teutel has been killed. That news is surely already spreading. What will people think if they hear just as quickly that it is a lie?'

I stared at her. 'Who cares what people think?'

But I knew that Teutel would care, when he was restored to himself. He was so proud of his family's good name; among the most trusted and respected of all the merchants trading up and down the Tane and the Dore.

'We must learn what is wrong discreetly,' Astrial insisted. 'Then we can share the truth with our partners when they come to call on Father.'

I shook her hand off my forearm. 'The Horned God's priests are sworn guardians of both truth and secrets.'

Teutel's hollow voice interrupted whatever she might have replied.

'To call on Father.' He went striding towards the open front door.

'Where are you going?' Astrila rushed after him.

'To call on Father.'

'Of course,' Astrila said with relief.

He hadn't been answering her question. He had merely repeated her last words. Couldn't she see that?

But somehow those words had caught and held his attention. Something prompted him to leave. I grabbed my own shawl and my keys, catching up with Astrila on the doorstep to hold her back.

'Wait. Let's see if he knows where to go. That will tell us something of what he's forgotten and what he hasn't.'

I was such a fool. Though I had no way of knowing it back then. As I locked the door and hurried after Astrila, I was only considering which of the Horned God's shrines was closest to Master Menore's house. I would go and explain to the priests myself, while Teutel was safely within his father's doors. Meantime, Mistress Menore's physician was welcome to hum and haw and wave vague hands and pocket her husband's gold.

No. First we must see if Teutel could even find his way to his parents' house. I grabbed Astrila's wrist. 'We will follow but we must not guide him, if we're to see how badly his wits are impaired.'

She tried to free herself, anguished. 'I would rather get him into a hireling carriage and away from all these gawkers.'

'No.' I shook my head. 'See, no one is even giving him a second glance.'

Astrila couldn't deny it. As Teutel strode purposefully along the street, men and women busy about their own business paid him no heed at all.

'He is taking the right road,' she said breathlessly.

'Come on.' I released her and we followed. The two of us drew more attention than Teutel as we scurried along; shawls askew, no baskets in hand and skirts flapping around our ankles.

He followed the usual route as steadily and unerring as water flowing downriver. As he turned the final corner Astrila was smiling tearfully. 'See, he knows his home.'

'He knows his old home.' I swallowed a choking lump in my throat. Why couldn't he remember the life we had built together?

Astrila seized my hand, torn between her own relief and her wish to comfort me. 'His memories will all come back to him. I'm sure of it.'

I wished she had something more than goodwill to convince her. While we were hastening through the city, I had recalled a girl a little older than me who I'd known as a child. Living among the tanneries was hazardous and one day she was trampled by a dray horse. Although she had lived, her head was left dented by an iron-shod hoof. Where she had once been an amiable, biddable child, now she fought with her brothers and sisters in the narrow streets. She lashed out, screaming, at her mother and father as they sought to keep her fed and clean.

One day the Horned God's priests had come to take her away. No one ever saw her again. No one dared ask her grieving family what had become of her. I hadn't thought of her in twenty years. Perhaps I could wait just a little while before finding the nearest Crescent Moon shrine—

Astrila broke into a run as Okem's startled shout rang down the street. 'It's all right, truly,' she frantically assured the gatekeeper. 'Master Teutel is not himself but we'll soon see him restored.'

I twisted the fringe of my shawl around my trembling hands. Okem was looking askance at Teutel, as well he might. Teutel was glaring at him with the ugly aggression I'd seen when Astrila arrived at our door.

'Quickly, open the gate!' she scolded Okem. 'Send the hall boy for Master Fyrid. At once!'

Shocked and bemused, the gatekeeper lifted the latch. Astrila ushered Teutel through the thatched archway. Thankfully there were no morning callers waiting on the bench seats within the four sturdy brick pillars.

'See,' Astrila urged. 'You know our father's house.'

'Our father's house,' Teutel murmured as he followed the path to the door.

'Mistress—?'

Okem looked to me for answers but I had none to give him. I could only echo Astrila.

'Send for Master Fyrid, if you please'

Okem thrust his fingers between his lips to send an ear-splitting whistle ripping through the dewy morning.

The household's youngest servant came running around from the tradesman's door. He skidded to a halt, gaping at Teutel and Astrila going up the entrance steps.

I snapped my fingers to get his attention. 'You, boy!' To my embarrassment I couldn't remember his name. 'Do as Okem bids you and not a word to anyone, do you hear me?'

The boy flinched, not from my urgent words. We were all skewered by the piercing scream from within doors. I was surprised the windows didn't shatter.

'Hurry up!' I left the boy to Okem and ran after Astrila and Teutel. Steward Gelar was dithering in the hallway, pale and incoherent.

'Where is your master?' I demanded. 'Send a lackey to fetch him back at once!'

'Yes, Mistress.' The steward was so completely knocked off balance that he was ready to take orders from anyone, even me.

As he yanked the bell pull to set a summons ringing in the servants' basement hall, I hurried to Mistress Menore's parlour. She had stopped screaming but the din had barely lessened.

Mistress Menore clung to Teutel, wracked with noisy sobs. Vari and Tracha flanked her, each eager to claim him with their own embraces and rival protestations that they had never believed he was lost. Astrila was trying to detach her mother's clutching hands from Teutel's coat front at the same time as explaining how she had found him at our house. Lessane pleaded with her sisters to withdraw, to give their ailing brother some air. The feathery black lapdog circled them all barking madly.

Astrila shot me a beseeching look. 'Deyris—'

That cut Mistress Menore's wailing short. 'You!'

She released Teutel and shoved Vari aside. Only the cushioned chair between us stopped her advancing to slap me. 'You were so ready to give up all hope. You faithless whore—'

'Mother!' Astrila pushed past Vari who fell backwards onto the sofa. 'Mother! You cannot say such things!'

Tracha seized her chance to seize Teutel in a rib-cracking embrace. 'I never gave up hope—'

She yelped as he wrenched her arms apart and brutally shoved her away. She tripped over Vari's feet which at least put an abrupt end to her sister's ostentatious sobbing. They spat at each other like cats as cushions spilled onto the floor.

'Enough!' Astrila sounded startlingly like her father as she thrust her mother into Lessane's involuntary grasp. I'd never seen her so angry. 'Can't you see that he isn't well?'

Indeed, now they had all left him alone, Teutel was swaying on his feet. His eyes rolled backwards in his head and his jaw lolled, slack. I skirted the chair to reach him, sure he was about to pass out. As I touched him, he shuddered and his eyes fixed on me, hard as agate.

He breathed a word so softly that only I could hear it. *'Whore.'*

I recoiled as though he had punched me in the face.

Mistress Menore pulled herself free of Lessane and made some effort to reclaim her dignity. 'Teutel, my dearest boy, you must sit down. Get up and make room for your brother!' she snapped at Vari and Tracha who were both still sprawled on the sofa. 'Shut Jet out of here, Lessane!'

The lapdog yelped as Lessane scooped him up. He squirmed in her arms, still barking furiously at Teutel. I was surprised to see how he bared his teeth, his hackles bristling. The little beast wasn't just driven to hysterics by the uproar. If he could have reached Teutel, he'd have savaged him.

As Lessane shut the parlour door on the little dog's wrath, Mistress Menore took Teutel's hand and drew him down to the sofa.

'My darling boy, what befell you? Was it footpads? Thieves from Usenas's back alleys or some River Folk sneaking ashore from their foul barges? Were you badly hurt, my love? You must have been knocked senseless—'

'River Folk,' Teutel said slowly. 'Knocked senseless.'

'Worthless flotsam,' Mistress Menore hissed.

'At least we cannot blame the Castellan for failing to keep Usenas's streets safe,' Astrila interjected.

I saw her glance across the parlour to Mistress Menore's writing desk. Costly sheets of paper were piled as high as autumn leaves and quills were scattered around the ink-stand. Not content with accusing and abusing anyone within earshot, she must have been spreading the blame for Teutel's loss as widely as she could.

'Or Captain Stryet,' Astrila continued firmly, 'who has always been a friend to this house.'

'A friend to this house.' Teutel nodded.

Mistress Menore took both his hands in her own. 'What happened? You travelled to Usenas and went ashore to conduct do business with Master Jedante—'

He nodded again. 'I went ashore—'

I interrupted. 'He's just repeating what he hears. We must stop prompting him if we're to learn what he truly remembers.'

I could see that Astrila knew I was right, even though she longed so fervently to believe that Teutel was safely home.

'Mama, he isn't well. We have sent for your physician—'

'Nonsense.' Mistress Menore waved her impatiently away. 'He's as fit as when he left, you stupid girl.'

'Teutel!' He looked up as Astrila addressed him. 'How did you lose your purse and rings? Captain Stryet brought them here—'

'He was attacked and robbed!' Mistress Menore cried. 'We all know that.'

Teutel nodded but this time I saw that eerie gleam of purpose in his dark eyes. 'I was attacked and robbed.'

'The body they found in the river must have been one of the villains, killed when they fell out over the spoils.' Mistress Menore swiftly found an explanation to satisfy herself. 'There is no honour among thieves.'

'Why throw a dead man into the river with a full purse and rings still on him?' Lessane challenged

'He fell in before they could rob him.' Mistress Menore waved that objection away.

I stepped forward. 'What happened to your wedding bracelet?'

He looked at me, eyes narrowing. 'I don't know,' he said slowly.

That chilled me. He wasn't just echoing those words. What did that mean? I fought to restrain a shiver and pulled up my sleeve to show him the twin bracelets beneath, one so grievously tarnished and one as bright as my love. 'How did you lose this?'

'I lost it—' he began, uncertainly.

'Did you?' I darted forward and shoved his crisp linen shirt cuff back to reveal shining silver. 'Then where did this come from?'

He seized my hand before I could retreat. 'I don't know.' Now those words were harsh with anger.

'Tell me something of our wedding day,' I demanded. 'What colour was my gown? What flowers were in my hair?'

Teutel had always sworn he would take those memories to his deathbed.

'I cannot recall.'

That wasn't an echo either but I couldn't think what to make of it with his grip crushing my fingers so brutally. 'Let me go!'

'Teutel!' Astrila's sharp rebuke distracted him.

His hold slackened and I pulled free, withdrawing to the far side of the cushioned chair.

'Mother,' Astrila insisted. 'We must find out what ails him.'

Mistress Menore looked at me with barely veiled satisfaction. She didn't think her son had lost his wits, I realised. She thought he had come to his senses, if he was so hostile to me.

Everyone in the room jumped as an uncertain knock on the door followed a scuffle in the hallway as the snarling lapdog was dragged away.

Steward Gelar knocked again. 'Mistress Menore? Master Fyrid is here'

'Enter!'

Gelar opened the door and a man wearing a long black coat over grey velvet breeches and a silver brocaded waistcoat bustled in. Expensive lace frothed beneath his chin and around his wrists. His fussily patterned stockings were silk and smoky topaz shone on his shoe buckles.

'Good day to you, mistress, and—' he barely paused for breath as he registered everyone else's presence in the room '—good day to you, Master Teutel and Mistress Deyris. Well now, I see that you have all decided to discuss this matter openly, which is to say, with immediate family. Naturally, I won't breathe a word outside this room. My discretion is guaranteed.'

To my surprise, he hurried to my side and cupped my shoulders with his hands. Close to, I could see the sheen of pomade holding his artfully brushed locks in place to conceal his receding hairline. His barber had used a citrus astringent after shaving him this morning.

His eyes searched my face, his expression and words alike fervently sympathetic. 'Mistress Deyris, I have seen time and

142

again how distressed a woman becomes when she fears that she is barren. But you are young and healthy and with the right regimen of diet and my special tonics, there's every hope that you will hold your own darling baby before a year has passed—'

I knocked his hands away, hard put not to slap his scented face. 'What are you talking about?'

That threw him off his stride. 'Mistress Menore—' Turning, he saw belatedly that she was looking daggers at him.

'You were summoned to tend to my son,' she said icily. 'He has returned to us, safe and sound, despite some fool of a Castellan sending word that he had been murdered. But it seems that he cannot recall precisely what befell him.'

'He is very confused,' Astrila added. 'He could barely speak when he first returned.'

Master Fyrid recovered his poise in an instant. 'A head injury, without doubt.'

'Best treated by the Horned God's priests,' I insisted.

'Let us see the damage first,' he suggested to Mistress Menore. 'May I examine him?'

So that was how it was going to be, I realised. If I wasn't to be his patient, I was of no more account.

Fyrid reached out to search Teutel's head with deft fingers. I waited to see the hostility which Astrila had provoked. It would serve the smug physician right to be knocked onto his plush arse.

But as Teutel's shoulders stiffened, Mistress Menore held his hands down on his thigh. 'Let Master Fyrid tell us how to help you.'

I saw Teutel shudder. He blinked once, twice, thrice. Then he looked at his mother and at the physician with that same wary assessment which I had seen when Astrila first embraced him.

Master Fyrid frowned as he concluded his examination. 'There is no hint of a wound.' He waved a hand at Lessane, standing by the fireplace. 'Light a spill and bring it here, girl.'

Lips tightening at being addressed like a maidservant, Lessane nevertheless plucked a sliver of wood from the jar on the mantelshelf. She took flint and steel from the metal box beside it and striking steel on stone, she dropped a spark into the tow in the same box. It was the work of a moment to kindle the spill from the burning fibres.

I saw Teutel stiffen, his eyes wide with apprehension. Whatever else he might have forgotten, I realised that he knew enough to be afraid of fire. Like any animal.

Mistress Menore must have felt some tremor running through him as Lessane carried the flame carefully across the room. She squeezed his hands, reassuring.

I saw him shudder again, and blink, once, twice, thrice. Now, as Master Fyrid took the burning spill, I saw a gleam of cold calculation in Teutel's eyes as well as the flame's golden glow.

Fyrid waved the spill back and forth. I watched Teutel's gaze follow the flame. The physician drew it back and then moved it forwards, closer to Teutel's nose.

'Well?' Mistress Menore demanded.

Master Fyrid waved the spill to extinguish it, leaving a twist of smoke hanging in the air. I watched Teutel watching the faint blue trail dissipate. The merest crease appeared between his eyebrows and my heart twisted in my chest.

I'd seen that look so often on my own beloved's face as he mused on some puzzle. For an instant I allowed myself to hope that he might be restored to me. Even if he had forgotten these past six years of his life entirely, we had learned to love each other before. If I could nurse him through this crisis, then surely we would learn to love each other again.

'There is no indication of any injury to the brain, which is very good news,' Fyrid added quickly. 'This confusion can easily be treated.'

'But what has caused it?' Mistress Menore snapped.

'An illness perhaps, some ague caught from river insects. Perhaps the draining effects of a vomiting flux brought on by spoiled food or tainted water.' The physician smiled, giving

Teutel's shoulder a jocular nudge. 'Some unaccustomed overindulgence in strong liquors in a wharfside tavern?'

Looking around the room and realising that no one else considered this remotely humorous, the physician hastily swallowed his chuckle.

'I prescribe bed rest in a quiet and darkened room, with daily doses of a mentally-strengthening tonic which I will provide. Amid familiar surroundings—'

'Very well.' Mistress Menore's dismissal was plain. 'We'll expect your boy before noon.' She jerked her head at Lessane. 'Ring for Gelar. I want Teutel's room cleared of Tracha's things. Set up her bed in Vari's room for tonight. Mistress Deyris will require the guest chamber,' she added, begrudging.

'Mama!' Both girls protested hotly. Evidently joy at her brother's return didn't outweigh their outrage at being forced to share a room even temporarily.

'We have no need of such hospitality,' I said firmly. 'My husband can recover in his own home.'

He could regain his memories untainted by his mother's venom poured into his ears. He had echoed her when he'd called me 'whore'. That wasn't going to happen again.

Mistress Menore's lip curled. 'You cannot—'

'Our street is a quiet one, our shutters are sturdy and there will be no interruptions from visitors or barking dogs.'

I jerked my head towards the hall where Jet was scrabbling at the door again, growling. We had all heard the successive of furtive knocks as Okem brought notes or enquiries from callers at the gate. Half the street must have heard that Teutel had returned by now.

Mistress Menore sprang to her feet, wrathful. 'Do not think, my girl—'

The parlour door flew open to bang against the wall and bounced back to hit Steward Gelar's outstretched arm.

Master Menore ran into the room. 'My boy, oh, my boy,' he sobbed.

Teutel stood but he had no chance to resist as his father embraced him. They were as tall as each other and Master Menore was still a man in his prime.

He blinked once, twice, thrice. 'Father.'

For a moment, I couldn't breathe. None of the girls had offered a greeting so Teutel wasn't echoing them. This must surely be honest recognition.

Master Menore took a step backwards, still gripping Teutel's shoulders. 'What befell you, my lad?'

'I travelled downstream and went ashore,' he said slowly. 'I was attacked and robbed.'

Golden Goddess and Horned God alike help me. Was this the beginnings of a true memory or still stitched-together fragments of what he'd overheard.

Mistress Menore pawed at her husband's arm. 'Master Fyrid says his skull is whole. He advises rest and a revivifying tonic—'

'No doubt.' Master Menore spared the physician a sceptical glance.

I seized my moment. 'He can rest at home, Father.'

'Deyris, my dear.' Master Menore turned, mortified. 'Forgive me.'

'There is nothing to forgive.' I spread emphatic hands. 'But I beg a favour of you, Father. Master Fyrid says that Teutel needs peace and quiet. Can your coach carry us home as soon as convenient?'

Master Menore nodded, looking at the physician with rather more goodwill. 'If that's what you think best.'

Master Fyrid hesitated, his eyes darting between Mistress Menore who so often summoned him and the master of the house who paid his bills. His smile twisted into a grimace as he sought to ingratiate himself with both. 'Peace and quiet is most crucial.'

'You spoke of familiar surroundings?' I challenged the physician before Mistress Menore could speak. 'Then he will fare much better in his own home, not in a room where he hasn't slept for three years, full of his sister's furniture.' I appealed to Master Menore 'You know for yourself how confusing it can be, to wake in a strange bed.'

I spoke from childhood experiences of shifting to new lodgings when my father fell behind with the rent or more rarely, won us the funds to enjoy more space and light before the inevitable return to squalor.

A well-travelled man for far better reasons, Master Menore nodded. 'Very true.' He raised his voice. 'Gelar! Call the carriage back – and shut that moon-struck dog in the cellar if you can't shut it up!'

'I'll look after Jet.' Lessane hurried out as the steward opened the parlour door.

'Teutel.' Steeling myself, I stepped forward and held out my hand. I wanted to get him out of here before Mistress Menore's barely-restrained outrage at being confounded got the better of her.

He looked thoughtful for a moment and then stood up. This time he took my hand more gently.

'My dear boy, can you remember nothing?' Master Menore studied his son's face intently, before turning to me, baffled. 'Take him home and see him settled. I will call as soon as I can. Our business must not suffer through all this confusion—' he shook his head.

'I will go and make up my tonic,' Fyrid said quickly. 'I will get directions to your house from the steward.'

He scuttled away before Mistress Menore could catch his eye.

'Master, the carriage is at the gate.' Gelar reappeared, so dishevelled that I guessed he had run down the street himself, shouting at the coachman before he could turn the fine bay horses into their stable.

'Teutel?' I pulled gently and he came with me, biddable. I saw that faint, familiar and beloved crease between his eyes again.

'Astrila, comfort your mother,' Master Menore said quickly, seeing his wife advance to block our path to the door.

'Come and sit down.' Once again, Astrila sounded uncannily like her father as she seized her mother's elbow. 'I will ring for some cordial.'

So thoroughly baulked, Mistress Menore burst into angry tears. I felt Teutel flinch. Did he remember some such display? He had told me long ago how hysteria was one of his mother's favourite refuges when events displeased her.

'So much for peace and quiet,' Master Menore muttered as he escorted us to the gate and saw us settled in the carriage.

Teutel sat opposite me. He was still looking thoughtful. I wondered what thoughts or memories were stirring inside his head. Then I wondered what sensations might be gripping his belly. As the coachman whipped up the horses, I realised that I was ravenous.

'We will go home and have something to eat.' I leaned forward to touch Teutel's knee.

'Home,' he said slowly. 'Eat.'

'That's right,' I smiled encouragement. 'What would you like?'

He didn't answer as something caught his attention through the carriage window. I was content to let him gaze on the city as the carriage carried us along. The more things he saw to prompt recollection, the better surely?

The coachman knew our swiftest route home through the morning press of vehicles clogging the city streets. I opened the carriage door quickly, before we felt the jolt of him jumping down from the driving seat.

'See to your horses,' I called up as I kicked the folding step out and descended. 'I'll see to my husband.'

'Very well, Mistress.' The coachman's expression veered between hope and concern. 'So good to know he isn't lost but it's sad to see him ailing.'

'Not for long, Goddess and God willing,' I said briskly. 'Teutel? We're home.'

'Home.' He followed me out of the carriage.

'The master will see you later,' the coachman called out before he set his horses on their way again.

Teutel was shoving at the locked door, his expression clouding. Had he expected to find it swinging open?

'Wait a moment. We need the key.' I fished in my skirt pocket, trying not to be too discouraged.

As soon as I unlocked it, he pushed past, knocking me into the door frame.

'Eat.' He headed straight for the cold, spilled soup and the buttered bread strewn across the floor.

'No!' I protested. 'You can't eat that.'

But he was on his knees, scooping up the food and whatever dust came with it. I keep my house clean but there is always a fine drift of ash from the fireplace.

I heard a crunch as some fragment of broken basin shattered between his teeth. I hurried over and took hold of his shoulders, trying to draw him away. If he swallowed some razor-sharp shard, it would tear through his innards.

Now I know better of course. If only he had. Then his agonies would have forced us to call for the priests. Everything would have been so very different.

'Eat! Hungry!' He flung out an arm, not to hit me but to stop me getting to the spilled soup and bread. He crammed another double-handful into his mouth, so hasty that he gagged. He retched and spat, like his mother's lapdog choking on a sweetmeat.

I ran to the kitchen. There was bread in the crock from the day before yesterday, past its best by now but clean and wholesome. I found a knife and a board and carried them into the living room. I fetched glasses and a precious bottle of wine from the dresser shelf. Teutel preferred beer but I kept none in the house while he was away.

Wine would quench his thirst, and I hoped, it would incline him to sleep, drunk on an empty stomach. I was still clinging to that foolish hope that sufficient rest would restore my husband.

'Teutel! Here's bread and something to drink.' I stripped the wax from the bottle and worked the cork free.

'Drink.' Teutel scrambled to his feet.

'Here.' I poured a generous glassful and began cutting slices.

'Eat.' He crossed the room with swift strides and wrenched the knife out of my hand.

'Careful!' I squealed.

He looked at the knife and then thrust it at the loaf. I remember thinking how it seemed for all the world, he had never cut bread before. Then I saw how deeply he had cut into his forefinger.

What I saw in the next instant drove every other thought out of my head. The gash had nearly severed his finger but not because he had cut through the bone or a joint. There was no flesh or blood beneath his skin, just some unearthly substance as pale and white as tallow.

I screamed but Teutel didn't make a sound. He didn't appear to feel any pain as he raised his mutilated hand and studied it, bemused. He poked at the greasy white wound with his other forefinger. Then he smoothed over the cut, drawing the sliced skin back together. The edges knitted together and the ugly gash vanished to leave no trace.

'What are you?' I gasped. 'Where is my husband?'

This unearthly creature wearing Teutel's face smiled that calculating, cold smile. He pointed the knife at me.

'I am your husband. You are my wife. This is my home.'

He was between me and the front door. There was no escape through the kitchen except into the back yard where the gate was locked. He would catch me before I could open it.

I fled up the stairs to our bedchamber and dragged the heavy clothes chest across the floorboards to bar the door. Heedless of soot and cinders, I wrenched the fire-basket out of the little hearth. Now I knew for certain that this uncanny sham of a thing wasn't my husband, I could use such a weapon against it.

Whether I would be able to escape it was another challenge entirely. I waited, trembling and terrified, for the first sound of its foot on the stair.

Chapter Three

After a while the iron fire basket weighed so heavy in my hands that I had to put it down. I didn't put it back in the bedchamber hearth though. Fearful of making a noise to draw the creature's attention, I lowered it to the floorboards at my feet as gently as possible. I could only hope that terror would give me the strength to snatch it up again if I had to defend myself.

I stared at the closed door barricaded by the clothes chest, forcing my breathing to shallow silence. What was this uncanny thing masquerading as my husband doing if it wasn't following me up here? Straining my ears I could make out faint sounds downstairs but could make no sense of what I was hearing. Were those footsteps going to and fro?

I waited, and waited some more. Was the sham creature pacing like some caged beast in the Paramount King's menagerie? More than once, Teutel and I had paid our silver pennies to pass through the palace park's gate, to marvel at the exotic animals and birds which traders ferried upstream and down, netted on the high plateau to the north, trapped in the grasslands to the west or snared in the forests to the south and the vast unbounded marshlands to the east. The Paramount King paid handsomely for any creature not yet known to the Horned God's priests, whether it was a beetle as small as a thumbnail or a bird with wings spreading wider than a grown man's arms.

Haphazard memories assailed me as I speculated fruitlessly as to what was happening below. Teutel and I had once seen a brindled bear break off from idly swaying from side to side and attack the confining bars. In vain hopes of freedom or lusting to feast on human flesh? Onlookers had offered their guesses, loudly and unsought, but Teutel and I had agreed that none of us could hope to know.

I stood there trembling, with skirts and hands soiled with ashes and soot. Would the creature below suddenly launch itself up the stairs and batter down the bedroom door? I couldn't guess what it wanted with me. Was there anyone who might know what the vile thing was or where it had come from?

At long last, though still before I could gather my scattered wits, I heard a sharp rat-tat below the window overlooking the street. Someone was using the brass heron knocker on our house's front door. I hurried to press my face against the leaded glass, desperately trying to see who was standing on the step. All I could glimpse was tousled brown hair. I only realised that the front door had opened when whoever it was offered a courteous greeting.

'Good day. Are you Master Teutel Menore?' This unexpected visitor must be a barely whiskered youth. His voice was breaking on his uncertainty. 'Master Fyrid—'

Of course. The physician had promised Mistress Menore he would send a tonic to strengthen Teutel's wits. I didn't wait to hear more. I cared nothing for that now. In an instant, I decided I had to escape this creature's clutches.

That meant I must get downstairs before the physician's boy departed. If the creature tried to stop me leaving the house, I could demand the youth's help in the Golden Mother's name. On pain of the Horned God's displeasure damning any man who would turn a blind eye to a villain abusing those weaker than himself.

Frantic, I hauled the clothes chest clear of the bedroom door. Hitching my skirts and petticoats high, I ran down the steep stairs so fast that I nearly fell headlong.

'Wait!' I shouted as I stumbled down the last step to appear by the kitchen door.

'Mistress?' The physician's startled boy took a pace backwards and nearly fell off the step. The basket he carried rattled as he recovered himself.

I was abruptly conscious of my dirty hands and dishevelled dress. No matter. I squared my shoulders. 'I require your services as my escort, to—'

Words failed me. Not merely because I couldn't think where I might find help or sanctuary. Mostly because I had belated taken in the scene before me.

A new laid fire was burning bright in the hearth, bringing warmth and cheer to the room. All the mess on the floor, the spilled soup, the broken basin, had been cleared away. Only the last dark smear on the drying flagstones showed where the floor had been freshly mopped. The bread and the cutting board which I had fetched from the kitchen were still on the dining table. Now there was also a jar of cherry jam with a sticky spoon laid carefully on a plate beside it. There were two more plates and a toasting fork besides. A slice of bread fixed upon its prongs already showed one side crisp and golden brown.

'Darling?' The thing wearing Teutel's face turned towards me, holding a brown glass bottle, freshly stoppered and sealed with wax. It had shed its green coat and rolled up its shirtsleeves.

'I—' I choked on the beloved familiarity of his broad chest, on the way he had unbuttoned his shirt to reveal a smudge of dark curly hair. Then I looked into its eyes. What I saw chilled me like a deluge of icy water spilling from a wintertime gutter.

This was not my husband but nor was it the senseless beast which could only echo other people's words like a fen crow. This wasn't the witless thing which had grovelled on the floor to fill its belly with spilled food like a dog. Not any longer. Somehow it had conquered its fear of fire. Some new understanding had guided it to making this pretence of domestic harmony.

I recalled how I had caught glimpses of low cunning kindle in the creature's gaze when Astrila and their mother had embraced it. Now unmistakeable intelligence shone in its eyes. But I still saw no hint of the man I loved in the creature's dark gaze. I assuredly saw no mercy.

'I must go to the market.' I forced myself to smile sweetly at the physician's boy before gesturing at the toast on the table. 'As you can see, I have no food in the house fit for my husband. But he must rest, as your master bid him. You can accompany me in his place.'

154

'Gladly, Mistress.' Though the boy looked utterly baffled, as well he might. Why should I need a chaperone to buy mutton and onions in the middle of the day? Not even a woman as censorious as Mistress Menore would insist on that.

'One moment.' I steeled myself to go into the kitchen and fetch my basket. I could do nothing about my ash-smudged skirts but I seized my chance to wash the worst of the soot from my hands with the last of the water from the pail beside the hearth. The creature hadn't refilled that, I noted.

For an instant, indecision wracked me. I didn't want to leave this bloodless sham of my husband in possession of my home. Perhaps, if I could persuade it to go to the well at the end of the street, I could bolt the doors against it. But where would it go then? Besides how would that help me, to be locked inside this once-beloved house with no food and no water and assuredly, no answers? I seized my basket and left the kitchen, my knuckles as white on the wicker handle as the eerie substance beneath the creature's nerveless skin.

'You should take a measured draught each morning, noon and night.' The physician's boy was dutifully instructing it how to swallow Master Fyrid's doses. 'See, each one is marked on the label.'

'I see.' The creature nodded but I saw no understanding as its eyes slid over the painstakingly even flourishes of the physician's handwriting.

'You'll find it more palatable than anything from the Moon God's gate.' The boy grinned amiably.

Teutel had once told me that he considered Master Fyrid's success was largely built on his fragrant potions, sweet with honey. Severe in their silver masks, the Moon God's priests said that a medicine's taste was of no consequence as long as it was effective.

'Thank you.' The thing answered with a smile that mimicked the boy's but still without a hint of warmth in its eyes.

'Let's be on our way.' Sweeping up my shawl, I sidestepped the creature, anxious to stay beyond its reach.

It made no attempt to stop me. Light-headed with relief I ushered Fyrid's boy down the step into the street and I walked quickly away. He scurried after me, torn between the courtesies he'd been reared with and the duties he was paid for.

'Forgive me, Mistress, but I have other deliveries.' He offered up his basket as evidence, his eyes wide with worry.

I heard the door close behind us and risked a glance over my shoulder. Seeing no sign of the creature following us, I breathed a little easier.

'Very well.' I nodded at the boy. 'Be on your way.' I draped my shawl around my shoulders and hung my basket in the crook of my elbow like any other respectable wife about her daily routine.

Fyrid's boy gave up trying to fathom my peculiar behaviour. 'Very good, Mistress.' As we reached the end of the street, he turned south for the leafy Doreward districts.

Heading north as swiftly as I could, I reached through the slit seam of my skirt. Did I still have any coin in the pocket hidden within my petticoats? Alas, I could only find a few thin coppers. Not nearly enough to pay a hireling gig to take me to the Taneside wharfs where Master Menore's sail barges would be tied up.

I thought desperately of the well-filled strongbox beneath our bed. If I had only had my wits about me earlier, I could have taken a fat purse of coin before I fled the house. But no, that was nonsense. Master Fyrid's boy wouldn't have waited any longer. Besides, how could I have gone downstairs, found the keys and gone back up to the bedroom to drag the strongbox out of its hiding place without attracting that creature's attention?

What was done was done. So I would just have to walk. I quickened my pace still further. I had more than half of Hurat to cross and that was some considerable distance even here as the land narrowed swiftly towards the city's point.

No one gave me a second glance as I strode briskly through the thriving central districts where folk bought and sold all the comforts and luxuries of life in our thriving city. It was only when I reached emptier streets that I drew curious looks from the women standing on their doorsteps to watch over their children playing in the gutters or to swap gossip with their neighbours. I could readily imagine what they were asking each other. What business did a young woman in a fine blue gown have amid the wharfs and warehouses where their husbands worked?

I steeled myself to answer blunter questions once I reached the river. At least I could call on the coarse oaths and belligerent manners which had surrounded me growing up if needs be. More than that, I realised belatedly that I had other resources to call on.

As the rows of houses steadily yielded to workshops and storehouses I began to look from side to side, searching the lesser streets and alleyways as I passed by. As soon as I saw what I sought, I broke into a run. Vital though it was, I didn't want this detour to cost me any more time than it must.

This Golden Mother's shrine was smaller than the one where I worshipped most often. There was no outer courtyard ringing the circular building and I was startled to see the wide windows above my head were barred. Were there truly thieves so desperate that they would risk the Mother's displeasure by robbing her handmaidens?

The Goddess's statue set out front was of stone rather than bronze. I greeted her with a brief curtsey before tugging on the bell pull beside the heavy wooden door carved with wheat sheaves.

'Yes, my daughter?' The grey-haired priestess who answered my summons betrayed more than a little curiosity at finding a breathless young woman on the threshold.

I folded my hands at my waist. 'Good day to you, mother. I wish to draw on my household's funds.'

The priestess's swift glance took in every detail of my appearance, from my creased and soiled gown to my fingernails still grimy with soot to my costly shawl and the empty basket at my elbow. She studied my face for a long moment. 'You do not keep your coin in our coffers.'

She wasn't refusing me; merely stating incontrovertible fact.

'No, mother,' I agreed. 'Our family ledger is kept by your sisters at the shrine where Longstick Lane meets Cuffe Street. I was there just yesterday, as they greeted women and children uprooted by the whirlwind to the south.'

That should help convince her of my good faith. It was well known that the Golden Mother's evening messengers circulated the city's latest news between their shrines, along with the daily tallies of coin received and disbursed, so that every ledger could be updated and all accounts reconciled before dawn.

The priestess nodded. 'Come in, my daughter.'

The shrine's lobby was wedge-shaped, blunted at the far end by the door opening into the Goddess's sanctuary at the heart of the building. A handful of priestesses looked up from their needlework as I entered. Waiting to offer support and succour to any women who rang the bell, they put their idle time to good use remaking clothes casually discarded by the likes of Mistress Menore into garb for the destitute such as I once had been.

'This way.' The priestess led me through the door in the right hand wall to the next of the rooms ringing the sanctuary.

Shelves from floor to ceiling were packed with black leather-bound ledgers, all alike. Only the sisters could read the ciphered names within. Only they knew whether the books were shelved by family name or street or using some other system.

The priestess who had greeted me took a chair on the far side of a table set with paper, pens and ink. At her gesture, I took a seat opposite.

'Your full name and your residence?' She looked at me, pen poised to dip the nib in the inkwell.

I told her and she carefully wrote everything down. She glanced up again, her faded eyes thoughtful. 'How much coin do you need?'

I bit my lip. Initially I had only thought of asking for enough money to win a bargeman's favour with the means to buy an evening's drinking, as I asked where I might find Captain Stryet. Now I realised that I would need more than that. I couldn't go home, not until this mystery was resolved and we were rid of that sham creature. I would need to pay for a bed in a boarding house and to buy daily necessities from clean underlinen to a brush for my hair. I had left everything behind as I fled.

I swallowed. 'Ten silver marks.' A sum which Mistress Menore would spend on a gown she might only wear three times. Equal to half the rent which Teutel and I paid for our house every month. Enough for someone raised in penury like me to live on for two full turns of the moon around the sky.

The priestess's goose-feather pen hovered over her paper without writing down the sum. 'Is there anything more we can do for you, my daughter?'

'Perhaps later, mother.' When I had heard Captain Stryet's tale, he and I could decide whether this mystery was better laid at the Golden Mother's feet or related to the Horned God's priests. Would sun magic lay bare the truth, plain for all to see, or must moon magic search out the source of this evil deceit?

I had no doubt that the barge captain would want his good name restored just as desperately as I longed to know my beloved husband's true fate. I also hoped he would know more of magic than I did. I had only the usual, trivial acquaintance the shrines' everyday cantrips to ensure good faith and the occasional encounter with a masked priest's healing charms.

The priestess made a neat note on her paper. 'Blessings upon you, daughter, and may the sun's radiance show you your best path.'

She rose to her feet before I could thank her and went through the inner door to the goddess's sanctuary where the coin chests would be concealed behind unrevealing stones and further warded with divine power.

But should I tell her what had happened? I wondered as I waited. Except it would take quite some time to relate the whole story. I'd be delayed still further if she insisted on calling some priestess in authority over her to hear my testimony and debate what to do about it.

I wanted to find Captain Stryet as soon as possible. I had no idea how long the creature would be content to stay by my usurped fireside. Would it come in search of me? Would it return to Teutel's parents' house? Would it go out into the city to work some other mischief? Each was a chilling prospect. No, I could not afford any delay.

The priestess returned with a small bag of coin. 'How do you propose to carry this securely?' she asked tartly.

'I have a pocket.' I showed her the discreet slit in my skirt.

She pursed her lips but didn't argue. Even if the coin's chinking wasn't muffled by my petticoats, there was no way that a thief could know I was carrying silver marks rather than copper pennies.

She offered me her empty hand and I laid my palm atop her own. 'Do you swear by the Mother of us all that you have every right to this money?'

This time I answered without hesitation. 'I swear.'

'Very well.' As her sunburst pendant shone brightly to attest to my truthfulness, she handed over the coin.

'Thank you.' Not for the first time, I wondered what happened to those foolish or desperate enough to try hiding behind twisted dissembling in some vain attempt to steal another household's coin. Everyone knew that the Golden Goddess's magic would find them but what punishment inexorably followed was one of the Horned God's closely guarded secrets. No one I had ever met had ever known someone who had faced such retribution.

'You can always find help here, my daughter, or within any circle's sanctuary.' She looked searchingly at me again.

'I know,' I assured her.

An infinitesimal shrug betrayed her acceptance that there was nothing she could do until and unless I chose to confide in her. She led me through the entrance lobby and waved me on my way. 'Blessings upon you, daughter.'

'And to you, mother.'

I headed for the wharves with new purpose in my step. Warehouses soon loomed high above me, black with pitch to preserve their wooden walls and casting shadows just as dark over the narrow lanes between them. I could smell the tang of the river, that hint of the countless dead leaves which stained the Tane's flood as it cut through the wooded hill country between here and the high plateau. Voices shouting warnings and summons to each other mingled with the hollow thuds of barge keels bumping against the sturdy oak pilings. The sharp snap of ropes on deck and dockside planking cut through the flap and rustle of canvas.

Those uncaring noises continued as I walked out of a sheltering alley but the men closest to hand fell silent, all looking at me askance. I looked upstream and down, seeking any sign of the Menore trading house colours flying from the stubby pennant masts at every barge's stern.

'What business brings a pretty girl like you here to brighten our day?' A man appeared at my side, stealthy on his bare feet. That marked him as one of the River Folk as surely as his yellow hair and those eyes as dark as the Tane. His kind travelled far beyond the towns which the Paramount King ruled, where Captain Stryet and his ilk plied their trade. River folk voyaged upstream through the high plateau's gorges and navigated the maze of the Nilgeh Mire on the barges where they lived, loved and died without ever sleeping a night on solid ground.

'Thank you but my business is my own,' I answered him politely.

I had never really believed my father's drinking companions who insisted that these river-born traders stole settled townsfolk's babies and dogs along with pretty much anything else which wasn't nailed down.

On the other hand, Teutel had told me often enough that the yellow-haired men and women, clad alike in coarsely woven breeches and sleeveless leather jerkins with no shirt

161

beneath, snagged and sold dockside rumours as readily as the fish they caught in their nets.

A wise man guarded his tongue around them, so his father had always told him. The wrong word in the wrong ear could ruin a merchant's livelihood more swiftly and more surely than a talon cloud striking down from a summer thunderstorm.

'Can I help you, mistress?' A bargeman approached, glaring at the River man.

I walked forward to meet him, keeping my voice low in hopes of going unheard. 'I am seeking Captain Stryet, newly returned from Usenas.'

I didn't offer my name. I didn't want to add to whatever gossip was already swirling around the wharves about Teutel's uncertain fate. The bargeman's eyes lit with curiosity all the same.

'I'll show you his mooring, and gladly, mistress.' He ushered me upstream. 'I'm sorry for Master Menore's – troubles.' His voice rose in unmistakable query.

'Thank you.' What else could I say?

I wanted to know if he recognised me or if he merely assumed that I was in the trading house's service like Stryet and his crew but I couldn't see a way to ask without provoking further questions. Refusal to answer would prompt both curiosity and ill-will.

Goddess be thanked, it wasn't far. As we rounded the river bank's curve, I saw the Menore colours of bright red and dull tan; four stripes on the forked pennant fluttering in the breeze.

'Thank you.' I turned to my escort with a nod of farewell.

'I'll see you into Stryet's care,' he insisted.

'Thank you.' Once again, there was nothing else I could say.

'Halloo Menore!' My inconvenient helper shouted out as we approached.

'Who—?' Stryet appeared on the small deck at the sail

barge's stern with surprising alacrity.

I was even more startled by his hostile scowl though that was momentarily replaced by a look of utter astonishment as he recognised me.

'Thank you, and good day to you.' I pressed the few coppers I had into the bargeman's hand. Not overly generous but a silver mark would have been such excessive payment, it would have started a whole new flurry of gossip.

Hurrying across the plank walkway onto Stryet's barge without a backward glance, I fixed my eyes on the captain. 'I want to know everything which happened in Usenas.'

'You and me both,' he said fervently, before turning to yell at the crewmen gawping from the foredeck beyond the vast hatch-covered hold. 'I want that mast checked from top to bottom, every rope and pulley! Get to it!'

He opened the door into the cabin and ushered me down a flight of ladder-like steps. Bunk beds lined the walls, for sleeping and as I quickly saw, for use as seats when the table hinged against the far wall was lowered to rest on its folded leg.

'The wharf rats are saying Master Menore's son has returned home safe and well,' he said without preamble. 'Calling me a liar for saying he was dead. Wondering what fraud I was trying to work; for the master or against him.'

'Something came to my door wearing Teutel's face.' Heedless of the rumpled blankets and the all-pervasive reek of unwashed men, I sat down on the closest bunk. 'Whatever it might be, it isn't my husband,' I assured Stryet grimly.

Even in the dim light through the meagre portholes I saw sour satisfaction on his weather-beaten face.

'I couldn't see how such a story could be true,' he growled.

'How so?' I leaned forward, urging him to continue.

He ran a rope-scarred hand over his grey hair. 'His gear is yours by rights.'

Before I could ask what he meant by that, Stryet disappeared through the narrow door beside the hinged table.

163

A few moments later he returned from whatever room lay between the cabin and the hold. He was carrying a leather bag. The bag which Teutel had always taken on his travels. The bag that the creature hadn't brought home.

'Mind yourself.' His voice rough with emotion, Stryet lowered the cabin's table. He dumped the bag on it with a thud. 'Forgive me, I couldn't bring myself to wash anything.'

He pulled out a green coat and a crumpled, bloodstained shirt. The garments had evidently dried before they were stowed away but the reek of river water still clung to them.

'I never got a chance to tell you before Mistress Menore started calling me a liar.' That clearly rankled with Stryet. 'The sign of a knife in his back is plain as sunlight.'

I laid out the coat as he spoke. The stained rent in the fine wool showed the course of the fatal blade. I laid the linen shirt over it and the torn fabric, stiff with dry brown blood, gaped like a wound in precisely the same place.

'Underneath the shoulder blade, straight into the heart,' Stryet was saying. 'No man could survive such a stabbing. Whoever this murdering bastard might be, he knows how to use a knife to kill quickly. But I'll go long and slow if I ever meet him with a blade in my hand,' he added savagely.

I looked up and he took a step back, stricken. 'Forgive me, Mistress Deyris.'

Belatedly, I realised that tears were sliding down my cheeks. I wiped them away with the back of an impatient hand. 'We must take these clothes to a temple. To the Golden Goddess's throne or more likely the Horned God's pulpit itself.'

Walking towards the wharves, I had become even more convinced that only the Moon God's cold gaze would penetrate this deception to explain whatever evil had been foisted upon me.

Now I had this evidence before me, this tangible proof of murder, I would go to the heart of the city, to the great temples honouring sun and moon where the Paramount King himself worshipped. High Priestess and High Priest, between them they would surely have the magic to reveal the truth of Teutel's death and to uncover the nature of this creature taking his place.

'I told Master Menore when I told him the bad news, that this was no accident,' Stryet insisted. 'I said he should come fetch Master Teutel's gear and see the proof for himself. He said he would be here this morning. I've been waiting for him all day.'

'He'll have his hands full with the mistress,' I said tartly. 'She's near as hysterical as she was yesterday, now that she's convinced that her son's returned.'

'This masquerader is so convincing?' Stryet shook his head, disbelieving. 'But how did he get here ahead of us, all the way from Usenas?'

I was about to try explaining that this was no ordinary man attempting to pass himself off as Teutel but Stryet had turned away to open a narrow cupboard concealed in the panelling.

'See what I mean.' He shoved the clothes aside and un-furled a map he'd taken from the cupboard. He traced the wriggling line of the Dore with his forefinger. 'Usenas is three hundred leagues downstream, near enough. The road cuts across some of the twists and turns but all the sizeable towns between here and there are guarded by loops of the river so the land route is barely twenty leagues shorter. A barge will make thirty leagues a day, even heading upstream. A man on a good horse would do well to cover twenty. How did this masquerader arrive in the city so hard on our heels?'

He glowered at the tragic garments on the table. Before I could tell him more about the creature wearing Teutel's face, Stryet went on. I guessed he'd been asking himself these questions and searching for answers since first light, waiting for his chance to put them to Master Menore. For the moment, I would suffice.

'We spent five days looking for the young master,' he assured me. 'If this murder was planned ahead of time, I suppose the villain could have ridden out that first day. If he had known what clothes the young master was wearing—'

I shook my head. 'The visitor showed no sign of hard riding—'

I might as well have saved my breath. Stryet was still locked in debate with himself.

'But why come here at all? Why not head for Scefet if he wants to try stealing Menore gold? Why not go beyond the Paramount King's reach altogether and try defrauding our trading partners in the towns flanking the Nilgeh Mire?'

He looked at me, impatient, demanding.

'How can the scoundrel hope to pass himself off as Master Teutel in a city where so many know him? Where his family will see the deception at first glance?'

'This is more than a mere deception.' I struggled to explain.

Before I could find the words, a voice shouted from the wharf, close by the barge. 'Halloo Stryet!'

'It's the master.' The captain's face showed his relief.

I followed him out onto the stern deck.

'Deyris!' Master Menore was astounded to see me.

'Father, good day to you.' I stumbled over my greeting. Not because he wasn't really my father. Because that evil creature wearing Teutel's face stood there right beside him.

Master Menore looked from side to side, thin-lipped as he took note of avidly curious faces all along the wharf. 'May we come aboard?'

He didn't wait for an answer, already setting foot on the plank walkway. The creature followed, quite at ease.

'What—' Captain Stryet retreated into the cabin, gaping at this apparent marvel.

I was forced backwards into the musty gloom, unable to escape. At least I had Stryet between me and the sham thing.

Master Menore's gaze fastened on the clothes still spread across the table. 'These are the garments you were given by the Castellan in Usenas?'

166

'They are and I would know them anywhere,' Stryet insisted.

'But don't you know me?' The creature spoke with such a perfect echo of Teutel's voice that a shiver ran down my spine.

He was wearing a russet coat with silver buttons. He must have found it in the clothes chest in our bedroom. How did he know it was one of Teutel's favourites?

'You—' Stryet stared at him, dumbstruck.

I seized on the captain's earlier arguments, challenging the thing which had stolen my husband's face. 'Tell us how you got back to the city?'

No one paid me any heed. Master Menore picked up the stained green coat. He examined it closely, shaking his head. 'Broadcloth is much of a muchness, Stryet, whatever loom it comes from. I don't suppose this button maker only cast six of these.'

He flicked a tarnished brass button with a fingernail as he dropped the coat back onto the table. He spread his hands, beseeching the barge captain. 'A coincidence, granted, but you said yourself that you never saw the body.'

I realised that Master Menore was so desperate to believe that his son wasn't dead, he was ready to explain all this evidence away.

'Deyris, you must come home.'

I recoiled, startled, as the creature spoke directly to me. In the next breath I defied its fake solicitude.

'The captain spent five days searching Usenas. The Castellan roused the town Watch. How did they fail to find you? Why didn't you go back to the barge?'

But Master Menore answered. sympathetic yet chiding me. 'My dear girl, we've already established that Teutel was attacked. His wits were shaken loose until he returned home.'

'Master Fyrid found no trace of any head wound,' I protested. 'He found no reason—' I broke off, seeing the creature's gaze passing over the chart on the table. There was no more comprehension in its dark eyes than there had been when the physician's boy gave it the bottle of medicine.

'What does this say?' I slapped my hand down on the reed paper, the noise abrupt in the cramped cabin. 'Read me any word on this chart. Tell me the name of a single town between here and Usenas. '

'Deyris, what is this nonsense?' But the creature tensed and I for the first time I saw apprehension in its cold eyes.

The narrow cupboard held writing necessities. I pushed past Stryet to seize pen and ink. I set them on the table before the creature. 'Write your name.'

'Why are you asking this of me?' Now it was as fearful as it had been when it was first confronted with fire. Because the written word was a complete mystery to it.

In an instant, that fear was replaced with anger. 'Deyris, you will come home!'

I had come too close. Its hand shot out and seized my wrist. Its grip pressed painfully on the bruises that its first assault had given me. I yelped and tried to prize its fingers loose with my other hand.

'You will come home!' It raised its other hand, ready to hit me.

'Teutel!' Aghast, Master Menore seized its elbow, forcing its hand down.

'You still believe this is your son?' I cried out to him. 'You think he would abuse me so?'

'He – you are not yourself!' He tried to turn the creature towards him. 'Release her, for pity's sake!'

'She is my wife.' With a snarl, it shook off his hand.

'I won't go anywhere with you!' Desperately resisting, I grabbed at the cupboard as it pulled me towards the cabin door.

'My boy, my boy,' Menore begged, 'what is wrong with you?'

'This isn't your boy!' I yelled at him. 'Can't you see that?'

In the next instant, I saw the pen knife in the cupboard;

a blade salvaged from a good knife broken in some mishap. Too good to be discarded or perhaps valued for some sentimental reason. So the stub had been reshaped and kept sharp for trimming quills.

I seized it and drove the angled end deep into the creature's forearm. I ripped it back towards me, to lay bare the unearthly substance beneath its skin. They would have to believe me now. They couldn't deny the evidence of their own eyes.

But the blade grated on bone. Crimson blood gushed from the wound to soak into the sleeve of my gown and the creature howled with pain.

Stryet and Master Menore pulled us apart. Dumb with shock, I didn't resist as the captain forced me down to sit on the innermost bunk. Master Menore used the knife on one of the musty sheets to fashion a bandage to staunch the creature's wound.

Captain Stryet tore another strip of linen free. I was too slow to realise what he intended to do with it. Before I could resist, he had bound my hands tight together. I had no hope of escape now.

Chapter Four

They took me to the closest House of Restraint. It's been three generations since Heurat had a single Justiciar sharing quarters with his constables as is still the custom in vassal towns up and downstream. The Paramount King's grandfather appointed a Chief Justiciar to recruit as many constables as each district might need and to house them close at hand. I've known this for as long as I can recall, like any other child raised in the city. I had never imagined I would be hauled before a constable.

Seeing me dragged up from the barge's cabin, hearing the false Teutel's cry of pain, Captain Stryet's crew hurried aft from the foredeck to see what was amiss. As they called for explanations, heads turned all along the riverbank. The sight of blood, stark crimson on the pale linen wrapped around the creature's arm, rapidly prompted the idle and curious to draw closer to learn what had happened.

As the four of us left the barge, questions assailed us from every side. A sizeable crowd soon gathered and followed in hopes of further enlightenment even though none of us said a word. Master Menore was dragging me after him with one hand holding tight to the torn linen binding my wrists. Scowling, he waved his other fist to clear his path. Captain Stryet was supporting the creature wearing my husband's face, his own expression twisted in appalled disbelief.

The waterfront House of Restraint was none too far away; a fearsome building with solid, iron-studded doors and high, narrow windows criss-crossed with bars, all the better to put well-deserved fear of the Paramount King's justice into all those who visit our city.

I didn't resist until Master Menore tried to drag me up the steep steps. 'No!' I recoiled, resisting with all my strength. To no avail. I couldn't break his hold on the twisted linen any more than my struggles could tear the cloth apart. 'You cannot—'

Seeing my defiance, someone in the crowd yelled encouragement. 'Kick him in the nuts, flower!'

'What's the girl done?' another voice demanded. A swell of sympathy for my plight rose amid the commotion and the mob surged closer, jostling us all.

'Constable!' Master Menore's shout broke on his distress. He could barely make himself heard amid the clamour all around us.

'No!' I screamed as some nameless brute threw a punch, hitting him hard enough to split his lip.

Winning my freedom at the cost of seeing Master Menore beaten senseless was too high a price to contemplate. He wasn't the one at fault here. He was just as much a victim of whatever evil sought to deceive us, to convince us that my husband still lived.

'Constable!' Stryet roared loud enough to be heard the length of the Tane.

The double doors flew open as a handful of burly men in the Chief Justiciar's livery emerged to see what this hue and cry was about. Assessing the volatile crowd with a swift, glance, the senior constable didn't wait for explanations.

'Get them inside!'

As his men hurried down the steps, ash staves in hand, the gawkers hastily retreated. Now the Paramount King's men could flank Master Menore and Captain Stryet. They urged the four of us up to the door as though we were all now their captives. One tall youth twisted Stryet's hand to break his grip on the cloth restraining me. Before I could thank him though, the constable stooped and swept me off my feet. Not to carry me to safety with any dignity but to sling me over his shoulder like a sack of grain. His shoulder dug painfully into my belly and I pummelled his back fruitlessly with my bound fists.

The Teutel creature was the only silent figure in all this melee. Still more evidence to convince me, if any such proof were needed, that this thing was not my husband. Teutel would never have allowed me to be manhandled like this.

As soon as we were inside, the constables slammed the dark wooden doors on the rabble. Deprived of entertainment, the uproar outside quickly faded away. The man who'd picked me up dropped me back onto my feet. Dizzy, I pressed my bound hands to my abused stomach.

'What's going on?' The senior constable took his seat behind the wide lectern dominating the entrance hall. The men who had escorted us stood to either side while their watchful colleagues remained seated on the hard benches which ringed the walls. They were a sizable force, though barely half wore the Justiciar's livery. I guessed that the rest, dressed like any other man or woman on the streets, must be thief-takers for hire.

'This—' Master Menore struggled to speak. 'My daughter by marriage has assaulted my son—' He couldn't go on.

'It's a clear case of wounding by the woman.' One of the constables dragged the Teutel creature forward, displaying the blood-stained linen around its arm. 'Maybe she intended more.' The liveried man glowered at me.

The senior constable looked from Teutel to Master Menore and then to Stryet. 'Is this some vengeance for adultery?' he asked wearily. 'His straying or hers?'

'No!' All at once, I was furious. 'This is not my husband!'

'They have been wed three years at barley harvest,' Master Menore protested.

'My husband is dead,' I spat at him. 'I have no notion who or what this imposter might be!'

'I brought the news that her husband was dead.' Stryet cut across my words unhappily. 'As the Horned God is my witness, I swear I believed that it was so. We had travelled together to Usenas and he was lost—'

The senior constable ignored him, turning to the Teutel creature. 'What have you got to say for yourself?'

In an instant, I saw the cold cunning which so unnerved me come and go in the creature's eyes. 'I have no idea why she should attack me,' it said carefully. 'She is my wife and this is my home.'

I saw the constable frown at its lack of passion, as toneless as a child reciting a lesson by rote. 'Ask something about

Hurat,' I urged him. 'Ask how to get from here to our home without anyone else's guidance.'

Now the constable looked at me, bemused, but before he could ask me to explain, Master Menore stepped forward. 'My son was assaulted in Usenas. He has forgotten much—'

'We searched for him high and low!' Stryet objected as though he had been accused of something.

I shook my head in emphatic denial. 'The physician said he hadn't —'

'Enough!' The senior constable slammed both his hands down on the polished wooden slope of his lectern. 'Take them to separate rooms.' He jerked his head at one of his underlings before surveying all four of us with ill-concealed disdain. 'I will talk to you all one at a time.'

I raised my bound wrists. 'May I at least be untied?'

The senior constable looked at me, reflective, inscrutable. 'All in good time.'

Before I could say anything more, a lesser constable took hold of my elbow, urging me towards one of the two doors in the rear wall, on either side of the lectern. Master Menore, Captain Stryet and the Teutel creature were directed to the other with as little ceremony.

The door opened onto a short corridor with four doors along the left hand side and one more beside the window facing me at the far end. To the right, a stone stair led downwards to torchlit gloom. The sound of this door opening up above provoked a noisy outbreak of insults and wailing, rising with the reek of unwashed bodies and desperation from the cells below.

I baulked, turning to the constable. 'Please—'

'In here.' He forced me towards the first door, pushing it open with his free hand and then shoving me inside.

There was a window high in the wall opposite the door and a wooden bench solidly mortared into the ochre bricks below it, spanning the width of the narrow room. As I took this in, I heard the key turn in the lock behind me.

I barely managed to reach the bench before my knees gave way beneath me. I was shivering from head to toe, my heart racing and harsh breath catching in my throat. Tears flooded my eyes and nose. Pressing my bound hands to my mouth, I fought with all my will to swallow the sobs which threatened to overwhelm me.

Amid all this chaos, I was certain of one thing. If I yielded to my fear and grief, I would be lost in a storm of weeping until I was utterly spent. I couldn't afford to let that happen. No constable would believe a weeping, hysterical girl. I must tell my story as calmly as I could. I had to convince the constables to send for a Sun priestess. The Golden Mother's magic would prove I was telling the truth.

I sniffed and swallowed and wiped my face as best I could with the trailing end of the linen still tight around my wrists. I contemplated the cloth and considered trying to free myself by using my teeth on the knots. Then I noticed a smear of blood. My empty stomach heaved at the thought of that vile creature's substance touching my lips.

Some while later, I heard the rattle of keys outside. I sat straight-backed, head up, my fists clenching as I refused to give in to my dread. I was innocent. So I had nothing to fear. The Paramount King's proclamations said that was as certain as the moon following the sun.

A woman of about my own age and dressed in Chief Justiciar's livery opened the door. As she entered this holding room, another female constable followed, older and grey-haired with watchful eyes. She carried an ash stave, twice as thick as a thumb and chest high to a middling tall man. I had no doubt that she could and would use it as deftly as her male colleagues.

'Stand up,' the younger commanded.

I scrambled to my feet 'Of course. Forgive me.'

My wandering wits had been fastened on the sight of their breeches and boots. What must it be like to stride the city's streets unencumbered by skirts and petticoats? I was growing light-headed with hunger, I realised. I hadn't eaten anything since yesterday morning.

It was hard to believe that one day, a night and barely another day had thrown my life into such disarray. I felt as though I had been living in this nightmare for a lifetime.

'You took a blade to your husband.' The older woman sternly demanded my attention. 'Do you still have it?'

'That thing is not my husband,' I assured her.

She smacked the butt of her ash stave on the floor so hard that I feared for the russet tiles. 'Where is the knife?'

I flinched. 'I don't know.' Then I remembered Master Menore using it on the sheets in the barge cabin. 'I believe my father by marriage may have it.'

She nodded curt acknowledgement. 'Are you carrying any other weapon?'

'No.' I stared at her, bewildered. 'Of course not.'

'This constable will search you to be certain. If you're telling the truth, we will untie your hands.'

Her gaze held mine. I felt like
a mouse cornered by a ferret.

'Thank you.' I swallowed and found that my throat was as dry as the dusty floor. 'If you please, may I have some water?'

The older woman didn't answer, nodding instead to the younger constable who advanced a few paces before beckoning me forward.

'Stand in the middle of the room and raise your hands above your head.'

I did as she commanded, albeit awkwardly with my wrists still tied together. Her fingers searched all through my hair, then she turned her attentions to my bodice, her hands firm yet impersonal as she confirmed there was nothing concealed beneath my gown.

She knelt to search my skirts. Her hands halted as she found the shifting coin concealed in my petticoats pocket.

'It is my money, I swear it,' I insisted.

The constable removed the coin. Finding silver rather than copper her voice betrayed her surprise. 'Sergeant?'

As the older woman came forward to take the money, she narrowed her eyes at me. 'Why are you carrying such a sum along the wharfside?'

'I must find some new lodging. I cannot go home as long as that thing squats in my house.' I might as well tell her the truth.

The grey-haired sergeant pursed her lips, though I couldn't tell what she might be thinking. Taking my money, she retreated to the door once again. 'You can loose her.'

'Thank you.' I lowered my hands gratefully.

'Don't move,' the younger constable warned unnecessarily as she produced a sharp knife from some hidden sheath at her back. She sliced through the cloth and shoved the linen rags through her belt.

I rubbed at my wrists, profoundly relieved even though Stryet hadn't bound me painfully tight.

'Sergeant.' The younger constable frowned. 'You should see this.'

Letting the linen fall to the floor, she took my hand. I didn't resist as she pushed the sleeve of my gown upwards and drew the two wedding bracelets which I now wore down as far as she could.

The older woman came to look at the bruises on my wrist and forearm. The marks of the creature's fingers were now darkly clear, where it had seized me in our dawn encounter, before it had thrown me across the room.

'Did your husband do this to you? How long has this being going on?'

'Yes. No.' I shook my head. 'My husband has never hurt me. But this thing masquerading in his place, it gave me these bruises and worse. It's brutal if its will is crossed.'

The two constables exchanged a veiled glance.

'We will send you some water.' The grey-haired woman turned her back, striding to the door.

I sat on the unyielding wooden bench and contemplated the fading patch of sunlight falling through the cheap rippled glass to spread across one wall. This seemingly interminable day was turning inexorably towards evening. I had to fight an impulse to weep. Was I going to be shut in here all night, alone and so wretchedly hungry and thirsty in the darkness?

Dusk had assuredly fallen before I heard keys outside in the corridor again. I forced myself to my feet, only to hesitate, uncertain. Would standing up be a show of respect or would the constable think that I meant to attack her? I raised my hands in surrender even before the door was fully open.

It was the younger constable, carrying a sizeable wooden cup. 'Water.'

'Thank you.' Since she made no move to approach me, I walked towards the door. As she handed me the cup, I drank enough to quench a working man's thirst after a long day in the sun.

I offered the cup back but she shook her head and stepped backwards from the threshold. 'Come with me.'

The elder constable with the stave was waiting in the corridor. I followed the younger woman meekly towards the door at the far end. It opened onto a small brick-paved courtyard overlooked by more barred windows. Above, the first of the night's stars spangled the darkening sky.

The constables escorted me to the door on the courtyard's far side which opened onto a far larger room. Wood-panelled, it was furnished with rows of benches as well as a three-stepped dais running along the opposite wall. The senior constable sat behind a table there with a sizeable ledger open before him, pen and ink to hand. A Sun priestess sat to his right while a priest wearing the Horned God's mask of silvered wood sat to his left. Branches of fine white candles flanked them.

The constables led me to stand before the dais. There was no one else in the room even though the benches could have seated a hundred or more.

The senior constable looked at me, his face impassive. 'Tell me everything which has happened since you first got word that your husband was dead.'

'Leave nothing unsaid.' The priest's voice was stern and clear despite his mask.

I laced my fingers together to gather my strength and began to speak. I did my very best to recall every detail, as I told my sorry tale. Though I couldn't help stealing glances at the priestess's sunburst pendant. In the candlelight, it was hard to see if it was glowing to endorse my honesty against her saffron-gold, silk gown, so unlike the sanctuaries' every-day garb of unbleached linen.

The priest sat unmoving in his mask and costly broad-cloth robes, triple-dyed to a sable hue. If he was working any arcane magic, I could see no sign of it.

The senior constable paid close attention to me although his pen remained motionless. I had expected him to write something of what I said in that open ledger But as I related the past two days' events and gave all my reasons for not believing in my husband's return, my story sounded increasingly absurd in this empty room.

I faltered to the end of my desperate explanations. 'I wasn't trying to kill it. I didn't even think I could wound it. I wanted to show Master Menore and Captain Stryet what I had seen when it cut itself in my home. But this time, it bled.' I couldn't help an involuntary shudder.

The senior constable looked at me for a long moment. 'You may be seated.'

As the female constables led me to the closest bench, he raised his voice. 'Bring them in.'

I twisted around in my seat to see another door open, twin to the one I had been brought through. A handful of constables ushered Master Menore and Captain Stryet into the room. The Teutel creature followed with Mistress Menore hanging on its arm. The lesser constables retreated to stand along the room's back wall.

I turned back to the dais, too astonished to stay silent. 'What is she doing here?' All at once I was conscious of my creased dress, my stale linen and my dishevelled hair.

The priestess answered calmly, offering no hint as to what she had thought of my pleas. 'She has asked to be present in support of her son.'

The senior constable looked sternly at me. 'You do not deny that you wielded the blade. You cannot since there are witnesses to the deed. What remains to be determined is why you did such a thing. Then I can commit you for trial before the appropriate justiciar.'

I had forgotten that the constables had such discretion; to decide which of the Royal Justiciars was best suited to hear a particular case, depending on whether the offence was primarily one of theft, whether by robbery or deceit, one of violence of whatever degree or truly one of deliberate murder, attempted or succeeded. My father's dealings had only ever been with the justiciar overseeing debts and there had never been any question about his guilt.

'She must answer for murder!' Mistress Menore had been about to sit on the front bench on the other side of the room's central aisle. Instead she released the Teutel creature's arm and approached the dais, her hands upraised. 'She sought to kill my son! She must burn for it!'

I was too shocked to speak. No matter. Master Menore and Captain Stryet both shouted her down, appalled at the prospect of sending me to the executioner's stake and the Goddess's purifying flames.

The Teutel creature sat silent and unmoved. I turned quickly to search the senior constable's face, to look for the priestess's response, both to Mistress Menore's spite and to my supposed husband's lack of concern. Neither showed any more reaction than the masked priest.

He was the one to speak, catching everyone unawares. 'Why do you believe your daughter by marriage would seek to kill your son?'

'Blood will out,' spat Mistress Menore. 'She's the daughter of a drunk and a whore. She's wearied of my son's goodness, so she's stolen his money to flee down the river to some villain she has conspired with. That must be who left him for dead.'

Even though I knew she detested me, this accusation left me gasping.

'What are you saying?' Captain Stryet protested.

Mistress Menore rounded on him. 'Who's to say what truly happened in Usenas? We only have your word for events. Have you been spreading that harlot's thighs while my son travels and trades? She came straight to you with a fat purse of my son's silver.'

'Master!' Aghast, Stryet appealed to Menore himself.

The merchant hurried forward to seize his wife's arm. 'You have no standing here. Sit down and be silent,' he hissed.

She shook him off with a sweeping gesture directing the constable's gaze towards me. 'Where did that copy of Teutel's wedding bracelet come from, if this wasn't planned ahead of time?'

Her eyes glittered with triumph as all three of those seated behind the table turned to look at me; the priestess, the constable and the dark eyeholes of the priest's mask.

I didn't realise that I had clapped my hand over the bracelets I wore until after I had done so.

'See!' Mistress Menore shrieked. 'She tries to hide the evidence of her treachery!' Now she hurried back to grab the Teutel creature's coat sleeve. It sat, unresisting, as she lifted its wrist and pushed back its cuff to reveal the engraved silver circle.

'Silence.' The masked priest raised his hand.

Even though he hadn't raised his voice, Mistress Menore immediately sank down onto the seat, her lips pressed tight together.

'You, who claim to be Teutel Menore.' The priest leaned forward. 'What is the first thing that you remember?'

The creature looked puzzled. Then Mistress Menore seized its hand, clasping it between both of her own. I saw a subtle shiver run through the loathsome thing. It blinked slowly, once, twice, thrice and then it answered the priest.

'When I came to my senses I was in the street where I live with Deyris. I don't know how I came to be there but I know that I wanted to go home. When my wife rejected me, I sought refuge with my parents.'

I bit my lip so hard I tasted blood. The thing sounded so like Teutel now. Worse, it sounded wearied and sorrowful, as though I had truly turned my husband out of his own home. But this vile creature was telling lies.

I sprang to my feet. 'Send for Astrila Menore. She was at our house first thing this morning. She will tell you how strangely this – this newcomer behaved.' I shot a hostile glare at Mistress Menore as she fawned over the thing. 'Astrila will swear by the Golden Goddess that my account is the truth.'

'Master merchant.' The masked priest addressed Teutel's father as though I hadn't spoken. 'Do you believe this is your son?'

'I do,' he said unhappily. 'But do not blame Deyris for her confusion. We have all been left reeling. To have Teutel restored barely a day after we grieved for his loss?' He looked at me with honest pity. 'She has every right to be distressed by his strange behaviour. After all he has suffered, he still isn't in his right mind—'

'There's no sign of injury. Your wife's own physician could find no head wound.' Once again, I might just as well have saved my breath.

'Captain Stryet.' The masked priest turned towards him. 'Do you believe this is Teutel Menore?'

'I do, though I do not understand—' he shook his head, wretchedly confused '— how he returned from Usenas so quickly.'

'They are all telling the truth.' The priestess confirmed

'No!' As I took a step forward the female constables laid heavy hands on my shoulders. After an instant of rigid rebellion, I yielded and resumed my seat. 'Please,' I begged nonetheless. 'Send a messenger to Usenas. Ask the Castellan for a full account of his search.'

That would be easy enough to do. Every vassal town's constable was quartered in the Paramount King's garrison alongside the Castellan and his cavalry.

'Ask for every detail of the body his men dragged from the river.' I implored. 'That is my husband's corpse.'

'I know you are telling the truth too, my daughter.' The priestess looked at me, sympathetic.

'How—' Mistress Menore abruptly thought better of her protest. Even her arrogance baulked at challenging the Golden Mother's own representative.

The masked priest answered her all the same. 'You are all telling the truth as you believe it to be. You cannot all be correct but this does not mean that someone has to be lying.'

He turned his dark gaze on me. 'Men and women alike can become honestly convinced of things which have no foundation in truth. They find asylum within our gates until their vision clears.'

'You're saying Deyris has run mad? Out of her wits with shock and grief?' Master Menore's first doubt swiftly gave way to breathless relief. 'Then she must be pitied rather than condemned. She must be cared for till she comes to her senses, not punished.'

'She must be held under lock and key,' Mistress Menore insisted venomously. 'Witless or not, she's a menace, even to her beloved husband.'

The senior constable took up his pen. He looked straight at me as he dipped the nib in the inkwell. 'You are consigned to the care of the Horned God, for your own protection.'

Writing with precise, indelible strokes, he recorded my fate in his ledger.

'No!'

My protest made no difference. The lesser constables who'd been silently observing ushered Master Menore and Captain Stryet towards the rear door. The women who had escorted me went to insist that Mistress Menore and the Teutel creature follow. My mother-by-marriage was hanging around the sham thing's neck now, weeping and whispering into its ear.

I wondered how quickly she would convince it to dissolve our marriage. No matter that the creature couldn't read or write. She would delight in writing that petition for the Golden Goddess's High Temple.

I wouldn't grieve over that. I had no wish to be shackled to the uncanny thing. But to be left penniless, alone and disgraced? As I sat there alone, I closed my eyes, for all the world like a child trying to deny a nightmare. I felt myself sway, on the precipice of fainting.

'You're to come with us now.'

I opened my eyes to see two men in front of me. They wore the homespun tunics and loose trews of the Moon God's devotees, simply woven from the wool of the black sheep sacred to the night and its mysteries. They were servants, not priests though; neither wore a mask.

'Where are we going?' I looked for the man in the silvered mask but he was nowhere to be seen. Only the priestess and the senior sergeant remained on the dais, heads close together as they conferred.

'You just be a good girl and don't give us any trouble.'

The two shrine servants stepped forward and each one took hold of one of my arms. I was hardly about to fight back. They were surely strong enough to restrain a man twice my size rampaging through drink or fury.

They escorted me through the building to the entrance hall. It was now thronged with people who had suffered injury or injustice come to seek help from the constables, alongside those who had been caught attempting robbery, violence or other misdeeds under cover of night's darkness. Every face was a blur and every lantern's light was shattered like broken glass as tears of terror and mortification blinded me.

The Moon God's servants didn't let me stumble as they took me out through the door and down the steps. They lifted me bodily into a waiting carriage. One climbed in to sit beside me while the other sprang up beside the driver.

He promptly whistled up his horse and the animal sprang forward. Inside, I was jolted off balance, falling into a corner of the worn leather seat. Now I gave in to my misery. I curled up and sobbed until the carriage jerked to a halt, sooner than I had expected.

As I sat up, the Moon God's servant wordlessly offered me a handkerchief. Hands trembling, I wiped my face. He jerked his head towards the door as his fellow opened it from the outside.

I half stepped, half fell out of the carriage to find myself in a small courtyard dimly lit by lamps confined behind thick slabs of glass covering niches deep in the walls. The first servant was waiting beside tall gates of solid wood topped with iron spikes. As soon as the carriage departed, they would be secured with massive bolts.

'This way. Follow me.' A third servant was waiting beside the only entrance into the building looming on all three sides. The iron-bound door opened onto darkness within. He held a lantern with horn shutters dulling three of its four glass panes.

I did as I was told. What choice did I have?

The doorway opened onto a staircase. The servant climbed one, two, three flights, finally opening another door onto the topmost floor of the building.

I saw a long room divided by wooden partitions from floor to ceiling. Each cell was fronted with iron bars. Just as in the House of Restraint, the small, high windows were barred and wooden benches were fixed below. These evidently served as beds. I could glimpse shadowy figures huddled beneath blankets and hear faint snuffling and snoring.

'In here.' The servant swung a set of bars open.

I went inside the cell. All I felt now was dead inside, too numb to even feel despair.

As the bars were locked behind me, I walked to the window to find the bench padded with a flock mattress and covered with a softer blanket than I expected. I sat down and considered stripping to my shift and trying to sleep. But what would the morning bring when I woke? More grief and humiliation? No one believed me. No one would come to help me. Even if I could persuade these priests that I wasn't mad, I would only be cast out, destitute, onto the streets. Why should I wish the night away only to face that?

Did I want to endure any of the torments in store for me here? Was this life even worth living now that I had lost my beloved Teutel? Would I find him waiting for me between the dark of the moon and the sunrise? There were always those who whispered such things, whatever the priests and priestesses said about death being the end of all consciousness as body and spirit alike became one with the cosmos.

I folded my hands in my lap and considered my options. I still had my stockings and garters. I could fashion a noose for myself. That would be one way to escape this nightmare. Though glancing up at the window, it was easy enough to see that I had no hope of reaching those bars, even if I stood on tiptoe on this bench bed.

Besides, now I had considered it, I wasn't ready to die. I had escaped destitution and ignominy once before. I could surely do so again.

Though if I was to live, I would need more than resolve to sustain me. Hunger gnawed at my belly more fiercely than I could remember since the worst days of my childhood.

I hurried back to the bars, hoping to call to the servant, to explain I hadn't eaten for nigh on two days. 'Please—'

I froze. The man had gone but something else moved in the gloomy aisle between the rows of cells. At first I couldn't make it out, then it hopped into a shaft of moonlight.

It was hopping on bird-clawed feet but this was no fowl. The whole beast was scaled like a lizard, from the tip of its thrashing tail to its narrow serpent's head. As I watched, dumbfounded, it spread leathery wings. Flapping like a tethered falcon, it looked from side to side, forked tongue licking its arrow-shaped snout. Waist high to a tall man, it was easily big enough to be dangerous.

Startled out of my daze, I screamed. How had the monstrous thing got in here? Could it get through the bars into these cells?

Several women threw their blankets aside and rushed forward to see what was happening. The monster's head snapped around to fix me with unblinking eyes. It began to hop towards my cell, spitting belligerently.

I retreated quickly. As best I could guess, it would struggle to get its wings through the bars but it could still strike forward through the gaps to bite me.

'How do we call for help?' I shouted to the woman opposite.

What under the sun and moon was the creature? I had even heard tell of such a thing in tales. What was it doing in here, amid a dozen madwomen?

'What are you yelling about?' the woman opposite demanded, aggressive.

'Get to your bed, you selfish bitch,' another snarled somewhere on my own side of the room.

The monster bounced around in a circle, wings flapping and fanged mouth gaping as it hissed at them both.

I stared across the gap. 'Can't you see it? The creature?'

Shadowy in the gloom, the woman shook her head. 'What creature?'

'It's right there, in front of you.' I couldn't believe she couldn't see it.

The unseen woman to my left sneered. 'Another one who sees invisible prodigies and freaks.'

'Keep your madness to yourself,' the woman opposite advised, contemptuous. 'That's what passes for good manners in here.'

'No, please—' but she had turned her back on me, lost in the darkness.

'Go to sleep!' Another voice shouted, savage with anger.

I retreated to my bench bed. I stared at the creature now strutting and preening in front of my cell. I watched it as the rest of the room subsided once more into sleep. I closed my eyes and rubbed at them but it was still there when I looked a second time and a third. I could almost believe it was taunting me, knowing full well that I alone could see it.

'Perhaps I really have lost my wits.'

I didn't realise I had spoken aloud until a shadow appeared where my cell's bars met the partition with the next.

'Tell me what you see,' the servant who'd brought me here ordered quietly.

I was already locked up as a madwoman. What did I have to lose by an honest answer? 'The bastard offspring of a snake, a bat and a chicken?' I rose to my feet and drew closer to the bars.

'What colour is it?' As the man spoke again, the creature began hopping towards him. 'Softly, if you please. We don't want to wake anyone up.'

He unshuttered one glass pane of his dark lantern. The creature hopped into the pool of light falling onto the floorboards.

I had thought the creature was black or grey but the lamplight struck an oily sheen from its scales. 'It's all manner of colours,' I murmured. 'Like a rainbow.'

'So it is.' The servant held out his other hand and the creature nuzzled his fingers. As he scratched gently under its jaw, its tongue flickered and now it hissed with an unmistakeable note of pleasure.

I watched, incredulous. 'What under all the heavens is it?

The man looked at me. 'It's proof that you're not mad.'

Now I recognised his voice. 'You were the priest who condemned me to this.' I struggled not to start shouting and cursing him, rousing everyone in this whole building.

'No,' he corrected me. 'I am the priest who will teach you how to destroy the creature masquerading as your husband.'

Chapter Five

The mysterious priest retreated into the shadows before I could ask what he meant. The winged snake-beast hopped after him to be lost in the darkness. I stood alone in the silence, for a long moment. I couldn't make any sense of what had just happened. I couldn't make sense of anything which had happened over these interminable past two days

So I shed my dress and slid beneath the soft blanket and closed my eyes. I fell asleep before I took a second breath.

Sunlight woke me. The high barred windows had no shutters and the dawn stirred most of the women held captive here. Lying quite still, curled up on my side and clinging to the illusion of warmth and comfort in this humble bed, I watched the prison's morning routine unfold.

It wasn't in the least what I expected. An older woman in a plain charcoal gown and with a white scarf concealing her hair came to unlock all of the bar-fronted cells. The women within threw off their blankets and wearing only their shifts, they made their way to the far end of the long room. Somewhere beyond my sight, I heard the clink of glazed earthenware and the slosh of water. The women returned, some with quick purpose, others at a leisurely pace, all with freshly washed faces and trailing a faint aroma of perfumed soap.

Some carried fresh underlinen. One had a dark grey gown draped over her arm. As they returned to their cells, I realised that each one had a curtain which could be drawn over the open bars to secure privacy within. There was just such a heavy drape in my cell, tied back in the corner where the bars met the wooden partition which separated me from my unknown neighbour. I hadn't noticed it last night in the darkness, lost in my distress.

Some women pulled the curtains and dressed, modestly shielded. Others were unconcerned that someone might see them naked. Meantime, the older woman with the keys made the rounds, asking who had used their chamber pot during the night. Covering the vessels which required emptying with a discreet cloth, she carried them through to the washroom, presumably to a sluice.

One by one, the women left, all dressed alike in charcoal grey gowns and with their heads covered with white scarves. The older woman briefly tidied blankets and tied back curtains as she went from cell to cell, relocking each barred door when she was done. Then I realised not every woman had risen to wash and dress. She went into one cell and spoke, low voiced, to whoever was still within. Coming out a few moments later, she drew the curtain across and locked the door, leaving the woman within unseen.

I sprang out of my bed, terrified that I would be locked in too, with no way to know how soon the keyholder would return. 'Please—'

'Good morning.' The grey-gowned woman bustled over with a cheery smile. 'Are you feeling rested?'

'Yes.' I was surprised to realise how well I had slept. 'Please, tell me—'

'All in good time, my dear.' She raised a kindly but quelling hand. 'Brother Quirian will answer your questions. First, you'll feel much better for some clean clothes and some food.' As she spoke, she was unlocking my cell. 'Follow me.'

I did as she bid. What else could I do?

She led the way to what proved to be a well-appointed washroom at the end of the cells. Curtained alcoves offered privacy, each one with a washstand, basin and ewer. Once again, everything was plain and practical.

'There is some hot water left,' she assured me, fetching a dish of bell-flower-scented soap, a washcloth and a towel as soft as the blankets from a tiled table in the centre of the room.

When I took them she used both hands to carry a heavy copper jug over to an unused basin. 'If you please?'

I hastily set down towel and soap and lifted out the ewer of cold water so she could fill the basin for me. 'I'm sorry.'

'I'll fetch you a gown while you wash.' Without waiting for an answer, she drew the curtain behind me, the lightened copper jug in her other hand.

I stared at the gently steaming water for a long moment. So I was to be stripped of my clothes as well as my freedom? I looked down at my blue gown; creased and grimy and spotted with that false creature's uncanny blood. My underlinen felt sticky and stale against my skin. I had slept in my clothes for two nights after all. How badly must I smell?

Abruptly revolted, I stripped, hastily and heedlessly, not caring that I ripped seams and lace. With the discarded garments around my feet, I washed as thoroughly as I could, short of pouring the water over my head.

I was emptying the basin into the slop pail underneath the washstand when the older woman returned.

'I have clean linen and a gown for you.' She did me the courtesy of not pulling the alcove curtain open, draping the clothing over the rail so I could pull the garments down on my side.

'Thank you.' Once again I was surprised. The serviceable chemise and stockings were not the coarse, scratchy weave I had anticipated. The grey gown might be sufficiently shapeless to accommodate all manner of different women's bodies but the broadcloth was good quality and I could use the white rope girdle folded within it to draw the cloth neatly around my waist.

That left me with the white headscarf. I ran it thoughtfully through my hands as I emerged into the washroom. I had sworn no oaths which need be declared for all to see by covering my head.

'The others are breakfasting in the refectory but you deserve some peace and quiet on your first morning here.'

My unexpected guide to this place was standing in the doorway, a tray now in her hands. Small dishes of butter and jam flanked a plate with two thick slices of bread. A pottery beaker presumably held something to drink.

I don't know what she saw in my expression but her face fell. 'There is cheese or sausage, if you prefer? I can—'

'No.' Now it was my turn to gesture to silence her. 'That

will do very well. Thank you.'

I was about to ask where I supposed to eat but she had already turned, leading the way back to my cell. I tucked the scarf through my rope girdle and followed.

'You may take your time,' she assured me as she laid the tray on the bed.

Was that so? What then? I had a hundred questions clamouring in my head. Before I could voice a single one, she had gone.

I ate my breakfast. The first bite awoke my hunger and I finished every crumb. Wishing I could have twice as much again, I drained the beaker of tepid redmint tea. That was fortunate, otherwise I would have spilled it when the man appeared at the front of my cell.

'Good morning.'

'Are you Brother—' I couldn't remember the name the woman had mentioned. He was definitely the man from the night before though. I recognised his voice. Now I saw him unmasked in the daylight, I looked him up and down. I didn't care if he thought me rude.

He was middling tall and middling broad, neither handsome nor ugly with hazel eyes and close-cropped hair a shade or so darker. He was clean-shaven and he wore a long black tunic over loose black trews, belted with double-looped black rope.

'Brother Quirian.' He smiled.

I laced my fingers together in my lap so he wouldn't see my hands shaking. 'How long am I to be imprisoned here?'

He raised questioning eyebrows and pushed at the open cell door. 'This is not a prison. It is a place of safety. An asylum.'

'Very well then. I will leave.' I wanted to get to my feet but my knees betrayed me.

'To go where?' He angled his head. 'Penniless and with no family to offer you food or shelter? I cannot allow that. You have been consigned to the Horned God's care by the Paramount King's Justiciary,' he reminded me. 'If we fail in our duty, your husband's family will have every right to appeal to the Justiciary, to insist you are condemned to a prison.'

I bit my lip, refusing to yield to the tears stinging my eyes as I remembered my humiliation in front of the constables.

He turned his attention to reknotting the cord tying back the cell's curtain. 'I can see how these barred windows and locked doors might have confused you. We watch over the Paramount King's prisons after all. Here though, doors and bars are to keep the violent and vengeful out. This is a place where women who have suffered all manner of losses and sorrows may find respite and healing. Some choose to return to their old lives or to new ones outside these walls. Some, like Sister Nalisa—' he nodded towards the door to the stair where the older woman had gone '— choose to stay lifelong.'

'Why is this the Horned God's business?' I demanded. 'The Golden Mother cares for destitute women and orphaned children.'

Satisfied with the curtain's folds, he turned to me. 'So she and her priestesses do. However the Horned God has always been the keeper of secrets and many women wish to commit their shame and suffering to his keeping before returning to the Goddess's sunlit embrace. Don't forget he is also the scourge of sinful men.'

His tone was kind rather than chastising but I felt rebuked all the same. Only for a moment.

'You speak of secrets. Last night you showed me something that none of the other women could see. You said you knew the truth of the creature—'

I swallowed hard as the recollection of the vile sham thing wearing my beloved husband's dead face made me nauseous.

The priest looked at me, his face unexpectedly stern. 'We keep many different secrets safe under the moonless sky and we cannot discuss all of them here. Will you come with me to my quarters where we may talk in private?'

I had expected that he would order me rather than ask. I narrowed my eyes, studying his face. 'Is this to be my choice?'

He nodded. 'It must be.'

Those simple words evidently held some meaning which I couldn't understand. What was plain to see was the only way to find out anything useful was to go with him. The only way to destroy the false thing whose masquerade as my husband had shattered my life into shards. That was what he had promised last night. With everything else lost to me, that was all I had left.

I rose to my feet. 'Very well.'

He smiled and led the way to the door without saying anything further. I followed him down the same stairs which I had climbed so fearfully the night before. Where this vast building had been silent and ominous, now it was full of life.

The floor below the sleeping cells was a long workroom where women sat on either side of a long table, embroidering fine cloths with bright colours. The floor below that was divided between women sitting in circles of chairs to knit and those leaning over tables to cut dress fabrics. Not for the shapeless grey gowns every woman wore but costly silks and velvets. The ground floor shivered with the thump and rattle of looms at work.

Brother Quirian held the door to the courtyard open for me. He nodded at the scarf tucked through my rope girdle. 'I would ask you to wear that. It signifies beyond all doubt that you are under the Moon God's protection. No one may touch you without incurring his wrath and that of every priest in the Paramount King's realm.'

Meek, I draped the white cloth over my head and knotted it at the nape of my neck. At least it would cover my tousled locks until I could at least find a comb and Goddess willing, discover where I might bathe and wash my hair.

Outside, we crossed the courtyard to the central building which linked the other two and faced the spike-topped wall. The double-barred wooden gates looked different somehow, as I contemplated their worth as a defence instead of a means of detention.

The priest opened the door in the middle of the central building and led me up two flights of stairs and along a corridor to a narrow, plastered and lime-washed room. In some ways it wasn't so different from the chamber I'd known as a maid-of-all-work. Against one wall, a settle-bed was folded away for the day, flock mattress and blanket concealed within the high-backed seat's solid base. A tall, narrow cupboard stood beside it, presumably for clothes and other personal necessities.

A desk and a single upright chair were set beneath the window at the far end. A stack of tattered, age-darkened pages were bound with black ribbon beside a sheaf of pale new paper weighed down by a loop of white cord. Beside the inkstand at least a dozen books were held between twin statues of the Moon God and the Sun Goddess. Not ledgers like those in a shrine nor the flimsy chapbooks which entertain idle women like Mistress Menore with romances and adventures. These were solidly-stitched and leather-bound tomes of different sizes and thicknesses; the sort of books the Paramount King was reputed to pay for with their weight in gold, if they were a new addition to his library.

Two rather more comfortable-looking low chairs flanked a small fireplace which I didn't think could do much to relieve midwinter's chill. Fortunately we had no need of it in this balmy spring weather.

'Please, sit.' Brother Quirian took the chair with its back to the door and waved me towards the other.

I smoothed my grey skirts and did so. 'What—'

'First things first,' he said apologetically. 'Can you see the wyverning?'

'The what?' I stared at him.

'The creature you saw last night.' He leaned forward, elbows on his knees. 'Or did you? Perhaps it was a dream or some phantom of your weary and hungry imagining. Do you trust the evidence of your own eyes? Can you tell me if it's in this room? I have to know before we can go any further.'

'Where might it be?' I twisted to look behind me. There

was nothing to be seen hiding under the desk, nor anywhere else in this simply furnished room unless it was shut inside the cupboard.

'Deyris?' Quirian held my gaze with his own when I looked back. 'Cast your mind back to last night. Only you know what you really saw.'

Now I challenged him with unblinking eyes. 'What does that mean for me? What if I can see it now?'

He looked past me and through the window, as though seeking an answer from the empty sky. Coming to a decision, he answered with that same intensity I couldn't fathom earlier.

'If you can see the wyverning here and now, then I will know how far I can go to help you see your husband buried with honour and your home restored to you.'

The two things I longed for above all else. I stared at the priest. Why was he asking me this though? He knew full well I had seen the curious beast. I hadn't been imagining it and I certainly wasn't mad, whatever my hateful mother-by-marriage might wish.

I heard a faint noise beside me and looked down to see the beast. What had he called it? A wyverning? In daylight it looked even more bizarre; bouncing on its chicken's feet with thighs as thick as its snake's body. Its neck was weaving sinuously as it studied me with jewel-like eyes. Its head was snake-like and yet, somehow, unlike any serpent I'd ever seen pictured on an inn sign or a broadsheet of travellers' tales.

'What is it?' I studied it, incredulous. 'Some creature from beyond the northern plateau or the furthest reaches of the Nilgeh Mire?'

Though I had never even heard rumour of any beast which could appear and disappear at will. The strange little thing flapped its pathetic wings eagerly as it realised I was looking at it.

'Can it fly or not?'

'No, alas.' Quirian held out his hand as its head snapped around at the sound of his voice. As it sought his caresses, he scratched the scaled folds of skin under its pointed jaw, as he had done last night. 'What do you know of magic, Deyris?'

'Magic?' I was nonplussed. 'What everyone knows. The Sun Goddess grants her priestesses power to bring truth into the open and to share the bounty of light and life. The Moon God's province is tracing evil, whether that's deceit hidden in someone's head or sickness in their body.'

The wyverning turned towards me, forked tongue tasting the air as I spoke.

'But what has that to do with this creature?' I gestured without thinking, hastily withdrawing my hand as it hissed.

Quirian leaned back in his chair. 'The magics you speak of serve this great city's interests day by day. There are many other enchantments which are not so widely known but are still the magic of the tangible realm. This is the Sun Goddess's province.'

His voice grew stern again, as daunting as when he'd sat in judgement, unknowable behind his sacred mask.

'Powerful enchantments relate to an unseen world, to an intangible realm, just as surely as night follows day and the moon follows the sun. The existence and the nature of this intangible realm is the Horned God's most closely guarded lore.'

'I've no wish to trespass on such mysteries,' I said apprehensively.

His thin smile offered no reassurance. 'You have just proved that you must be instructed in the proper use of your inborn magic.'

Now I was startled as well as scared. 'I have no magic.'

He gestured at the wyverning which was looking from me to him and back again as we spoke.

'If you had no talent for magic, you could not see that. It's a creature of the intangible realm. Try to touch it.'

'No, thank you.' I folded my hands in my lap.

'That was not a request.' His mild tone belied his words. 'If you are ever to be able to leave here, with your good name restored and your husband's reputation unstained, you must do as I ask and learn as much as you can of the unseen world and its inhabitants.'

I still kept my hands in my lap. 'What damage could that false creature do to Teutel's reputation?'

'All in good time. Now, can you touch the wyverning or not?'

I pressed my lips tight together to keep my irritation to myself and reached out towards the creature's arrow-shaped head. Forked tongue flickering, it leaned towards me, clawed feet scraping on the floorboards.

As it bobbed and weaved my hesitant fingers passed straight through its neck, as though it were no more than a shadow.

I snatched my hand back. 'How can that be?'

Quirian leaned forward and tickled under its chin again. I could hear the rasp of scales and the creature's soft hiss of pleasure.

'How can you touch it? How can I hear it?'

'You can see and hear creatures of the intangible realm but you have not yet honed your skills sufficiently to touch them. That must be your first goal.'

'Please.' I pressed my hands to my face, closing my eyes as though that would make everything disappear, not just the wyverning. 'I don't understand.'

'Let's start with this little creature.'

I waited for the priest to continue. When he didn't I was forced to lower my hands and look at him.

'It was called into being in the unseen realm by one of our residents' sleeping imagination. Most magical talent is so weak that it can only manifest itself in dreams. But even a thin drip of water can eventually wear away a stone. This woman has dreamed so often of this curious beast that it has become a reality in the intangible world.'

He smiled ruefully. 'Do you know what a wyvern is?'

'No.' I shook my head.

'It's akin to a dragon but a wyvern's form is more like a bird. It has two wings and two legs though it's scaled like a lizard and has leathery wings. Whoever dreams of this beast has heard that much but she's never seen a picture and has no notion what size such a beast's wings must be, if it were ever to fly. This curiosity is the best that her sleeping imagination can contrive. So we have called it a wyverning.'

'Why does she dream of such a thing? Have you asked her?' Now I was lacing my fingers together to stop myself reaching for the creature again. Discovering I couldn't touch it made me want to try until I succeeded.

Quirian shook his head. 'We have no idea who dreams of it, and we wouldn't ask such questions if we did.'

'What's his name?' I studied the wyverning intently and was rewarded with its full attention, the creature's jewelled eyes glowing. 'Is it a he?' I wondered suddenly, 'or a she?'

'It's neither and it has no name.' Quirian spoke so sharply that I looked at him, startled. 'And you are not to give it one,' he added sternly.

'Why not?' I was more curious than affronted.

'If we give it a name, it becomes more real,' he told me solemnly. 'If we think of it as male or female, it becomes more real. It becomes a creature which needs a mate. If we discover who dreams of it and ask her questions, that will turns her thoughts to what it might mean to her. Every time she consciously brings it to mind, it becomes more real. If it becomes real enough, it might even make the step from the unseen realm into the tangible world. Who knows what it might do then? You've seen it has a snake's fangs. It might well have a snake's venom and who knows how potent that might be.'

A scant three days ago, I would never have believed that anything imaginary could become solidly real. But I knew my husband was dead and yet I had met something wearing his face. A creature which was solid enough for his family to embrace and strong enough to shove me off my feet and across a room.

'But surely you could stop it?' I looked at the wyverning and remembered the priest's promise to help me stop the creature which had ruined my life.

'Destroy it, you mean? An innocent beast which never sought to be called into being? Only trying to save itself or fleeing from the terror of being surrounded by hordes of unknown creatures? As far as it's concerned, this building is almost entirely empty. As long as it stays in the intangible realm, it can only see those of us who can see it in return.'

'But you said—' As I glanced at him, feeling confused and somehow guilty, Quirian gazed steadfastly back at me.

'As long as it offers no threat and stays safely unseen and insubstantial, we will leave it be. But if it crosses into this world, then yes, however undeserved its fate, we would unmake it with stronger and more practised magic than a sleeping woman's dreams. Just as you must learn how to unmake your husband's fetch which is a far more dangerous thing.'

'His what?'

The unfamiliar word prompted my question even though I realised what the answer must be before the priest spoke.

'The creature wearing his face.'

I couldn't help a shudder. 'What made it? Who made it?'

'Grief made it,' Quirian said with unexpected compassion. 'Your grief—'

'This is my fault?' I gaped at him, appalled.

He shook his head. 'No, it's not. Please, let me explain. There was your grief and your mother-by-marriage's and his sisters and Teutel's father's heartbreak. More profound sorrow besides, among the household who'd known him since birth. As well as grief, there was utter disbelief. His death was so unexpected.

'More than that, and forgive me—' his voice softened '—I have no wish to sound callous but you had no body to bury. Not funeral to plan to convince all of you that this calamity was real. Consequently so many of you were free to wish that it simply wasn't true, to long for news that there had been some mistake. Among such a large number there will always be one or two with unsuspected magical talent. Even weak potential all focused on the same thing increases the risk of a manifestation. When someone with a powerful talent—'

'My talent.' I felt sick at heart.

'Not alone,' Quirian said briskly. 'The strongest talent in this instance belongs to Mistress Menore. That's why I had all of you brought together in the House of Restraint. We have ways to see how long a shadow someone casts into the unseen realm.'

I stared at him and so did the wyverning. Astonished, I sat as mute as the creature.

The priest smiled his rueful smile. 'Hers is not a talent we would ever wish to train. This creature's sly and violent nature reflects the malice that runs through her like the grain through a piece of wood. Thankfully there's no sign that she has the least notion of what she could do. Evidently she's a woman wholly unable to see beyond her own wants and needs to appreciate anyone else's concerns in the real world around her. Contemplating the intangible realm would be utterly beyond her capabilities.'

I couldn't restrain a quiet smile of satisfaction. Even amid all this upheaval, it was good to know that someone else saw my mother-by-marriage for the selfish leech she was.'

'Of course, now that we are aware of her unrealised potential, we will keep a close watch on her, in case of further trouble. On the whole household,' he added, reflective, 'since she may well have passed some measure of magical talent to her daughters.'

'Magic runs in a bloodline?' I instantly wondered which of my parents had bequeathed this curse to me. It must have been my mother. The notion of my father's drunken dreams spawning imaginary monsters didn't bear thinking about.

'Sometimes,' Quirian temporised. 'In many cases, we can find no hint of magic if we trace ten generations back and follow every spreading branch of a family's line.'

'But if her magic is stronger than mine—' I couldn't go

on. Saying such things aloud made this seem all the more absurd.

'You will be stronger than her, once you are trained,' the priest assured me. 'Besides, she wants to believe in this fetch, to have her son restored to her. You know the creature for the sham that it is and want nothing more than to be rid of it. That will double and redouble your strength.'

'How can it be unmade?' I spoke aloud without intending to. But that was the only question that mattered.

Quirian hesitated and I saw something in his face which sent a shiver of unease down my spine.

'Tell me!' I demanded.

'The longer a fetch endures, the more real it becomes,' Quirian explained with studied calm. 'The more people who see it and believe that it truly is their lost loved one returned, the more real it becomes. It begins to draw on the memories of those who surround it, who knew the living person. It starts to learn who the lost loved one truly was and becomes ever more adept at mimicking them. The more real a fetch has become, the harder it is to be rid of it.'

This explained so much of what had happened over the past few days. So much of the creature's behaviour.

'Any number of folk have seen this thing,' I pointed out with growing concern. 'All Teutel's friends will have heard that he has returned, that he was never dead at all.'

Quirian nodded sombrely. 'Which is why it's now become so real that it even bleeds. Unmaking a fetch while it is still a creature of surface illusion over blank substance is difficult enough. When belief in it goes to the bone, destroying it truly is a challenge.'

'How did it come to this?' I was suddenly enraged. 'If you know all this, why didn't you act sooner? When—'

'We didn't know,' he retorted. 'We don't walk down every street and alley in all this vast city looking for such things. We don't peer into every house's windows from dusk till dawn in case we see some manifestation of magic. I told you that such talent is rare and an occurrence like this is rarer still. In any case, if the thing had been brought before the Horned God's gate when it first appeared, when it was still behaving so unlike the man you remembered, even a priest with no magic would have suspected something was seriously awry. He would have sent for one of us with the skills to see it for what it was.'

'I wanted to go to the priests,' I protested. 'Truly, but his mother insisted on calling in her own physician. The fool said there was no cause for concern and they all believed him, especially once the creature started becoming ever more like Teutel—'

Quirian raised both hands in apology. 'I didn't mean to accuse you.'

I bit my lip. That was generous, since I had accused him undeservedly. I set that aside. I had another question I must have answered.

'How like Teutel could it become?' If only I had believed in it at that first meeting, would it have reflected my love, not his mother's spite?

'It will never become the man you loved. It could never do so.' Quirian's words were both full of compassion and yet utterly merciless. 'If you cherish any such hope, however faint in your heart of hearts, abandon it now. This is a creature born of magic and darkest emotion. It has no spark of divine life within it. It does not live. It merely exists. As long as it does, it will only serve its own appetites; food and warmth first and foremost.'

He shook his head, dour. 'As it becomes more real those appetites will grow more complex, to encompass lust for women, for money or for power. It will learn the ways it can satisfy such desires without conscience or consideration for anyone. Fetches that have gone undiscovered have become bywords for brutality until they end up on the gallows.'

Recalling the way the creature had behaved towards me, now I understood what Quirian had meant about the threat to Teutel's reputation.

'How long—'

202

'We must be rid of it as soon as possible. These things can even become sufficiently real to marry and spawn children. As long as they have one human parent, killing those children would truly be murder but they will grow with a shard of darkness in their spirit and bring sorrow and pain to those around them.'

'Children?' As horrified as I was, I immediately saw how real a danger that was. Mistress Menore would be wilfully blind to any faults in her apparently restored son and now that I was safely locked away, she would seek to marry him off as soon as possible, to secure the grandchildren she craved.

While Master Menore, Astrila and Lessane, maybe even Tracha and Vari, would all be more and more troubled to see the brother and son they had loved apparently turning into a vicious brute.

'What must I do?'

'You must kill it.' Quirian said implacable. 'Now that it's a creature of flesh and blood, it can be killed with a blade, provided that is wielded by one of those whose magic helped make it. More than that, it must be killed in such a way that its body is there to be found, so Teutel's family must accept that he is dead and grieve for him accordingly.'

He leaned forward again, hands clasped together.

'If we were simply to unmake it, and that would be no easy task, believe me, Mistress Menore would be free to believe that her vanished son would somehow return a second time. Her belief would be all the stronger, since such a marvel had already happened once.'

He didn't need to tell me what would happen then. 'And it would come back.'

'Quite so.' He nodded.

'But everyone would believe I had murdered him.' I found my mouth as dry as dust. 'I would be condemned and burned.'

'Not at all.' Quirian surprised me with a smile. 'How could you be guilty of such a crime? You are safely confined within the Moon God's walls. There will be twenty women able to swear by the Golden Goddess that they saw you here when the crime occurred.'

'How?'

'You will leave a simulacrum of yourself here—' he spread one hand and then the other '—while you cross the city unseen to do the deed.'

He made it sound so simple. It seemed utterly impossible to me.

'Since time is of the essence, and I have a great deal to teach you, we should make a start today.' He rose to his feet and went to open the door.

I was about to follow when I realised something. 'Where is the wyverning?' The strange little creature was nowhere to be seen.

'It has faded into nothingness. It rarely endures past midmorning.' Quirian sounded as though this was nothing remarkable. 'We will see if it returns tonight. One day, sooner or later, it will cease to appear.'

I frowned. 'What would you have shown me, to convince me of my own magic, if yesterday had been the day it faded away?'

Quirian held the door open. 'Oh, it's far from the only such creature we keep watch on within these walls. You must start your training by learning to see them all.'

He left the room. I followed. What else could I do?

Chapter Six

What else could I do? Whatever other mysteries beset me, one thing was as clear as daylight. I would never leave the Moon God's sanctuary without Brother Quirian's permission. Trying to hide my apprehension, I followed him to the topmost floor of the central building which linked the two wings. This was no dormitory partitioned into sleeping cells like the one where I had spent the previous night. The whole floor was a vast empty room with white-washed walls and plaited-rush matting underfoot.

A door opposite presumably opened onto the further wing. On one side, broad, unbarred windows overlooked the central courtyard, though there were none facing whichever street skirted the building. What street was it? I realised that I had no idea whereabouts I might be in the city.

Quirian walked into the room and turned around. Seeing me still standing on the threshold, he beckoned. 'Close the door.'

I only advanced a few steps, searching this apparently empty room. Was there some intangible creature from the unseen realm lurking here, like the wyverning in his study.

Quirian smiled. 'There is nothing in here besides the two of us. I want you to study the courtyard and tell me what phantasms may be found down there.'

I joined him to lean on the windowsill, looking downwards. I saw his eyes flicker from side to side, and from the high wooden gates to the cobbles below.

All I could see were draymen unloading a wagon heaped with sacks and barrels while a black-garbed man sworn to the Horned God's service was closing the entrance.

I frowned. 'Why don't the creatures you speak of escape when the gates stand open?'

'Most leave, at least once,' Quirian was unconcerned, 'but for creatures like the wyverning, the further they stray from whoever's dreams spawned them, the more quickly they fade. Since all things strive for life, in the intangible realm as well as the one we're born to, such frail phantasms soon learn to stay within these walls. Those which have endured long enough to break free of such ties wander the city from time to time until they encounter something which scares them back to this refuge. We find that useful,' he added. 'It tells us there's some new manifestation we must locate and assess.'

I was left speechless by his matter-of-fact tone.

'Concentrate,' he ordered me, 'until you can see how the courtyard appears in the unseen realm.'

'You say there are phantasms down there.' I repeated this new word carefully, to fix it in my mind. Pressing my forehead against the leaded glass, I searched as much of the yard as possible. 'What exactly am I looking for?'

'I cannot tell you,' Quirian reproved me mildly. 'You might create what I'm describing out of your own imagination.'

I stared at him, unnerved. 'It's that easy? To unwittingly make such a thing?'

Was I going to have to guard my every waking and sleeping thought for the rest of my life? Had I been carelessly spawning unimagined beasts, all unawares?

To my relief, Quirian shook his head.

'Not as a rule but here and now, with all your concentration focused, your wish to succeed would most likely become self-fulfilling.'

That was some reassurance. I returned to the window and forced myself to study the courtyard. The only things I could safely ignore were the draymen unloading the wagon drawn by their patient horses.

'Oh!' I pushed myself back from the sill, startled.

'Well?' Quirian looked expectantly at me.

'They disappeared.' I leaned forward, still not quite believing it. 'The draymen and the horses. The Horned God's servant. Oh.' Now I was disappointed. As I looked down into the courtyard, they were all clearly visible.

'Well done.' Quirian's congratulation surprised me. 'That

was your first conscious glimpse into the unseen realm. The draymen and the horses have no knowledge of the intangible world, still less any power to influence it, therefore they have no presence there. That's why you couldn't see them.'

'But I couldn't see anything else.' I was caught between elation and frustration.

'Look again,' Qurian ordered.

I did, but not only because he said so. I knew my eyes hadn't deceived me. Everything else in the courtyard had remained as clear as day, lit by the Goddess's sun up above. For the first time, I truly believed I could do what the priest was asking.

As I concentrated I found I could continue searching the courtyard even as some fraction of my awareness noted the horses and draymen fading from sight. I caught a glimpse of something quartering the cobbles. Only a glimpse. Exasperated, I tried again. As soon as I caught fleeting movement in the corner of my eye, I refused to let it escape me.

'It's long and low, like a polecat.' Though I had never seen one so large. 'It would be waist-high to me, if it stood up on its hind feet. It's grey-furred like a rabbit with a brush of a tail like a squirrel.'

Qurian smiled. 'It's a petori. A creature from nursery tales in towns upstream on the Tane. As the forests were cleared, they were the first folk to rear orphaned marten kits to hunt vermin in cellars and attics. Stories soon invented mystical brethren for the real animals, to be blamed for lost socks and stolen griddle cakes. Children were told as long as they were good, these unseen guardians drove off the shade rats eager to bite naughty boys' and girls' toes.'

'Shade rats?' I had never heard any such tales.

'They're real enough in the unseen realm, though we seldom see any these days,' Qurian remarked. 'Most folk leave grandparents' tales behind, when they come from vassal towns to the city. Fewer still pass on old stories to the next generation.'

Watching the petori scurry round the courtyard, I was

filled with wonder. Truly, I could now choose to see into this unseen, unsuspected realm.

In the next instant I was beset with anxiety. The strange little wyverning and this curious creature; they were a world away from the evil thing wearing my dead husband's face. The fetch wasn't some insubstantial shadow, visible to only a few and unable to engage with the tangible realm. It had been strong enough to knock me bodily across our living room when it had first appeared. Since then it had grown daily more cunning and knowing. How could I possibly hope to attack it with a blade a second time?

The petori vanished and I saw the rough-coated dray horses shifting their feet and shaking their heads.

'You must remain single-minded to see both realms of existence.' Quirian sounded as though he was quoting some ancient wisdom.

'I need none of this magic to see the vile sham that's destroyed my happiness,' I retorted. 'It's walking the city's streets—'

'—and growing stronger by the day.' The priest interrupted, merciless. 'How many more lives will you let it ruin? Don't you wish to reclaim your home? You are the only one who can unmake that fetch.'

Qurian's sweeping gesture took in the empty room and the courtyard below. 'This is only your first step on that path. Will you give up so soon? Will you betray your beloved's memory so easily? Will you resign yourself to a life locked behind the Horned God's walls? At least you won't witness the fetch's misdeeds but I didn't think you were such a coward.'

His contempt scalded me. 'I am no such thing!'

'Then trust me, Deyris.' Quirian's voice softened. 'My mother used to tell me, one thing at a time and first things first. Truly, I believe that you can do this and remember, I know far more of this lore than you. You're not the first person I've instructed in these mysteries, little by little and step by step. I will help you learn what you must do to unmake the fetch. For the moment, don't try to run before you can walk.'

Did he think such trite proverbs would convince me? I gazed into the courtyard, resenting being beguiled like some fractious child. On the other side of that coin though, perhaps he was right. Since I'd already learned to see these creatures, perhaps I could do more.

More than anything else, I longed to go home. To rap the bronze heron knocker on our red-painted door and find Teutel opening it to embrace me. But I knew beyond any doubt that would never happen. Didn't I owe it to Teutel's memory to destroy this creature which would leave loathing as his legacy?

Wasn't attempting to kill the fetch my only hope of escaping this place? If it wasn't the prison I had first feared, the thought of living out my life within these walls, hemmed in by these wounded women was a dire prospect.

Could I trust Quirian's certainty? For the Moon God's sake?

I cleared my throat and schooled myself to see the unseen once again. I found the petori and a curious white bird with scarlet feathers trailing like ribbons from its wingtips and tail.

'Good,' Quirian approved as I described it. 'That's all there is to see at present. Now, do you prefer to knit or to embroider?'

'Why do you ask?'

'Every woman within these walls works to earn her keep.' The priest explained further. 'Your next lesson is to hone your skills at seeing the unseen while you go about your everyday business. So will you join the women who knit or those who embroider? This evening you can tell me what you have seen in the work room.'

I thought quickly. 'I'll knit.'

Truth be told, I was more proud of my needlework. Even Mistress Menore had grudgingly admired my precise stitching. But I'd been knitting since I was a child, when my father brought home discarded, moth-eaten garments for me to unravel and salvage the yarn. Once a piece was established on my needles, my hands could work on it with barely conscious thought. I could turn all my attention to whatever might lurk beneath tables and chairs.

'Very well.' Quirian headed for the door.

I went to follow and tripped headlong over something. As I sprawled on the rush matting, the harsh fibres scoured the palms of my hands. The dog I had fallen over yelped and the second priest in the room knelt to reassure his affronted hound. It was a sandy-coated mongrel with long ears and feathery tail.

'Who are you?' I scrambled to my feet, scarlet with embarrassment.

'This is Brother Jatier.' As Qurian nodded, the older man rose stiffly to acknowledge me with an expressionless bow.

'I'm sorry if I hurt your dog.' The poor thing was looking up at me with deeply offended brown eyes.

'He's used to it.' Brother Jatier spared Qurian a look of veiled rebuke before walking away towards the far door. As the dog followed, limping where I had trodden on its paw, I realised that entrance was now standing ajar.

'I didn't see or hear—'

'You didn't look or listen,' Brother Quirian corrected me. 'You must always reacquaint yourself with the real world after gazing on the intangible realm. Any number of things could have changed around you. You had no idea that I had rung this—' he took one hand out of a pocket to show me a little bell muffled within his fist '—or that Brother Jatier and his dog had come in.'

'You could have warned me to look.' Now I was more indignant than humiliated. For my own sake and the dog's.

'You have a great deal to learn and quickly. Forgive me but experience teaches more thoroughly than words alone.'

Quirian continued walking towards the door we had entered by.

'You must learn to look between the two worlds with the blink of an eye. Practise in the knitters' work room. The women will ask you where you have been this morning, so tell them that you have been making your peace with the Horned God. They won't enquire further. I will call on you this evening and see how you have progressed.'

He didn't say anything more as we went down the stairs. I stayed just as silent, wondering how far I could trust a man accustomed to wearing the Moon God's inscrutable mask. Evidently Quirian had no qualms about using his superior knowledge to teach me a hard lesson rather than an easy one. He had shown he was as ready to wound me with cutting words as he was to coax me with promises and reassurance.

At least I found congenial company in the work room. As Brother Quirian left me at the entrance, the closest circle to the door obligingly shifted to open a space. One grey-gowned woman set down her knitting and fetched another chair from the far end of the room while another brought me a plain willow-woven workbasket holding wooden needles and the undyed black wool.

'We're making winter tunics, my dear.' As she spoke, her swift fingers were casting on the stitches for a sleeve to match some other woman's work.

The circle ranged from my much own age to those old enough to be grandmothers though I guessed they had no living kin to care for them, or none whom they cared to acknowledge, to end their days here.

'What do we call you?' The woman handed me the needles.

'Deyris Menore.'

To my relief, no one seemed to have heard my name or my disgrace. No city gossip at all appeared to scale the Moon God's walls. The women's talk was all about the tasks in hand in the various work rooms.

'Where will these tunics go?' I asked as needles clicked around the circle.

'The Horned God's schoolboys,' a thin-faced woman

explained.

I tried not to look at the burn scars striping her fingers. 'They will certainly be warm.' The wool was thick and strong and knitted quickly into a sturdy weave.

'Some for the first time in their lives.' A motherly woman smiled.

'Those used to lording over the rest will be suitably humbled,' the girl sitting beside me remarked with cold satisfaction, 'when no one can tell them apart by their garb.'

There was a tale to be told there but no one prompted the girl to continue. So I curbed my own curiosity as conversation resumed, flitting from subject to subject without ever settling on anything of substance. I need only offer the occasional nod and smile, a few words here and there.

By the time the sun outside the windows told us midday was approaching, I found I needed no more than a thought to look from the circle of women into this room as it appeared in the unseen world. There were no creatures to be seen so I considered other aspects of the intangible realm. Tables and chairs stood in the self-same places but there was no sign of the garments the women were making. I wondered why that might be so and resolved to ask Brother Quirian.

My fingers swept black wool around my needles only to feel the yarn resisting. I leaned forward, reaching down to free the snagged yarn from some frayed willow-wand.

The phantasm squatting by my feet and clawing the wool looked up at me. I couldn't tell if it gaped with glee or menace. It was an ugly little beast, resembling a toad though with longer arms and legs and manlike hands and feet. I've no idea what a real toad has in its mouth but I wager it's not the snaggled fangs I was looking at.

'Are you all right?'

The thin-faced woman looked at me with concern as I recoiled.

I managed a rueful smile. 'A cramp in my back from sitting so long.'

As I looked down, the phantasm stared up unblinking. Its gaze was as eerily manlike as its hands. I remembered what Quirian had said. If I could see a creature in the unreal realm, then it could see me. I stared back, defiant and twitched the strand of wool out of its reach.

The creature's tongue lolled at the corner of its mouth as it hissed with annoyance. How could the other women not hear this? As I blinked I could see them sharing some amusement, oblivious.

I stiffened as something stabbed, needle-like, into my ankle. Summoning all my self-control, I looked down at the warty creature. This time I would swear I saw amusement curve its gaping maw. It had extended a single finger and driven its talon through my stocking. I could feel the tickle of a trickle of blood as it withdrew its hand.

I tried to kick it away under the pretext of stretching my legs. The scuffed toe of my shoe passed through it, as readily as my hand had swept through the wyverning's neck.

The toad-manikin's jaw flapped with silent laughter as it dug its talon into my ankle a second time. I gritted my teeth against the pain. How could it wound me when I couldn't even touch it?

When the noon bell sounded, all the women set down their work.

'The refectory is in the building across the courtyard,' said the girl who hadn't smiled all morning.

'Thank you.'

I followed the other women out of the room but I didn't go to the refectory. I went straight to hammer on Brother Quirian's door.

'There is a phantasm in the work room tormenting me,' I protested as soon as he opened to my knock. 'I cannot even touch it.'

'The gremian.' His expression was as amiable as his words were implacable. 'You must focus on it sufficiently to see it, while remaining clear in your own mind that it is an intangible creature and that you are of this physical realm. Once you are certain of that distinction, the creature will be unable to reach across the void to touch you. Come and tell me when you've succeeded.'

With a brisk nod, he closed the door. I was left staring at the blank wood, lost for words.

It took me the rest of that day and most of the two that followed. By noon of the following day, I was well on my way to hating the gremian but I also began to see that the more anger I felt, the more solid it appeared and the sharper its claws became.

What I must summon up was detachment; to regard the capering thing as though it were no more than a painted picture, or one of those wax arrangements of fruit and flowers that were all the fashion when Teutel and I wed. Once I was armoured with such aloofness, the gremian's claws couldn't even snag my stockings. Though by the time my dogged defiance was proof against it, my ankles were spotted with pinpricks that itched as fiercely as fleabites.

I hurried to Brother Quirian's room, on the evening of the day I succeeded. I wanted to tell him the trick I had found, of likening the creature to those wax creations. Mistress Menore had presented us with one, when Teutel and I had set up home together. Goddess forbid that she actually give us something of use. The unwanted gift even cost us coin we could ill-afford; to buy a glass cover to protect the ugly thing from becoming dull with dust. It wasn't that Teutel liked it but he would dutifully cherish it for his mother's sake.

I could be rid of it now, I realised. Once I was rid of the fetch, when I reclaimed my home, I could hurl the ghastly ornament into the gutter, or throw it on the fire and watch the improbable blooms melt across the coals.

Though smashing it in the open road would leave glassy shards to injure people and horses alike. Consigning it to the flames would fill my home with stinking smoke. A more practical solution would be selling it. While Teutel and I had banked a substantial sum at the Goddess's shrine, I would have to find some way to earn my own bread and meat in the days ahead.

Looking ahead in such a fashion was helping me tolerate the other women's inconsequential chatter and the enforced closeness of the night time dormitory. I reminded myself hourly that the sooner I mastered the puzzles of the unseen realm, the sooner I would be leaving this place.

Meanwhile, I could see for myself that I was making progress with these arcane skills. While I still didn't want to contemplate the awful task which stood between me and freedom, I reminded myself time and again that Brother Quirian believed I could kill the fetch. All in good time.

I rapped impatiently on his door.

'Enter!'

I snatched my hand back. That hadn't been the priest answering.

'Deyris?' Qurian opened the door and beckoned me inside. 'This is Alace.'

The priest looked as uneasy as Teutel had, when he'd first introduced me to his parents. Apprehensive that I would be unfairly found wanting, or nervous lest they look at him with disappointment, or perhaps both.

I offered the unknown man a brief curtsey, though nothing about him suggested he warranted such deference. He was a short and skinny man, old enough to be my father. Bandy legged in leather breeches and a grimy shirt, smelling powerfully of horses, he seemed to have just come from a stable.

He looked me up and down as though I were a promising filly. 'How fast is she progressing? How hard are you pushing her?'

The priest turned to me. 'What have you achieved today?'

I answered proudly. 'The gremian can no longer touch me and I was able to drive it off with my knitting needles.'

Only that afternoon I had realised I could see the handiwork I was holding whenever I glanced into the unseen world. Quicker than thought, I jabbed the wooden needles at the gremian's flank. I don't know who was more surprised, me or the creature as it yelped. It scuttled away to crouch under an oblivious seamstress's table, rubbing its bruise and chittering with indignation.

I'd had to explain away my sudden laughter with a garbled tale of mistaking a curl of discarded fabric for a mouse.

'Well done,' Qurian approved.

The older man, Alace, snorted. 'It's something, I suppose. Very well,' he addressed me directly before jerking his head towards the doorway. 'Let's see if his faith in you is justified.'

Qurian obediently took his black priest's cloak and silvered mask from a hook inside the room's tall cupboard.

'Where are we going?' I retreated nervously.

I wanted to ask who this stranger was and what authority he had over me. Seeing Qurian's meekness in his presence, I didn't dare.

'If you please.' The masked priest's gesture told me to follow the bandy-legged man. He followed close behind. So I couldn't run?

A plain carriage was waiting in the courtyard, like the one which had brought me here. The skinny man opened the door and ushered me in. As Qurian followed, I realised Alace had climbed onto the driver's seat. As he urged the horse on with a whistle, I heard the gates opening.

'Where are we going?'

'I don't know.'

Was Qurian telling the truth? With his face masked and his voice muffled, I couldn't tell.

We didn't go far, though I had no idea where I had been taken. I was little wiser when the carriage stopped and the old man opened the door so we could step down.

I stood beneath a pillared canopy sheltering a great house's double door. I glanced over my shoulder but the horses blocked my view.

'In here.' Alace opened the small porter's door cut into the main entrance. Even he had to duck his head as he went through. The hinges squealed a petulant demand for oil.

Hitching my grey skirts high, I stepped over the sill to follow him. I found myself in a vast empty entrance hall. Magnificent as this house was, it had been stripped bare of all furniture and decoration except the ornate carvings on the doors and banisters. Though the house hadn't been neglected, I noted, despite the door's stiff hinges. The red and white chequer-tiled floor was swept clean and the cornices were free of cobwebs.

Alace strode towards double doors across the hall and threw them open to reveal a withdrawing room whose walls were hung with rose-pink silk. An ornate white marble fireplace reached from the elaborate plaster ceiling to the polished wooden floor and blood-red velvet curtains shrouded the windows against the dusk outside.

Lamps had been lit in the wall sconces but there was no furniture. That didn't mean that the room was empty. A great hill lynx sprawled in front of the hearth though no fire was lit.

As Quirian ushered me into the room, the tawny beast raised its head, black-tufted ears pricking with curiosity. Alace snapped his fingers as he walked towards it and it rose to its feet in leisurely fashion. As it yawned to show lethal white fangs, I backed into Quirian.

'Don't worry,' he said quietly. 'Alace has drawn it here from the unseen realm.'

The skinny man leaned against the marble fireplace and folded his arms. 'Show me you're proof against this.'

The lynx was trotting towards us, padded paws silent on the floorboards. It looked at me as though I were a helpless fawn cowering in some grassy glade. My father had once painted such a scene for a wealthy patron commissioning a reminder of the forested estates he preferred to the city's paved streets.

I felt Quirian's hands on my shoulder blades. He pushed me forward. The lynx crouched, its bobbed tail twitching.

'Move, girl!'

As Alace's shout echoed around the room, the lynx rounded on him and snarled.

'What do you want me to do?' I could barely whisper, my throat was so dry.

'Walk to the window,' Alace ordered. 'Open a curtain.'

'Remember—' Quirian began.

'Silence!' Alace snapped.

I clenched my jaw in a vain attempt to stop myself shivering and took a first, fearful step.

The lynx's head whipped around, its golden eyes intent upon me. As I took another step, it turned its whole body to face me.

Out of the corner of my eye, I saw a fold of Quirian's black cloak as he withdrew to the corner of the room. The lynx's gaze didn't waver. I still had all its attention.

'If you ever hope to be free of the Moon God's dominion, you must open those curtains.'

I heard Alace's cold certainty that I would never meet either challenge. The lynx heard the man who had brought it here and turned its head to snarl at him a second time.

I seized my chance to hurry across the room, heading for the wall opposite the fireplace, hoping to stay as far away from the beast as possible.

It darted across the empty room. Now it stood between me and the window. I froze. The lynx took a step forward. I edged a little further along the wall. It moved closer. I tried a pace away from the wall but moving backwards. Perhaps if it thought I was retreating...

No. The creature drew closer still. I stood motionless. The lynx kept coming, wary but purposeful.

Perhaps if I didn't move, it would see that I was no threat. I stood there like a statue while I longed to run with every fibre of my being. The great cat came close enough to sniff at my skirts. It was a solid bodied beast, broad across the haunches and deep in the chest. I could see its whiskers bending as they brushed against my grey dress. As it circled me, its shoulders nudged my thigh.

Over by the fireplace, Alace hissed with derision. 'She cannot do it.'

As the Golden Mother is my witness, I tried. With every breath, I told myself that the beast wasn't real. That it was merely some phantasm. But it was so hard. Disbelieving a creature as comical as the wyverning, or something so self-evidently unnatural as the gremian was one thing. Convincing myself that this fearsome animal couldn't touch me, when all of us in the room could see it, large as life? When I could smell its musky scent and see the hairs it was shedding on my gown? I had no doubt that it could kill me as easily as any woodland deer.

The lynx reared up and swiped at me with vicious claws. I barely got a hand up to save my face. As it was, the beast's talon tore into my forearm.

I screamed with shock and pain. The lynx yowled and sprang, heavy forepaws thudding against my shoulders. It knocked me off my feet. As I landed hard on the wooden floor, I was nose to nose with its fur-ruffed face, its hot breath on my cheek. It was standing on my belly, its weight an agonising burden. I sobbed, incoherent with terror.

'Enough!'

Alace's hand passed through the lynx's head and the beast melted away like mist in the sunshine. He stood over me, looking down with scant sympathy.

'It was too much to hope for.' He extended a calloused hand. 'Let's see that wound tended.'

I realised my forearm was still blazing with pain, my gown's torn sleeve sodden with blood. I clutched it as I sat up, biting my lip in a vain attempt to stem shocked tears.

'Sanife!' Quirian opened the door, shouting into the entrance hall.

A green-gowned woman hurried into the room.

'Oh, my dear,' she said with warm sympathy. 'You're Deyris?'

219

I could only nod. If I tried to speak, I knew weeping would overwhelm me.

Alace was helping me to my feet, his hand beneath my unwounded elbow. I say helping. Forcing would be more accurate.

The woman shooed him away, wrapping one arm around my shoulders. Her perfume was as costly as her dress. I tried to pull away to avoid smearing blood on the watered silk. She had no such concerns. 'Don't fret, my dear.'

She was handsome, chestnut haired, perhaps ten years my elder, and with the precise grooming afforded by a lifetime's wealth. I let her usher me out of the room and through the hallway to an antechamber. The room had a small sink and its walls lined with shelves. Though it was grander than any I had worked in, I recognised it for a servery. Doubtless some grand dining room lay beyond the other door.

Gauze and bandages were laid ready on the scrubbed table along with an array of apothecary's jars.

'He knew I would fail.' My voice quavered.

'No, but we came prepared for anything short of complete success.' The green-gowned woman sat me on a stool and gently laid my forearm on the table.

I looked away as she began cutting my blood-soaked sleeve with silver surgeon's shears. 'What does this mean? That I have failed this test?' I winced as she cleaned the gash in my arm with a fragrant lotion.

'I'm sure you will do better next time.' Sanife leaned closer to study the gory slash.

Something in her voice made me horribly uneasy. I grabbed a bandage and wrapped it tight around my forearm to stem the blood. 'I need to talk to Quirian.'

'Wait—'

But Sanife didn't try to restrain me. As I reached the withdrawing room' doors, I heard shouting within.

'She will succeed if she's given time.' Quirian was furious. 'Besides, how else are we to be rid of it?'

'We know all of those involved in its making.' Alace's cold answer only served to inflame the priest's wrath.

'We can only guess,' Quirian spat. 'You would kill innocents on mere suspicion?'

'If we must, to weaken the thing sufficiently so we can unmake it!' Alace wasn't to be dissuaded. 'I have seen what these things can do. You haven't. One way or the other, we must act and swiftly.'

'Deyris? The mother?' Quirian objected. 'All four of the daughters? How are so many women in one family to die without drawing every eye in the city? Especially when the gossips are already chewing over Teutel's supposed return?'

'Houses burn and whole families die.' Alace sighed with genuine regret but I heard no hint that he would shirk such dire necessity.

I gasped as a hand clasped my shoulder.

It was Sanife. She turned me around, pressing a finger to my lips to silence me. Mute with shock, I let her lead me back to the servery and seat me on the stool once again.

'This will numb the wound.' Discarding my hasty bandage, she smeared a thick white paste along the bloodied gash.

'Why bother, if they're going to kill me?'

Sanife was pouring pungent liquid from a black glass bottle onto a length of folded gauze. She paused. 'Do you want to die? Are you going to give up and let Vari and Tracha be killed? Astrila and Lessane?'

'No!'

Sanife smiled as she laid the gauze along the wound and began to bind my forearm tightly with a fresh bandage. 'Keep that in mind as you face your next test. It will help you succeed.'

'I must face the lynx again?' I tried to steel myself. 'Or some other creature?'

Sanife looked at me, thoughtful. 'Would you like to try a different test first? While Alace and Quirian are still arguing?'

'What—' I set my jaw. 'Yes.'

Sanife deftly tied off the bandage around my wrist. 'Come with me. Quickly and quietly.'

She led me into the entrance hall and up the stairs. With every step, I expected the door below to open, to hear Alace or Quirian demanding to know where we were going. But their loud disagreement continued.

Sanife opened a door to a bedchamber, where I was surprised to see there was indeed a bed, along with a tall looking glass propped against the wall.

'Did Quirian explain the two-fold challenge that faces you? That you must leave a simulacrum of yourself within the Moon God's walls, so no one can accuse you of murdering the fetch?'

I nodded. 'How?'

She gestured towards the bed. 'Picture yourself lying there asleep. Use the mirror to study every detail of your face, as though you are a stranger seeing this young woman Deyris for the very first time. Create this illusion in your mind's eye and then convince yourself that it is real. Succeed in this and that will help convince you and Alace both that you will be able to face down the fetch.'

My first thought was that creating such an illusion was impossible, that these vague instructions were meaningless. An instant later, I reminded myself that I would have dismissed the mere notion of the wyverning and the gremian a bare handful of days ago.

Besides, I had heard the implacable resolve in Alace's voice. I had to master this magic if I was to save my own life, and Teutel's sisters, and Goddess be my witness, even Mistress Menore deserved better than being sacrificed for the sake of killing the fetch.

I looked at the empty bedstead and marked every detail of the linen, the blanket and counterpane. Turning to the looking glass I studied myself as dispassionately as I could. I closed my ears to any distractions and thought of nothing else but picturing myself asleep on those pillows.

'Deyris.' Sanife laid a gentle hand on my unwounded arm.

'Deyris, see what you have done.'

Distantly, I realised that she had already spoken my name twice, trying to reclaim my attention. Then I realised I wasn't afraid to turn and see. I knew beyond any shadow of doubt what was lying in that bed. I looked on the thing I had made and smiled. Just as the fetch was wearing Teutel's face, my own features overlaid this lifeless imitation.

Perhaps I could do this because I was already used to making things from needle, cloth or wool. Perhaps my father's legacy was some unsuspected artistic talent. I don't know and it didn't matter.

'This will more than make up for the lynx.' Sanife couldn't hide her relief. 'Alace is a fair man. Now he must give you all the time we can spare to meet the rest of this challenge.'

'How long?' I demanded.

'The fetch must die within five days.'

I didn't ask Sanife why. I had no time for such irrelevancies if I was to learn what I must do to kill it.

Chapter Seven

They had told me that the fetch must be destroyed within five days. Then this nightmare would be over. The creature masquerading as my husband would be gone. I could return to the home which Teutel and I had shared. I would scrub away all traces of the vile thing which had drawn its semblance of life from my grief. I would be able to mourn, honestly and openly, for my murdered beloved.

All could be set to rights within five days. As long as I could wield the blade that would kill the thing. As long as I could plunge a dagger into something wearing Teutel's face and speaking with his voice. Doubts still beset me. So I reminded myself time and again of the creature's unnatural waxy, white substance, revealed when it had cut itself. I recalled the bestial way it had scavenged food spilled on the floor. I remembered its lifeless eyes when it had turned on me, hand raised to attack.

I swore to Brother Quirian that I could do this. I prayed to the Sun Goddess to forgive me if that was a lie, and to the Golden Mother and the Horned God alike that they would give me the mental and physical strength which I would need to see this through. To see my life restored.

Every morning I worked in the knitting circle with the other women under the Moon God's protection. After every noon bell, Brother Quirian took me to the empty mansion where he and Sanife made me practise seeing into the unseen realm and banishing the natural and unnatural creatures which they made manifest with their own arcane skills. I don't know where the other women thought I was going. They didn't ask and I didn't say.

Five days. Perhaps the prospect of an end to my imprisonment helped focus my thoughts. I had perfected the sleeping phantasm by the evening of the first day. No one looking at my bed on the upper floor of the Horned God's sanctuary would be able to tell that this wasn't me lying beneath those blankets. Indeed, I added some touches of my own, only to be harshly rebuked by Alace when he arrived at dusk to assess my progress.

'It's breathing.' He scowled at Quirian. 'You know better than that!'

The priest paled. 'I didn't notice.'

'I thought you wanted it to be as convincing as possible,' I objected.

'Convincing, yes. On the threshold of life, not at all.' Alace shook his head emphatically. 'You have no idea what the cost to yourself would be if it were to shift from simulacrum to phantasm. Be rid of it, now!'

He stalked out of the room without saying anything further. I looked at the bed and banished the sleeping figure, more annoyed than chastened.

Later, before I was returned to the asylum, Sanife explained a little more. She was redressing the wound I'd suffered from the lynx which Alace had first summoned up to test me. At least the injury was healing well, and cleanly.

'If you inadvertently created a phantasm of yourself, you would be left exhausted by the strain of destroying it. If one of us were to banish it, you would still suffer a brutal backlash. We cannot risk that when you'll need all your strength to kill the fetch.'

For the first time, I noticed dark smudges of weariness beneath her eyes. 'Then you, and Quirian, while you're testing me—'

'As with so many things, such skills grow with practise.' Sanife smiled, reassuring. 'And the further from reality a creature is, the easier it is to dismiss it. The closer a phantasm is to humanity though, the harder it becomes.'

'I see.' Which was to say, I trusted Sanife was telling me the truth, even if I didn't really understand.

So I limited myself to giving the sleeping simulacrum softly flowing hair. Those wisps would catch any passing breeze and make the counterfeit look more lifelike.

The next time Alace returned, dusk was deepening outside the unshuttered windows. He stood in the grand entrance hall and summoned us all with a bellow echoing through the emptiness.

'Come on!' Quirian sprang to his feet and threw open the drawing room door. He'd been as tense as a tight-wound lyre string all day.

I followed, knotting my hands together to hide their trembling. This was the fifth day since I'd been eavesdropping outside this very room. When I had learned of Alace's implacable resolve, if needs must, to kill those of us who'd been closest to Teutel. Wife, sisters, mother, father, even the Menore household's servants. Anyone whose grief might have played some part in creating this fetch, all unaware that their intolerable longing to see Teutel restored could somehow summon this ghastly counterfeit.

Then Alace and Quirian and Sanife could try to destroy the fetch without me. That's what they would be forced to attempt, if I failed to master this eerie magic which I'd never dreamed I possessed.

Sanife knew that I had overheard Alace's determination to kill the fetch, whatever the cost in innocent blood. I didn't know if she had betrayed me to Quirian and I hadn't dared ask the priest. Seeing the strain in his face this evening though, I guessed that she must have told him I knew what Alace had threatened.

The skinny old man stood in the chequer-floored hallway, holding a horse by its bridle. As before, he was dressed like a groom fresh from the stables. The bay horse stamped its feet and shook its head irritably, black mane rippling against its glossily muscled neck.

I flung a hand out and it vanished. Alace looked at me with measured approval.

'Good. How did you know?'

I gestured towards the lofty double doors. 'We didn't hear its hooves on the tiles and you would never have got it though the porter's door. You'd have had to open the house up properly to lead it inside and we would have heard that too.'

Also I had been expecting some trick as soon as I'd heard his summons. I'd been determined to escape without injury this time.

'Very good.' He nodded at me before turning all his attention to Brother Quirian. 'We will make sure it leaves the drinking den at midnight.'

Before I could ask what that meant, Alace turned his back on us all and left through the narrow porter's door set into the mansion's imposing entrance. I looked at the priest.

'This way.' Sanife appeared at my side.

She led me through the kitchens, as empty as every other room in this great house. A plain carriage waited in the servants' yard. Quirian climbed onto the driver's seat as Sanife went to hold the horse's head.

'I'll see you tomorrow.' She smiled at me.

I wished I shared her certainty. I climbed into the black-painted carriage, shivering. The fifth day was done. Would I see this fateful night through to success? Doubts tormented me on the drive back to the asylum.

I tried to tell myself that was simply because I was riding back alone. Though Quirian and I rarely talked as we travelled to and fro, the satisfaction I had seen on his face each evening had bolstered my confidence.

When we arrived back at the Moon God's sanctuary, he jumped down and left the care of the horse and carriage to the servants.

'I will fetch you an hour before midnight. Shape the sleeping simulacrum when you hear the quarter bell before that, no sooner. Now, go to dinner.'

He shooed me away with relentless hands before I could ask any questions. As he donned his silver mask and strode away, the door to the workrooms' building opened and the sanctuary's women streamed into the courtyard. I was carried along with them to the refectory on the opposite side.

I ate my serving of bread and pottage, thick with beans and greens and shreds of bacon. Now that I was surrounded by cheerful chatter, I found I was strangely calm at the prospect of the trials ahead. Before tomorrow dawned, the nightmare I'd been living would be over.

After eating I did my share of clearing the tables before helping to wash up and put away the wooden bowls and horn spoons in the scullery beside the kitchen. Some of the women stayed in the refectory, carrying the benches over towards the broad hearth to keep warm as they chatted. I followed the others who preferred to retire to their solitary beds, to sleep or to write letters by candlelight.

I snuffed my own candle and feigned sleep, only to be seduced by the treacherous warmth of blankets and mattress. As the bells startled me awake, I sat up with my heart pounding.

What was the clock striking? I recognised the three-quarter chimes with a mixture of relief and anxiety. But was this a quarter to midnight or an hour earlier? Quirian had warned me against making the simulacrum too soon, though he hadn't told me why.

Did any of these secretive magicians ever explain anything properly? Even Sanife only offered me answers which I had an immediate need for.

While I was still dithering, a black-clad shadow appeared by the bars at the front of my sleeping cell. Two shadows.

'Deyris?' One was Quirian.

'One moment.' I hastily filled the rumpled bed with a sleeping simulacrum.

'Here.' Quirian passed a bundle through the bars.

It was asylum servants' clothes; loose trousers and a shapeless tunic woven from undyed black wool. I pulled my grey gown over my head and kicked it under the bed before dragging on the disguise. The feel of thick cloth sheathing my legs was most peculiar. I tried to shake that off as I donned the short black cloak. I pulled the hood up and forward to hide my face.

Quirian unlocked my cell. As I reached the bars, the dark outline beside him melted away into the shadows. So any wakeful woman seeing us pass would note that two servants had entered the dormitory and scant moments later, two had left. Though it was anyone's guess what they might think the men had been doing there.

I followed Quirian to the door and down the stairs. There was no carriage in the yard. Instead the iron-bound gates were standing just a little ajar. The priest ushered me through the narrow gap and strode swiftly down the road, as hooded and anonymous as me. I followed as quickly as I could, still disconcerted by the unfamiliar sensations of trousers.

We didn't have far to go. This was a middling-prosperous neighbourhood of houses with fine gardens not too different from Master Menore's house. Though my father-by-marriage would have never allowed his gate to be left unattended through the night. There was no one keeping a watch here as we passed through.

Brother Quirian hurried along the flagstone path which skirted the building and we arrived at the rear servants' door. A woman answered to the priest's knock. She was dressed in a housekeeper's plain gown.

'This way.' She led us to a basement room filled with racks of clothing and a table strewn with cosmetics. The walls were ablaze with candles.

'We must hurry.' Quirian stripped off his tunic and bare-chested, reached for a mirror and shears.

I stood there, stupefied as he began clipping his curly hair so close that I could see the pale skin of his scalp.

The unknown woman measured me with a practised eye and began sorting through a rack of dresses. 'Here.'

The purple gown she shoved at me was stale and stained around the hems. It was also scandalously low cut in the bodice.

'I can't wear that!' I protested.

'Do you want people remembering your face or more interested in your other charms?' the housekeeper demanded.

'Please, Deyris, just do as we ask.' Quirian turned his back to give me some semblance of privacy.

'You don't have time to waste.' The woman clapped her

hands impatiently. 'I won't answer to Alace for you.'

I don't know if she meant that as a threat but it spurred me into action. I stripped off the tunic and trousers, thankful that at least I still wore my shift beneath them.

The woman shook out the purple dress and held it ready for me to step into. It was even worse than I had imagined as she laced it tight in the back. The grubby frill of lace around the neckline barely covered my nipples.

I blushed as I looked down to tuck the edges of my shift out of sight. 'I must look like a trollop.'

She laughed, not unkindly. 'Not yet, flower, but you will soon enough.'

As I looked around, astonished, I saw her taking a blonde wig out of a calico bag.

'Sit down.' Her firm hand on my shoulder guided me to a stool.

I sat numb as she swept my own hair into a tight knot and fixed the wig securely to it with a substantial handful of pins.

'Turn around and look up.'

Obeying, I saw Quirian, now dressed in muddy topboots, faded scarlet breeches and a soiled, white silk waistcoat over his shirtless chest. I closed my eyes as the woman began painting my face.

'Up you get,' she said a few moments later.

As Quirian took my place on the stool, I caught a glimpse of myself in a looking glass; extravagantly rouged with painted lips and eyes. The wigs ringlets, as falsely gold as brass, were now dressed with dyed poultry feathers, I looked entirely the whore which Teutel's mother had called me, though Mother Menore would never recognise me, any more than I would have known Brother Quirian if I had passed him on the street. The priest now had a false black beard gummed to his jaw and around his mouth. So the fetch wearing my husband's face shouldn't recognise either of us.

Quirian grinned as he stood up. 'Visari works in the song-and-supper halls in the tapestry district.'

'Thank you.' I curtseyed to her, not knowing what else to say. I had no wish to insult her but my father had always forbidden me to mix with the songstresses or their dressers. Any girl who paraded on a stage to entertain men getting drunk led a perilous life, he insisted.

Amused at my hesitation, Visari handed me a thin silk cape with a capacious hood. 'You'll need a cloak.'

'One moment.' Quirian raised a hand as I swirled the flimsy silk around my shoulders.

Before I realised what he was doing, he drew a finger down from my bare shoulder to nestle between my breasts. 'What—?'

I saw that he had traced the coarse line of a scarcely healed scar across my pale skin. I gasped but as I pressed my hand to my chest, I could feel no trace of a blemish.

'It's merely a guise,' he assured me, 'to draw eyes away from your face. Then if the constables do come asking, they'll spend the rest of the year trying to trace any girl so badly cut in a knife fight.'

'Which will explain you carrying a blade tonight.' Visari handed me a scabbarded blade as long as my forearm. 'It goes in here.'

She showed me the slit in the sideseam of the trollop's skirts where a narrow pocket had been especially sewn to accommodate just such a weapon.

'Come on.' Quirian belted a short sword on one hip and dragged on a heavy russet coat with tarnished silver buttons. He looked as disreputable as I did.

'This way.' Visari opened a door to the servants' stairs and led us up to the front hall. This dwelling wasn't as empty as the mansion. Cloaks hung on the pegs by the front door and a tantalising savoury scent lingered in the air.

Quirian opened the front door and I saw a two-wheeled gig waiting by the gate, a boy holding the horse's head. I had to hitch my skirts indecently high to clamber in and was barely seated before Quirian stirred the horse to a trot with a slap of the reins on its rump.

Goddess only knows what any neighbours still awake must have thought, seeing two such ne'er-do-wells leaving the house.

I clung to the side of the gig with one hand and made sure I hadn't lost the blade hidden in my skirts with the other. I shivered and not merely from the inadequate cloak.

'Where are we going?'

'Beyond the southern wharfs, upstream from the bridge.' Quirian glanced at me as the sound of the horse's hooves on the cobbles rang through the night. 'Are you ready to do what you must?'

I wasn't but I dared not admit it. 'I must stab it in the heart.'

He had told me time and again, him and Sanife both. I could only pray once more that the Golden Goddess would guide my strike, straight and true.

'Good.' Quirian focused on the road ahead, stirring the horse to a quicker pace.

We soon reached an area of the city where I had never been. The road was following the river now, running alongside a down-at-heel pleasure garden that reached to the water's edge. Quirian turned the gig into a hard-packed gravel track, leaving the cobbled thoroughfares behind. I began to catch glimpses of the Dore through the trees, silvered by moonlight. The kingdom's second river was far broader than the Tane, its far bank completely lost in shadow.

A barrel organ's raucous song echoed among the trees. I saw lantern light and could soon make out the canvas roof and wicker-hurdle walls of a drinking den. This pleasure park seemed a surprisingly public place for the unsanctioned sale of liquor but perhaps it was far enough away from the established taverns and outraged householders who would normally insist the Justiciar's men enforced the rule of law.

Or perhaps the constables turned a blind eye, preferring to keep all the local rotten apples in one barrel. My father had once told me that was why the particular den that he favoured endured, untroubled, by the tanning yards. I realised my wits were wandering and checked for the blade hidden in my skirts once again.

Quirian reined the horse to a halt. As the gig swayed, Alace stepped out of the darkness beneath the trees and caught hold of the beast's bridle.

'He'll be coming out any moment.' He scowled at Quirian. 'You cut it fine.'

'This way.' Quirian ignored the skinny old man, reaching up to set his hands firmly around my waist and lift me down from the gig. 'Leave that.' Stripping off the flimsy silk cloak, he tossed it back in the gig before cupping my elbow with his hand to usher me over the garbage-filled ruts in the gravel.

'How are we to leave?' I tried to turn to look over my shoulder, glimpsing Alace leading the gig away.

'Never mind that.' The priest was searching the crowd of men and women swirling around the drinking den. With his seedy disguise, he fitted right in and to my embarrassment, so did I.

A good number of couples were dancing to the barrel-organ's jaunty music. Others had claimed the mismatched chairs and tables scattered among the trees. My childhood home had been furnished with such discards, scavenged from the detritus of debtors' house-clearance sales.

Others were slinking away into shadows beyond the reach of candles fixed to the tables with their own molten tallow. Men and women went hand in hand, men with men and women with women, to indulge in illicit delights. Would-be onlookers loitered, waiting for the sounds of rutting to start in the darkness.

'Can you see it?' Quirian demanded.

'He's over there.'

The fetch was wearing my dead husband's best blue silk coat as well as his face. Ale had spilled down the front of the costly garment and stained his fine waistcoat and shirt besides. A splash on Teutel's neatly tailored breeches made it look as though the fetch had pissed itself.

Or perhaps it had. The creature looked as filthily drunk as

233

I had ever seen my father. It was swaying as it sat on a bench, legs widespread to accommodate the slut perched on one knee, his arm circling her waist. Her dress was as indecent as mine and her trailing locks just as counterfeit.

I recalled what Quirian had said about the unnatural creature being ruled by pleasures of the flesh, without conscience or scruple.

The whore leaned close to the fetch's ear and whispered something as her fingers toyed with his shirt laces. The creature threw back its head, laughing uproariously before it plunged its face between her breasts, licking and nuzzling. It waved the hand holding its slopping flagon, trying to find the table top to set the ale down. The cheap earthenware shattered against the wooden edge and ale cascaded over the furniture and the fetch's feet. It didn't care, tossing the useless handle aside. Now that its hand was free, it could grab a handful of the whore's skirt and drag her petticoats up to reveal her pallid thigh. She wasn't wearing any stockings.

Now I understood what the priest had said about the fetch ruining Teutel's good name. There was no way of knowing if anyone here recognised his face but the first time that the creature behaved so atrociously in some decent quarter of the city, such gossip would pass from servant to servant quicker than counterfeit coin was palmed off.

I would cut out this creature's heart sooner than see my beloved's memory so foully soiled.

Quirian's hand on my arm restrained me. I hadn't even realised I'd taken a step.

'We must wait. We have to catch it unawares.'

'When it's spreading that whore's thighs to tup her against a tree?' I looked at him aghast.

His reply was even more appalling. 'Perhaps. I don't imagine she'd bear witness against us. But I'd prefer to corner it on its own.'

Before I could protest, the midnight chimes rang out from some distant shrine. A handbell inside the drinking den echoed their call. Whoever was in charge within had the sense not to provoke the constables beyond the closing time for licensed and tax-paying inns.

The crowd still lounging outside was joined by those being ushered out of the flimsy doorway by hard-faced women with painted smiles. A handful of burly men in leather jerkins followed, spreading out among the tables and chairs.

I realised those with wine, ale or liquor still in hand were being allowed to remain, though clearly encouraged to drain their cups. Those without a drink to show were unceremoniously rousted from their seats. Some went willingly enough. Others protested, to no avail. The drinking den's henchmen wouldn't take no for an answer.

The whore stood up, hands swiftly raised to show her understanding so that the approaching man need not manhandle her. The fetch was inclined to argue but we soon saw it was too drunk to raise more than a wavering fist. Another henchman instantly joined the first and the two of them hauled the fetch to its feet, sending it on its way with a shove.

Quirian and I were mingling with those lingering between the candle light and the cobbled road. Plenty of folk were waiting for old friends or the evening's chance-met companions to finish the drinks they had paid for or to return from the shadows under the trees, lust slaked.

'Follow me.' Brother Quirian squared his shoulders, his falsely-bearded face intent.

The whore was still hanging on the fetch's arm as the creature cursed the drinking den's master and all his hirelings. Its face was ugly with anger, its insults vile. Teutel would never have been so foul-mouthed.

'Come, come, my friend!' Quirian waved a placating hand at the nearest henchman who'd snapped his fingers to summon a colleague with a club. The priest slipped a hand through the unsuspecting fetch's other arm and clamped his elbow to his side, holding the creature close. 'Let's get you home to bed.'

'He's promised to me till morning, sack-arse,' sneered the whore.

I saw her sly hand searching the fetch's waistcoat pockets for whatever purse of Teutel's coin it had stolen. I dragged her away. 'Get lost, you thieving bitch!'

'I know you.'

Before the whore could insult me in like fashion, the fetch's dull eyes fixed on me. Shaking Quirian off, it lunged, hands crooked like claws and reaching for my throat.

The priest hooked an arm around its neck to hold it back. He barely slowed the monster. I scrambled backwards, tearing at my skirts to free the hidden blade.

The whore got caught between us. The fetch smashed a backhanded fist into her face, knocking her clean off her feet. She fell to lie as motionless as a discarded doll. I heard a yell of outrage from one of the drinking den's henchmen.

'Now!' Quirian was still struggling to hold the fetch off me.

I had the blade in my hand. I thrust, as hard and fast as I could. I missed its chest completely, driving the steel through its forearm instead. As I ripped the blade free, blood gushed and the fetch roared with pain, more like a beast than a man.

'Behind you!' I screamed.

One of the henchmen was swinging his club at Quirian's head. The priest barely managed to escape a blow which would have knocked him senseless, if not killed him outright.

The fetch seized its chance to shake Quirian off. It ran. I tried to step into its path, bloodily glistening blade ready to try again. It dodged around me with startling speed. As I turned, I saw it vanishing into the crowd of people fleeing this sudden eruption of violence.

'Where is it?' I yelled, furious with myself.

'Run!' Quirian caught hold of my arm and we both took to our heels to escape the henchmen's wrath. We didn't slow till we reached the edge of the cobbled road.

'Where has it gone?' I choked on frustration as I saw the

crowd ahead scattering in all directions.

'Look properly.' Quirian stood stock-still, his eyes unblinking.

I realised what he meant in an instant but it took a long moment more before I could regain my composure and peer into the unseen realm.

The horde of trollops, drunkards and whoremongers were nowhere to be seen. Now I could search the road running alongside the river and the entrances to the lanes threading through the houses on the far side.

Not all the corner buildings had lanterns hung outside but enough complied with the law for me to see the running figure wearing Teutel's best blue coat. 'There!'

'I see.' Quirian gestured and I yelped.

A gryphon reared up to block the fetch's path, its eagle wings flapping wide and taloned forefeet clawing the air. As the fetch scrambled backwards, the impossible beast crouched low, lion's tail thrashing as its haunches quivered, ready to spring.

Quirian raised a hand and the gryphon screeched with frustration, cruel beak agape. But the fetch didn't realise it was being held back; any more than it realised no one else could see the murderous mythical beast. It simply ran headlong in the opposite direction, desperate to escape.

'Make sure you see where it goes.' Quirian's attention was still all on the gryphon. 'We have to get this done before any constables arrive.'

I blinked for a brief moment and saw men and women hurrying down the lane, never suspecting the gryphon's intangible presence. Then I blinked again and watched the fetch return to the cobbled road and cross over towards the pleasure garden. 'It's heading into the trees.'

'We mustn't lose it.' The priest grunted with effort. I saw the gryphon was still fighting to escape his control.

'I'll follow it.' I surveyed the reality all around me; most of the drinkers had now fled but enough were left that I must be careful not to barge into them. With the next step, I searched the intangible emptiness for the fetch.

It had reached the trees already, heading into the darkness, but it was still reeling so drunkenly that I was sure I could outpace it. I followed a gravelled track which should cut across its path. Now that I had left the night's crowd behind, I risked running. Hitching my drab's gown high above my knees, I snatched glimpses of the tangible realm in case anything unexpected lurched into my path. I still had the blood-smeared blade in my hand.

I halted at a skewed junction where three of the gravelled tracks met deep in the trees. I could see the sliding silver of the river so turned my back to face the city. This must be the way the fetch was coming. I strained my ears, trying to make out any sounds from the unseen realm.

I couldn't hear the gryphon's screeching. Did that mean that Brother Quirian had banished it or did I need to see intangible creatures for my other senses to register them? I'd never thought to ask Sanife such a question.

Then I heard staggering footsteps on gravel. I moved to get the clearest possible view of the path coming towards me. Was this some innocent mortal, guilty of nothing more than pursuing cheap liquor's oblivion? I blinked to be quite certain that the shadow stumbling towards me manifested in both the seen and unseen realms.

It did. It was the fetch. It saw me and stopped dead.

'You,' it breathed, hoarse with hatred. 'I know your voice.'

I said nothing, waiting, bloodied steel ready. I had already wounded it once. I wouldn't fail a second time.

It surged towards me with a roar, fists flailing. I held my blade tight with both hands, my gaze fixed on the point to the right of Teutel's best silver buttons and on the line from the point of his shoulder where Quirian had told me a man's heart was found.

The fetch barged into me, knocking me to the ground. I fell hard with all the creature's weight pressing painfully down on me. Its breath was foul with rancid ale and old food. It was trying to batter me around the head but Teutel had been taller than I was by quite some measure. With my face pressed into its shoulder, it couldn't strike any effective blows.

I held on tight to the knife's hilt. I could feel warmth seeping between my fingers. The fetch's attempts to hit me grew more and more feeble. The steel I had thrust between its ribs was doing its work. I had driven the knife home with all the hatred I felt for this creature. With all the grief that beset me, for all that I had lost; my loving husband's embrace and all hope of children born from our devotion.

I had done what they had demanded; Quirian, Sanife and Alace. Now Teutel's sisters were safe along with my lost beloved's shrew of a mother. Though they would never know the debt they owed me, as they mourned him a second time.

But how long would the monster take to die? Crushed beneath it, I was gasping for breath. As the fetch gurgled wetly in my ear, I was on the verge of falling senseless.

'Deyris!' Qurian arrived and hauled the creature off me. 'Are you all right?'

'I think so.' I sat up and shivered as the night's chill struck through my blood-soaked bodice, the cold cutting through to my skin.

'We must make this look like a robbery, when they find the body.' In his vagabond's disguise, Quirian ransacked Teutel's pockets and tore my dead husband's rings from the fetch's fingers. 'Get up. We must get away, and quickly.'

I blinked and in an instant, the fetch vanished.

'Where is it?' I screamed.

'Deyris, look at me, look back to the tangible realm.' Quirian reached for my hand and gripped my fingers so hard they hurt. 'You have killed it, truly. The magic which spawned it is broken. All that's left is the outer husk.'

It took me a moment to make sense of what he was saying. Then I realised. Now that I had killed it, the fetch would have no presence in the intangible realm. That's what I had seen disappear.

I blinked again and saw Quirian leaning over the corpse

239

which was all that remained of the monster. The corpse which would convince everyone that Teutel was truly dead, so no such revenant could ever return.

I still couldn't catch my breath. Pulling my hand free of Quirian and drawing my feet up beneath me, I tried to stand but my head was spinning. I was shaking from head to toe though I didn't feel cold any more. I was feverishly hot, sweat beading my brow and soaking through my shift.

'Deyris?' Quirian's concern echoed strangely in my ears, as though he was on the far side of the great entrance hall in the deserted mansion.

I slumped on the blood-stained gravel. What had Sanife said about the cost of destroying a phantasm? Especially a phantasm that I'd had a hand in making. The closer such a thing was to human, the worse the consequences would be. Hadn't she said that too?

'Deyris!'

I could feel Qurian's arms cradling me and hear the anguish in his voice. I couldn't answer him. I couldn't even raise a hand as numbness spread from my fingers and toes to leave all my limbs useless.

Was Mistress Menore being struck down with the same mysterious malady? That would be some petty satisfaction.

Was killing the fetch to be the death of me though? I could find no answers as my senses faded and the darkness claimed me.

Chapter Eight

'Deyris?' The soft voice repeated my name, hesitant. 'Deyris, are you awake?'

Teutel? Back from his trip to Usenas so soon? I struggled to throw off my drowsiness. Why was I so weary? Even with my eyes closed, I could sense the sunlight flooding the room. What would my beloved think; to find me idling so late in bed? I should be up and ready to welcome him home.

I opened my eyes and saw Master Menore. 'Oh, my dear girl.'

He stretched out a shaking hand before snatching it back. Fresh tears trickled from his reddened eyes to be lost in his grizzled beard.

Teutel's voice had always been an echo of his sire's, I remembered, suddenly heartsick for no reason that I could explain. And why was Master Menore at my bedside?

My mouth was as stale and sticky as if I'd just woken from a five day fever. Was that why I felt so feeble? I couldn't even lift my head. Though I could see enough to know I wasn't at home. This narrow, whitewashed room had a single barred window and a small table beside the bed where I lay, helpless. The only other furniture was Master Menore's chair.

I cleared my throat. 'What—? Where—?'

'You are in the infirmary.' A hooded priest moved to stand behind the weeping man. He laid a comforting hand on the merchant's shoulder. 'Alas, your father by marriage has grievous news.'

'Teutel—' he choked on his anguish. 'My dear girl, Teutel is dead. There's no hope of a mistake this time. He was robbed and murdered. His body—'

He couldn't go on, burying his face in his hands. Racking sobs shook him from head to toe.

'He's in Usenas,' I said, bemused. 'He's coming home any day now.'

Baffled as well as distressed, Master Menore turned to look up at the priest. 'She doesn't remember?'

'She has been grievously ill.' The Horned God's acolyte shook his head, sorrowful. 'A subtle and insidious infection, so hard to detect before the crisis strikes. If only she had been brought to the Crescent Moon Gate when her behaviour became so erratic.'

'Then she was never truly at fault?' Hope lifted Master Menore's hoarse voice.

'She is more to be pitied than condemned.' The priest patted his shoulder, reassuring. 'Just as your wife must be forgiven her vicious suspicions. Just as you must forget the sordid excesses of Teutel's last days. They were none of them in their right mind.'

I closed my eyes as they talked about me as though I wasn't even there. My memories were returning, albeit piecemeal and confused. I was certain of one thing though. Teutel was dead. He was dead in Usenas, robbed and murdered just as his father had said.

But that wasn't what Master Menore had meant. Somehow I was sure of that. As I groped for recollection through my exhaustion, everything became clear with shocking abruptness.

Eldritch magic which I had never suspected had created a vile creature in the guise of my dead husband. Learning the secrets of that magic, I had been the one who must kill it. I had been forced to stab the unnatural thing in order to save myself, and to save the lives of all those whose grief had unwittingly spawned the monster.

I had done so and that meant that everyone must now accept that Teutel was dead, beyond any doubt or dispute. Now I could finally grieve for my husband. Tears slipped through my eyelashes.

'Brother Quirian?' A new voice spoke, respectful yet firm. 'You said this would be a short visit.'

'Of course.' Now the priest, gentle yet inexorable, addressed Master Menore. 'Let me escort you home, to offer what consolations I may to your family, and to assess your wife's condition.'

'You can throw that physician tending her out on his pompous arse.' Wrath momentarily burned through the merchant's misery. 'Charlatan pocketing my gold.'

I felt a faint pang of sympathy for Master Fyrid. He might be a pretentious dabbler in medical matters but the prissy little man didn't deserve to be tangled up in whatever yarn the priest was spinning to explain away recent events.

Though I could understand Brother Quirian's reasons and even agree with the necessity of such a tale. To cleanse Teutel's reputation of the fetch's sins. To brush aside his mother's hysterical accusations, calling me a whore and worse. To explain away my attacks on the monster wearing my husband's face. Best for everyone if that whole slate was wiped clean.

Above all else, the priest's lies would make sure there was no need to admit to the hidden magic which had provoked these upheavals. No one would doubt Brother Quirian's pronouncements, spoken through his silvered mask and all the dark authority of the Horned God himself.

I lay motionless, my eyes still closed, as the two men left the small room. Then I felt the weight of the woman who'd spoken taking a seat at the foot of my bed. I rolled my head on the pillow and looked at her. 'Sanife.'

She was plainly dressed in a grey dress, with a neat headscarf concealing her hair, like any other woman housed within the Moon God's walls.

'I said I'd see you soon.' She smiled wryly. 'Though it's been two full days since you killed the fetch.'

'You never said I would suffer like this.' I tried to sit but could barely shuffle a little higher up the pillows.

'I said you would need all your strength.' Though she was sympathetic, she showed no remorse. 'I warned you about the backlash that comes from destroying a creature your magic has made.'

So she had. As my wits were clearing, I recalled our conversations. But while I had heard what she'd said, I assuredly hadn't understood and that must have been clear to them all;

243

Sanife, Quirian and Alace. They'd made no effort to make sure that I knew what I was facing. That was a lesson I would take to heart.

She was still speaking. 'The funeral is tomorrow, or the next day, as soon as Mistress Menore can leave her bed. Even if you feel well enough though, I really would advise against attending—'

'I've no interest in seeing that monster buried.' I waved that repellent notion away and managed to sit up straighter in the warm and comfortable bed. 'How soon can I go home?'

Sanife shook her head. 'Don't you remember? The Justiciar's constable committed you to the Horned God's care for your own protection.'

I shivered as I remembered that dreadful night, standing all alone before the implacable official, accused of attempting a murder. 'But that was before—'

'Where would you go?' she demanded.

'Home.' I looked at Sanife, confused.

'To the home you shared with Teutel?' She shook her head again. 'Your mother by marriage has already paid an advocate to petition the Royal Justiciary, to deny you any rights in Menore family property. She secured the fetch's signature on a petition to dissolve your marriage, or forged it herself, most likely.' Sanife shrugged as though such a trivial detail was of no particular consequence.

'But that was before.' I clenched my fists. 'Now Quirian is spreading this tale of some infection curdling all our wits—'

'Do you have any money to hire an advocate to argue your cause?' Sanife challenged. 'Do you honestly believe that your mother by marriage will abandon her plea once she's recovered from her own collapse? Now that her son is dead, she need not hide her true contempt for you for his sake. She hated you long before this, and now she has four daughters to dower and marry to best advantage, to secure the family name and trade. She will want that house of yours and all Teutel's money for his sisters.'

'I—' Tears of misery stung my eyes. Sanife was right. Mistress Menore would be my enemy till the day she died.

Rallying, I shook my head, defiant. 'Master Menore won't see me disinherited. Astrila is my friend and so is Lessane.'

'Perhaps.' Sanife looked sceptical. 'Is that the life you would choose? Given a garret room out of charity in a household where you're detested by half of the family? You'll be at their beck and call, expected to be endlessly grateful for your daily bread and whatever other favours they care to grant you. You won't even have a servant's wages, or be able to walk away from the humiliations which Vari and Tracha are sure to devise.'

'I will live on my own, in my own house!' I insisted.

'If you can find an advocate to persuade the Justiciary to grant it to you.' Sanife angled her head. 'What happens after that? How will you earn the coin to feed yourself? What will you say to your neighbours as they watch you come and go and whisper behind their hands? Do you suppose any respectable man will ever dream of courting you? Brother Quirian can draw a veil over the truth of these past days but you know how gossip lingers and spreads. There'll always be someone to recall that you once stabbed your husband, and he was found dead a few days later. They'll say there's no smoke without fire.'

'It's not as though that's your only problem.' Her voice hardened. 'What will you do in the dark and silent watches of the night, when you hear something scrabbling at your door? Something too big and too full of purpose to be a mouse on the stairs. Because now you know that monsters can truly step out of the shadows.

'Oh, you can lock your doors and bar your shutters.' She waved a dismissive hand. 'But you must still to keep a tight rein on your imaginings. Otherwise you may even find that you've created the very monster you feared. It'll be right there beside you, summoned inside your locked room.'

'No.' I shook my head in furious denial. Weak though my body might be, my mind was now crystal clear. 'How do you know about Vari and Tracha?' I demanded. I hadn't told her about them.

'I'm sorry?' Whatever response Sanife had hoped for, this wasn't it.

'Why do you assume my husband's sisters would be so unkind? How do you even know their names? Why are you trying to frighten me with the prospect of living alone, when I barely have the strength to get out of this bed?'

Though I silently vowed to myself that I would try to walk to the window and back as soon as I was left on my own. That should give me some idea of how long it would take to regain my strength. As to what I would do then—

'I told him you were no fool.' As Sanife laughed, it was my turn to be startled.

'Who? Qurian?' I guessed he must have been telling her about Mother Menore's spite towards me.

Sanife shook her head. 'Alace.'

I shrank back into the warm comfort of pillows and blankets. 'He told you to terrify me?'

Sanife folded her hands in her lap. 'No. He simply says that you must accept you can never go back to the life you knew. For so many reasons, not merely because Teutel is dead. Once you've accepted that's impossible then you will see the sense of joining us.'

I stared at her, astounded. 'Join you? I don't even know who you are, beyond a mismatched handful of deceivers.'

'That's harsh.' Sanife seemed genuinely wounded. 'But you deserve to know more, now that this crisis is past.'

She waved a hand towards the window. 'Garrisons and cavalry defend us all, from humblest to highest, against raiders who might ride in from the northern plateau or the southern forests, from boat-borne threats in the unknown lands upstream or down.

'We are the hidden guardians of this kingdom. We keep those who only see the tangible world safe from monsters from the unseen realm. We discover how and why phantasms and simulacra arise. We watch them and we destroy

them when that proves necessary. Above all else, we find
ways to stop such terrors manifesting again.'

'By killing innocents?' I interjected. 'Alace was ready to do
kill Mistress Menore, Teutel's sisters, that entire household!'

'Only as the very last resort. Only if there had been no
other way to rid this city of a monster which could destroy
countless lives. But what of it? We didn't come to that. You
succeeded in killing the fetch.'

She looked steadily at me. 'I swear to you, we do a great
deal of good to balance such rare, grim necessity. We help
constables and justiciars to keep the peace, and to track down
the guilty, in the towns up and down the kingdom's rivers.
When outlying villages are menaced, we conjure creatures
of our own to protect the weak and helpless until the Paramount King's cavalry can come to their defence. We serve
the Paramount King himself with stratagems which would
astonish you.'

Sanife grinned and the glint in her eye invited me to ask
her to continue, to draw me deeper into her world.

I folded my arms, hugging the blankets to me. 'How many
of you are there?'

Sanife shook her head, apologetic. 'I cannot share such
secrets until you are sworn to our service.'

I drew my knees up, to get my feet away from her. 'You're
so sure that I'll agree, because you tell me I have nowhere
else to go. Why is that so? When it would only take a word
from the Horned God's temple, or from the Golden Mother's high priestess, and the Justiciary would throw out Mistress Menore's plea, condemning the malice behind it.'

While she'd been speaking, I'd been searching my rec-
ollections of all that Brother Quirian had said, when he had
first explained the mysteries confounding me.

'He said magic talent is rare. Strong magic talent is
rarer still and even then, not all those who possess it can be
trained. That's why you're interested in Teutel's sisters, you
and Alace and whoever lurks behind him. Quirian spoke of
searching family trees for ten generations in hopes of finding

unsuspected abilities.'

I looked at her, defiant. 'You need me more than I need you. I've lived without money and family before. I grew up going to school not knowing if the rent had been paid or if I would come home to find all our belongings thrown into the street. I will scrub floors again if I must, to keep myself from the gutter.'

'I said you were no fool.' Though Sanife wasn't laughing now. 'So you cannot imagine that we'll let you loose, knowing what you know, and knowing what you can do.'

'No,' I agreed, fighting to keep my voice level, 'and I have no wish to be locked up here for the rest of my life thanks to yet more lies laid before the Justiciary. So yes, I would be willing to use this magic I seem to be cursed with, to serve the kingdom. Provided Alace meets my conditions.'

Sanife pursed her lips. 'You want your house and your savings secured.'

She didn't sound surprised or even doubtful that this could be done. So I was right. Whoever these people were, they could compel the Justiciary to do their bidding.

'To begin with.' I nodded. 'Then I want to go to Usenas, with you or Brother Quirian or whoever else has some magical means to uncover the truth of what happened to Teutel. Don't tell me it can't be done because I won't believe you. I don't demand that you succeed, but I will see you swear before the Golden Mother that every effort has been made. Then I will join your—' I had no idea what the right word might be, for a gathering of people with these unearthly talents.

'Cabal. A group of magicians who work together is called a cabal.' Sanife sat still for a long moment, studying my face.

I set my jaw, summoning all my resolve to match her, stare for stare.

She was the first to look away. 'I don't know if Alace will agree.'

'Then ask whoever instructs Alace.' I wasn't going to be dissuaded.

Sanife looked back at me with cold amusement. 'No one instructs Alace, not in questions of magic. In matters concerning the kingdom, he answers only to the Paramount King and advises him daily.'

I tried to hide my shock. That shabby little man had the Paramount King's ear? All I could do was shrug, trying to make believe that was no concern of mine.

Sanife looked at me for a while longer, then got up and left the room without another word.

I shrank back beneath the covers, exhausted. Overwhelmed by sudden grief for Teutel, I cried myself to sleep.

It was eight days before I was strong enough to leave the asylum's infirmary. But I left wearing my own clothes, and not the bloodstained blue gown I had arrived in. Sanife had brought a pink dress from my home as I'd requested. It wasn't one which I particularly favoured, so with the journey we had ahead of us, I wouldn't grieve if it got travel-worn.

Brother Quirian entered my little whitewashed room as I was buckling my shoes. I hastily smoothed my skirts and reached for my shawl. My travel bag was ready by the foot of the bed, with all the personal necessities I'd asked Sanife to fetch for me.

The priest had a sheaf of papers in one hand and a slender black pen box in the other. He set them all down on the table. 'You need to sign these for the Justiciar for Property before we leave the city.'

'Thank you.' I waited for him to unsnap the stiff catch on the pen box and unscrew the silver-topped ink bottle slotted securely into one end. As he went to look out of the window, I sat on the chair and studied the official documents.

'We are pressed for time,' Quirian said testily some moments later.

'I won't sign anything without reading it first.' Truth be told, I wasn't going to dip the pen nib into ink until I could be sure that my nervous hand wouldn't shake black blots all over the paper and my skirt besides.

I still couldn't quite believe this had happened. That I was confirmed in all my widow's rights to my home and to the money which Teutel and I had so diligently entrusted to the Sun Goddess's shrine.

But these carefully scribed clauses made it clear that was so. Now I must decide if I was ready to sign my name to this document. It might just as well have been an apprentice's binding indenture; committing me to serve Alace and his cabal. For how long? At least an apprentice was only bound for five years.

Or would I rather scrub floors by day and spend my nights, hungry and fearful, in some squalid boarding house down by the tanneries of the Spearhead district? What would I do then, if I found myself facing monsters, without allies and untaught in this magic?

I didn't look at Quirian as I took a pen from the box. 'This is only my first condition. I won't promise my allegiance to Alace until we return from Usenas.'

'Then the sooner we go, the sooner you will be satisfied,' the priest snapped.

I signed my name on all three copies of the documents with smooth, swift strokes. For some reason, his irritation at not having the whip hand heartened me.

'All done.' I used the neat little blotter tucked into the other end of the pen box to dry the glistening ink.

'Thank you.' Quirian left one copy on the table for me and picked up the others along with his pen box. 'I must see these are sent to the Justiciary. I'll meet you and Sanife in the yard.'

He left without another word, leaving me to pick up my bag and carry it down the flights of stairs myself. This was how I discovered the infirmary was on the middle floor of the asylum's central building, above the sparse chambers for the priests and below the vast empty room where Quirian had first instructed me in the unseen world's mysteries.

Sanife was indeed waiting in the yard, beside a smartly liveried carriage drawn by well-bred chestnut horses. She wore a violet silk gown and a dark velvet cloak that must have cost more than all the silver in the purse safely stowed inside my bodice. The coin which the women constables had taken from me in the House of Restraint had been returned to me late last night by a young man I didn't recognise, who didn't say a word. Another of Alace's cabal?

'There you are.' Sanife smiled warmly and snapped her fingers. The coachman jumped down from the carriage to take my bag and stow it safely up on the roof, alongside Sanife's many valises.

I looked at her coldly. 'I am only masquerading as your maid.'

Still smiling, she nodded. 'Let's see how well you can do that. If you choose to join our cabal, you'll need to play any number of roles.'

She turned her attention to the coachman who was now holding the door open so we could get into the carriage. As I followed, I noted that at least Sanife still considered my joining the cabal was open to debate.

Would she support me if I refused? Or would Alace throw those documents I had just signed into a fire, to leave me destitute once again? Would that be my punishment?

Quirian arrived a few moments later, in his priestly robes and mask. The coachman whipped up his horses and we travelled swiftly to the wharves on the Dore where passenger barges waited on either side of the great bridge bearing the Paramount King's highway southwards. Half as wide again as the boat Captain Stryet commanded, these boats carried no cargo but were fitted out with comfortable cabins and boasted tall masts with broad sails to sweep the wealthy between Hurat and the kingdom's vassal towns, upstream and down.

Our journey to Usenas was uneventful, and Sanife was an undemanding mistress, though her ease at being waited upon convinced me she had been raised with servants at her beck and call.

More than once, I was tempted to ask about her life before she had been drawn into Alace's circle. How had she first encountered the unseen realm?

Every time I reminded myself that I wasn't yet committed to their cabal. Such questions could wait till I had made that choice. Besides, Sanife never volunteered anything about her past.

She never sought to teach me anything further about this magic I was now burdened with. I couldn't decide if that was a relief or not. Meanwhile, all I could do was keep the tightest possible rein on my imagination. I didn't even try to see into the intangible world, in case some terrifying river monster appeared.

Brother Quirian kept himself to himself. He had quarters at the front of the long, wide, barge while Sanife and I shared a stern cabin. Allotted different tables in the dining salon amidships, we barely exchanged nods as we came and went from our meals.

I had plenty of leisure, with little more to do that to sit beside Sanife on a comfortable chair on deck and watch the kingdom pass us by. It was an education. I knew Sharow and Masecal to be the principle vassal towns between Hurat and Usenas but I had never imagined that so many hamlets would be strung along the riversides like beads on a thread. They nestled in curves in the banks where the waters slowed to swirl through reed beds or sheltered behind stark outcrops of rock churning the Dore's flow to foam-crested eddies.

Small boats came and went at dawn and dusk, bringing fresh food to the sail barge's galley. I didn't see a wharf large enough to take our vessel though, not until we reached Sharow itself. The vassal town's moorings were thronged with cargo boats of all sizes.

As we halted at noon for the overnight stop, to allow passengers to depart and to board, I watched the Sharow Castellan's liveried officials at work. They were collecting the Paramount King's tariffs from local merchants and ensuring the quality of the goods to be traded. Masecal wasn't much different, though the liveries were russet and grey, not ochre and blue.

We arrived in Usenas early on a fine, clear morning. After I'd delivered the spiced apple tea which Sanife liked to drink before rising, I went up on deck to watch the barge crew guide their vessel towards its designated berth.

Busy officials wore grass green trimmed with pale yellow. I wondered if any of those men and women on the waterfront had helped pull my husband's murdered corpse from these rubbish-strewn waters.

'We must visit the Castellan first.' Brother Quirian's words were muffled by his mask.

His voice made me jump regardless. I hadn't heard him approach across the barge's planking. I turned to see Sanife was at his side. She was elegantly dressed and bejewelled, with her hair and cosmetics as pristine, as if I had laboured over her appearance since dawn.

'I should see to your luggage, Madam,' I said hastily.

'That's all in hand.'

As Sanife smiled, I saw crewmen emerging from the deck hatch, laden with her valises and my own modest bag.

'I'll hire a carriage.' Quirian stalked down the gangway as soon as it thudded onto the wharf.

His priestly robes and gleaming mask commanded instant attention from the closest functionary. A snap of the liveried man's fingers sent a skinny youth running to summon a single-horse gig.

I looked at it doubtfully. 'Will there be room?'

'Our luggage will be taken to the castle separately. That's where we'll be quartered.' Sanife lowered her voice as she followed me close, going down the gangplank. 'From now on, as far as anyone here is concerned, I am a close friend of Master Menore's late sister, and consider myself as good as Teutel's aunt. You must keep quiet, watch and listen. Hopefully all will be revealed.'

I nodded. I didn't need anyone here to know I was his widow. I had no interest in their sympathies, however well meant. I simply wanted to know what had happened.

I was coming to terms with my loss. Not that my grief had lessened but it was no longer so raw. It seemed I had wept all my tears in the Moon God's infirmary. These past ten days with little to do beyond sit and watch the kingdom pass by had given me time to remember better days with Teutel. The horror of the fetch's presence in my life was fading, like the memory of a nightmare.

It was a tight squeeze for the three of us on the gig's seat, with the driver on his perch in front. Fortunately it wasn't far to the brick-built castle standing four-square with its pinnacled towers overlooking both the river and the highroad. The gig was allowed to cross the outer moat's drawbridge, passing beneath the gatehouse's toothed portcullis. That was as far as we rode. We had to get down and walk across the inner moat's footbridge to the Castellan's keep; a second hollow square of fortifications.

A liveried servant was waiting at the central entrance to greet us with a low bow. 'If you will follow me, please.'

Quirian led the way, black cloak billowing and silvered mask impassive beneath the shadows of his hood. I don't believe anyone criss-crossing the cobbled innermost courtyard spared Sanife or me a glance, as they wondered what dark secrets the Horned God's priest had arrived to share or to seek out.

The Castellan had his apartments in the northern corner tower. The ground floor waiting room was full of men and women. Quirian ignored them all, walking straight to the man guarding the stair. At the gatekeeper's nod, the guard stepped aside and three of us climbed the stone spiral to the audience chamber.

'Good day to you.' The Castellan rose from his chair behind a wide table covered with tidy stacks of ledgers and documents. Countless leather-bound books filled the shelves that lined the walls between the windows overlooking the water.

He was a broad-shouldered man with dark hair barely silvered at the temples. With his rein-calloused hands and weathered face, he looked as skilled at leading this garrison's cavalry as he evidently was at managing the town's administration.

'Good day.' The priest inclined his hooded head. 'You received my letter?'

'Indeed.' The Castellan reached for a sheaf of papers without hesitation. 'I believe I have the answers you need.'

'Let's hope so,' Quirian stretched out his hand and took the documents.

'Don't hesitate to send word, if you need anything further,' the Castellan said earnestly. His brow clouded. 'It is a wretched business. My men have done their best to shake answers from the local ne'er-do-wells but we still don't know who the dead man might be, or why he was mis-identified as Master Menore. Until we do, we can't find his accomplices.'

I couldn't help myself. 'Who—'

'Quite so.' Brother Quirian's forceful voice drowned out my half-formed question. 'I will make my own enquiries. Meantime, please see to it that our quarters are prepared. We will return later.'

Sanife was gripping my arm painfully tight, just above my elbow. I was so taken aback that she was able to wheel me around on the spot and march me back to the spiral stair. Her glare of rebuke was eloquent.

Qurian followed, his cloak blocking out the light from above as we descended to the ground floor again.

I shook off Sanife's hand before we passed the stair guard. Everyone in the room below was wide-eyed with curiosity. I saw no reason to give them something else to wonder about.

Quirian strode past us and the waiting men and women hastily parted to let him through. Sanife and I hurried in his wake. I braced myself for the two magicians' displeasure as we emerged into the cobbled courtyard.

Instead, Quirian turned aside to stand in a quiet corner and quickly read through the Castellan's papers. 'He's done well,' he noted, approving. 'He tells us where the body was discovered and where it most likely went into the water.'

'Where is he buried?' Sanife demanded. 'That's where we must go first.'

'Quite so.' The priest rolled the papers right together and walked towards the gate.

Sanife and I followed. I didn't need her warning glance to keep me silent. My throat was so tight with emotion that I couldn't have said a word. I hadn't imagined I would see Teutel's grave.

The gig was still waiting in the outer courtyard. As we climbed into the back seat, Quirian tapped the driver on the shoulder. 'The Woolgate.'

This turned out to be where the road to the hill country left the town, though the land hereabouts on this north bank of the Dore spread out flat in all directions, as far as the eye could see. The Woolgate itself overlooked a canal which I now realised ringed the whole of Usenas, backed by earth and brick ramparts. This was so very different to home.

Or perhaps not. Hurat's dead are buried in the cemeteries on the northward bank of the Tane, outside the city proper. Those who can afford it anyway. My father's shrouded corpse was tipped, uncoffined, into a pauper's charnel pit with the rest of that day's destitute and abandoned dead. Fresh tears prompted by that old memory surprised me as the gig brought us to the burial ground gate.

At least Teutel had been spared that dishonourable fate. Quirian consulted the Castellan's papers again and led us confidently through the gravestones to regularly spaced plots of turned earth. Unlike Hurat's crowded cemeteries with their grey cinder paths, this was a green and peaceful place, with flourishing trees here and there and fragrant herbs planted amid the grass covering the older graves. Birdsong sweetened the breeze.

A plain wooden marker bore my husband's name and the date of his death but I saw that the carved words had been scored through with a hot iron.

'He's dead and buried in Hurat, as far as everyone but us is concerned.' Sanife spoke before I could ask. 'That's how it must be, to put the fetch to rest.'

'So he must lie here, nameless and forgotten?' But though I longed to be angry, I knew that she was right. Besides, I knew the truth and now I had stood at this graveside to re-member my love. That would suffice.

I slid Teutel's wedding bracelet off my wrist and over my hand. His real bracelet. The one which Captain Stryet had returned to me, not the magic-wrought fake which the fetch had worn. I realised I had no idea what had happened to that eerie counterfeit.

I looked up to ask Qurian but his question forestalled me. 'What are you going to do with that?'

'Bury it with him.' I unsnapped my matching bracelet as well. 'Along with my own.'

'Before you do that—' Sanife reached out to cup her hands around mine, enclosing the engraved silver circles. 'Hold them as tight as you can. Think of Teutel. Think of him here in Usenas. Reflect on all that you have lost here.'

I looked at her, confused and scared. 'But the fetch—'

'The fetch is destroyed,' Quirian said with absolute cer-tainty. 'You know that. I know that. Sanife was there to see it buried.'

'You won't bring it back,' she assured me. 'But you may be able to glimpse something of Teutel's last moments if you look into the unseen realm with such thoughts filling your mind.'

Quirian nodded. 'Intangible time flows differently. Echoes of death and violence linger, like driftwood trapped in the roiling water at the bottom of a weir.'

'Sometimes.' Sanife shot him a quelling glance before looking intently at me. 'We may see nothing at all. But you asked us to try to discover what really happened. This is the best way to begin.'

'Very well.' I held on so tight that the marriage bracelets dug into my hands. I welcomed the pain if it would show me Teutel's killer. It was slight enough, compared to the agony of losing him.

Taking a resolute breath, I focused on the unseen world. That took a great deal more effort than I expected. Was it because I had shunned all magic since the fetch's death? Before I could ask Sanife or Quirian, I glimpsed some phantasm flitting between the graves. Relieved, I nevertheless turned my back on it, not wanting to give it any more substance.

I gasped as the sky darkened above us. Shadows coalesced all around to hint at buildings. I stiffened as I saw Teutel walking through this unnatural dusk. He seemed to be coming towards me. Then an indistinct figure appeared, following close behind him.

Before I could shout a warning, Sanife's grip tightened so cruelly that I thought she would break my fingers against the silver. But I understood. She was warning me not to speak. I swallowed hard and turned my attention to the shadowy killer.

He was a thin-faced man with dark, unkempt hair and a sparse beard. His sleeveless leather jerkin hung open over a pale shirt with torn cuffs. Shod in soft leather, he wore no stockings, his breeches flapping unlaced at the knee.

He carried a knife. He drew his arm back, half-turning his upper body. I bit my lip and tried to concentrate. The murderer's empty hand reached out to seize Teutel's shoulder, ready to throw all his strength into the fatal thrust which had pierced my husband's heart. Simply so this vagabond could empty a traveller's purse of safely anonymous coin, leaving more readily identifiable valuables behind.

No. I couldn't bear to see my love die. I screwed my eyes tight shut. When I opened them again, the sun was shining brightly and carefree birds sang in the trees.

'Good.'

Quirian's praise surprised me. I'd expected cold rebuke for my cowardice. I was even more surprised to see him sketching with a stick of charcoal on the back of the Castellan's papers. Within a few moments, I saw a likeness of Teutel's killer which my father would have been proud to draw.

'Well done.' Sanife stroked my hands.

Her touch reawakened my senses. I winced as searing cramp knotted my forearms and I had to make a conscious effort to uncrook my fingers. I flexed my hands, one after the other. 'What now?'

Quirian carefully laid another sheet of paper over his sketch to save it from smudging and rolled them loosely together. 'Now I go and ask who recognises this man.'

'Won't people want to know why?' I contemplated the defaced grave marker. 'How can he be held to account if everyone must believe Teutel died in Hurat?'

Quirian turned his silver mask towards me, the merest glint of sunlight catching his eyes behind the hollow dark gaze. 'Those of us sworn to the Moon God need never explain who we seek or why.'

His cold tone made me shiver, though he didn't seem to notice as he nodded to Sanife. 'I will see you both later.'

I watched him walk purposefully away. What was I supposed to do now?

'You wanted to bury your bracelets?' Sanife prompted.

I looked down at the mounded earth. 'Yes, I do.'

Slipping the hinged circle of my open bracelet through the unbroken ring of Teutel's, I secured the catch. Now they were linked as surely as the two of us had been in love and life.

I dropped to my knees, heedless of my pink dress. This late in the spring, there hadn't been very much rain so the soil was still easy to dig with my fingers. I scooped out a hole as deep as my hand and laid the interlaced bracelets gently down. After an endless moment, I brushed the dark earth across to cover the gleaming silver. I took a moment more to contemplate what I had lost.

Teutel was dead. All that he had been; son, lover, husband, was gone. All that he might have been; father, grandsire, trader and city worthy, would never be. His body would decay in this grave. The spark of divine light that had given him life, had been snuffed out. All that had made up his character was scattered like motes of dust in a sunbeam, drifting away to be lost in the void between the dark of the moon and the sunrise.

'Let me show you Usenas.'

Sanife's voice startled me. I had forgotten she was there. As I looked up, I wondered how long I had knelt there.

She offered me her hand. 'If you choose to join our cabal, you might travel the length and breadth of the kingdom. Shall I show you what you may need to know?'

I let her help me to my feet. 'You may as well.'

I didn't know what I was going to do. Questions of cabals or magic seemed utterly meaningless. What had mattered most in my life was Teutel and now he was dead. Whatever came next was scarcely signified.

So that was how we spent the rest of that day. Sanife clearly knew Usenas well and she showed me where to find food and lodging, fresh clothes and such necessities as a cobbler and an apothecary without paying the premium prices travellers were charged. At the time I didn't think I was paying much attention but afterwards I discovered I'd registered more than I had realised.

As dusk approached, we made our way back to the castle, laden with Sanife's purchases. We had taken a break for cakes and watered wine but I was surprised to find myself hungry when we were invited to share the Castellan's dinner in his private dining room, together with notable merchants of the town who wished to convey their condolences to the Menore family.

Quirian wasn't there, so I sat, meek and silent as a good maid should, and listened to Sanife skilfully drawing all manner of information out of these men while she evaded their enquiries with ease. I made sure not to betray my surprise at seeing just how much she knew of Master Menore's business and his relations, especially Teutel's aunt; a woman who I'd barely begun to know before she died scarcely a month after our wedding.

After sweetmeats and fine liqueurs had been served

and enjoyed, Sanife graciously said her goodnights and we left. Our room was in the western range of the outer ring of buildings. It was large and luxuriously furnished, with a truckle bed for me already made up beside the grander bedstead warmed and perfumed for my supposed mistress. As soon as my head hit the pillow, I sank into a dreamless sleep.

Perhaps that's why I thought I was dreaming when Sanife shook me awake. I looked up at her, startled. She pressed a finger to her lips and then walked to the window to open the shutters. I joined her to look across the wide outer moat to the broad thoroughfare beyond.

It was the dead of night and the town's windows were all dark. Every porch lantern had been doused long since. The new moon was barely a nail-paring among the countless stars in the cloudless sky. It was nigh on impossible to make anything out on the far side of the water.

Then pale radiance caught my eye. I leaned forward, unsure what I was seeing. At first I thought it was a horse. Then I realised the beast was armed with a ferocious, spiral horn, iridescent as mother of pearl. A unicorn.

I turned to Sanife, full of questions. She shook her head and pointed back across the moat.

The unicorn cast its own light, cold and merciless as the moon. As it cantered along the road rounding the moat, I saw a darker shadow just ahead of it. The beast was pursuing someone. Someone was fleeing for his life.

The man skidded to a halt as a cloaked figure emerged from the darkness ahead of him. The newcomer threw back a hood and as the unicorn approached, its eerie radiance burnished the silver of the Moon God's mask.

The fleeing man fell to his knees. He raised pale hands in supplication, trying to cling to the implacable priest's robe. Standing behind him, the unicorn shook its silver mane and stamped its feet.

I gasped as the creature lowered its head. It drove its horn clean through the kneeling man, piercing him underneath his shoulder blade. For a moment the man froze, pinioned, his arms outstretched in the shock of unexpected death. Then the unicorn shook him off and the corpse slumped to the ground.

The beast raised its hooves high to step across the dead man without treading on the corpse. It nuzzled the priest's shoulder and he embraced it. Even at this distance, I could see the affection between them.

I also saw the unicorn was as tall as any horse I had ever encountered but it was nothing like the heavy dray horses whose broad hooves pounded Hurat's streets. The creature was as finely boned and as elegant as the most expensively bred horse in the Paramount King's stables. It was also the most chillingly lethal beast I had ever seen.

'Justice is always done,' Sanife said calmly, 'even if it cannot always be seen to be done.'

She went back to her silk-curtained bed without another word.

I stood and watched until the Moon God's priest patted the unicorn's neck in farewell. It cantered away until its glow was lost amid Usenas's buildings. When I looked back across the moat, Quirian had gone and I could no longer make out the dead body of Teutel's killer.

I closed the shutters and felt my way through the darkness to my own humble bed. As I settled myself to sleep again, I realised I had made my decision. I had set Quirian and Sanife a challenge and they had met it. So I would honour our bargain and join Alace's cabal. For the time being. At least until I understood the magic of the unseen realm. Until I could keep myself safe.

So this is the story of how my life changed. I wonder how many more of these records there are; testimony to the magic and its secrets known only to the few blessed, or cursed, with this talent for seeing the intangible world.

Quirian tells me that this book will be bound with white cords, the knots sealed with black wax stamped with the Horned God's sigil, and stowed in a hidden vault deep within Hurat's great temple. I wonder who will ever read it.

JULIET E. MCKENNA

All I ask is you think kindly of me, whatever else I may have done in the Paramount King's service, by the time you turn these pages.

About the Author

Juliet E McKenna is a British fantasy author, living in the Cotswolds. She has always been fascinated by myth and history, other worlds and other peoples. After studying Greek and Roman history and literature at Oxford University, she worked in personnel management before a career change to combine motherhood and book-selling. Her debut novel, *The Thief's Gamble*, first of *The Tales of Einarinn* was published in 1999, followed by *The Aldabreshin Compass* sequence and *The Chronicles of the Lescari Revolution*. Her fifteenth epic fantasy novel, *Defiant Peaks*, concluded *The Hadrumal Crisis* trilogy.

She reviews for the web and print magazines notably *Interzone* and *Albedo One*, teaches creative writing from time to time and writes diverse shorter fiction. These stories range from contributions to themed anthologies such as *'Alien Artifacts'* and *'Fight Like A Girl'* to shared-world projects such as *Tales from the Emerald Serpent* and the serial novella *'The Ties That Bind'* for *Aethernet* magazine. She's also had the opportunity to write a handful of tales for *Doctor Who*, *Torchwood* and *Warhammer 40k*. Always enjoying the challenge of something new, she is currently exploring the possibilities and opportunities of independent ebook projects alongside traditional publishing.

www.julietemckenna.com

The Tales of Einarinn

1. The Thief's Gamble (1998)
2. The Swordsman's Oath (1999)
3. The Gambler's Fortune (2000)
4. The Warrior's Bond (2001)
5. The Assassin's Edge (2002)

JULIET E. MCKENNA

The Aldabreshin Compass
1. The Southern Fire (2003)
2. Northern Storm (2004)
3. Western Shore (2005)
4. Eastern Tide (2006)

Turns & Chances (2004)

The Chronicles of the Lescari Revolution
1. Irons in the Fire (2009)
2. Blood in the Water (2010)
3. Banners in The Wind (2010)

The Wizard's Coming (2011)

The Hadrumal Crisis
1. Dangerous Waters (2011)
2. Darkening Skies (2012)
3. Defiant Peaks (2012)

A Few Further Tales of Einarinn
(ebook from Wizards Tower Press)

Challoner, Murray & Balfour: Monster Hunters at Law
(ebook from Wizards Tower Press)

Lightning Source UK Ltd.
Milton Keynes UK
UKOW02f1230131016

285174UK00002B/6/P